THERE WAS
INSIDE HIM...

Nicholas Devine was a published writer, with an interest in the literary horror greats—Poe, Baudelaire, and others. On the other hand Patricia Lane was a social butterfly of great beauty and charm. Her intellect and vivacious nature attracted Nick and soon won his heart. A romantic entanglement followed. In Nick, Pat Lane saw a sweet and sensitive soul. Yet there were times she caught a glimpse of something different, something...darker.

Before long Nick Devine confessed a terrible secret: there was something inside him so mysterious, so evil that it was beyond his control. He and Pat could never be happy together. But Pat begged him to seek the help of her friend and father-figure Dr. Carl Horker, a renowned psychiatrist and neurosurgeon. But before long Pat and Dr. Horker realized they were dealing with something more than a simple case of schizophrenia. It was something fraught with a growing sense of inescapable horror...

FOR A COMPLETE SECOND NOVEL, TURN TO PAGE 153

CAST OF CHARACTERS

PATRICIA LANE
A beautiful, smart young lady. Previously fickle, but that changed after she met Nick Devine—there was something about him.

NICHOLAS DEVINE
This sensitive writer had won the heart of a beautiful intellectual butterfly. But deep inside Nick held a dark secret…

DR. CARL HORKER
Pat was like a daughter to him—his door was always open. Could he protect her from a sinister force beyond the realm of science?

MUELLER
This plain clothes man was hired by Dr. Carl to tail Nick, but could never find anything amiss until one ominous night…

MRS. LANE
She was a vibrant widow who adored her daughter. But she was too busy with bridge games to notice a mysterious growing threat.

MAGDA
A steady and reliable housekeeper who had been there for Pat her whole life. She tucked her in and told stories of good vs. evil.

THE DARK OTHER

By
STANLEY G. WEINBAUM

ARMCHAIR FICTION
PO Box 4369, Medford, Oregon 97504

CHAPTER ONE
Pure Horror

"That isn't what I mean," said Nicholas Devine, turning his eyes on his companion. "I mean pure horror in the sense of horror detached from experience, apart from reality. Not just a formless fear, which implies either fear of something that might happen, or fear of unknown dangers. Do you see what I mean?"

"Of course," said Pat, letting her eyes wander over the black expanse of night-dark Lake Michigan. "Certainly I see what you mean but I don't quite understand how you'd do it. It sounds—well, difficult."

She gazed at his lean profile, clear-cut against the distant light. He had turned, staring thoughtfully over the lake, idly fingering the levers on the steering wheel before him. The girl wondered a little at her feeling of contentment; she, Patricia Lane, satisfied to spend all evening in nothing more exciting than conversation! And they must have parked here a full two hours now. There was something about Nick—she didn't understand exactly what; sensitivity, charm, personality. Those were meaningless clichés, handles to hold the unexplainable nuances of character.

"It is difficult," resumed Nick. "Baudelaire tried it. Poe tried it. And in painting, Hogarth, Goya, Dore. Poe came closest, I think; he caught the essence of horror in an occasional poem or story. Don't you think so?"

"I don't know," said Pat. "I've forgotten most of my Poe."

"Remember that story of his, 'The Black Cat'?"

"Dimly. The man murdered his wife."

"Yes. That isn't the part I mean. I mean the cat itself—the second cat. You know a cat, used rightly, can be a symbol of horror."

"Indeed yes!" The girl shuddered. "I don't like the treacherous beasts!"

"And this cat of Poe's," continued Nick, warming to his subject. "Just think of it—in the first place, it's black; element of horror. Then, it's gigantic, unnaturally, abnormally large. And then it's not all black—that would be inartistically perfect—but has a formless white mark on its breast, a mark that little by little assumes a fantastic form—do you remember what?"

"No."

"The form of a gallows!"

"Oh!" said the girl. "Ugh!"

"And then climax of genius—the eyes! Blind in one eye, the other a baleful yellow orb! Do you feel it? A black cat, an enormous black cat marked with a gallows, and lacking one eye, to make the other even more terrible! Literary tricks, of course, but they work, and that's genius! Isn't it?"

"Genius! Yes, if you call it that. The perverse genius of the Devil!"

"That's what I want to write—what I will write someday," He watched the play of lights on the restless surface of the waters. "Pure horror, the epitome of the horrible. It could be written, but it hasn't been yet; not even by Poe."

"That little analysis of yours was bad enough, Nick! Why should you want to improve on his treatment of the theme?"

"Because I like to write and because I'm interested in the horrible. Two good reasons."

"Two excuses, you mean. Of course, even if you'd succeed, you couldn't force anyone to read it."

"If I succeed, there'd be no need to force people. Success would mean that the thing would be great literature, and even today, in these times, there are still people to read that. And besides—" He paused.

"Besides what?"

"Everybody's interested in the horrible. Even you are, whether or not you deny it."

"I certainly do deny it!"

"But you are, Pat. It's natural to be."

"It isn't!"

"Then what is?"

"Interest in people, and life, and gay times, and pretty things, and—and one's self and one's own feelings. And the feelings of the people one loves."

"Yes. It comes to exactly the point I've been stressing. People are sordid, life is hopeless, gay times are stupid, beauty is sensual, one's own feelings are selfish. And love is carnal. That's the array of horrors that holds your interest."

The girl laughed in exasperation. "Nick, you could out-argue your namesake, the Devil himself! Do you really believe that indictment of the normal viewpoint?"

"I do—often!"

"Now?"

"Now," he said, turning his gaze on Pat. "I have no feeling of it at all. Now, right now, I don't believe it."

"Why not?" she queried, smiling ingenuously at him.

"You, obviously."

"Gracious! I had no idea my logic was as convincing as that."

"Your logic isn't. The rest of you is."

"That sounds like a compliment," observed Pat. "If it is," she continued in a bantering tone, "it's the only one I can recall obtaining from you."

"That's because I seldom call attention to the obvious."

"And that's another," laughed the girl. "I'll have to mark this date in red on my calendar. It's entirely unique in our—let's see— nearly a month's acquaintance."

"Is it really so short a time? I know you so well that it must have taken years. Every detail!" He closed his eyes. "Hair-like black silk and oddly dark blue eyes—if I were writing a poem at the moment, I'd call them violet. Tiny lips, the sort the Elizabethan called bee stung. Straight nose, and a figure that is a sort of vest-pocket copy of Diana. Right?" He opened his eyes.

"Nice, but exaggerated. And even if you were correct, that isn't Pat Lane, the real Pat Lane. A camera could do better on a tenth of a second's acquaintance!"

"Check!" He closed his eyes again. "Personality, piquant. Character, loyal, naturally happy, intelligent, but not serious. An intellectual butterfly: a dilettante. Poised, cool, self-possessed, yet inherently affectionate. A being untouched by reality, as yet, living in Chicago and in a make-believe world at the same time." He paused. "How old are you, Pat?"

"Twenty-two. Why?"

"I wondered how long one could manage to stay in the world of make-believe. I'm twenty-six, and I'm long exiled."

"I don't think you know what you mean by a make-believe world. I'm sure I don't."

"Of course you don't. You can't know and still remain there. It's like being happy; once you realize it, it's no longer perfect."

"Then don't explain!"

"Wouldn't make any difference if I did, Pat. It's a queer world, like the Sardoodledom of Sardou and the afternoon-tea school of playwrights. All stage-settings and pretense, but it looks real while you're watching, especially if you're one of the characters."

The girl laughed. "You're a deliciously solemn sort, Nick. How would you like to hear my analysis of you?"

"I wouldn't!"

"You inflicted yours on me, and I'm entitled to revenge. And so—you're intelligent, lazy, dreamy, and with a fine perception of artistic values. You're very alert to impressions of the senses—I mean you're sensuous without being sensual. You're delightfully serious without being somber, except sometimes. Sometimes I feel a hint, just a thrilling hint, in your character, of something danger-ously darker—"

"Don't!" Said Nick sharply.

Pat shot him a quick glance. "And you're frightened to death of falling in love," she concluded imperturbably.

"Oh! Do you think so?"

"I do."

"Then you're wrong! I can't be afraid of it, since I've known for the better part of a month that I've been in love."

"With me," said the girl.

"Yes, with you!"

"Well!" said Pat. "It never before took me a month to extract that admission from a man. Is twenty-two getting old?"

"You're a tantalizing imp!"

"And so?" She pursed her lips, assuming an air of disappoint-ment. "What am I to do about it—scream for help? You haven't given me anything to scream about."

The kiss, Pat admitted to herself, was quite satisfactory. She yielded herself to the pleasure of it; it was decidedly the best kiss she had, in her somewhat limited experience, encountered. She pushed herself away finally with a little gasp, gazing bright-eyed at her companion. He was staring down at her with serious eyes; there was a tense twist to his mouth, and a curiously unexpected attitude of unhappiness.

"Nick," she murmured. "Was it as bad as all that?"

"Bad! Pat, does it mean you—care for me? A little, anyway?"

"A little," she admitted. "Maybe more. Is that what makes you look so forlorn?"

He drew her closer to him. "How could I look forlorn, honey, when something like this has happened to me? That was just my way of looking happy."

She nestled as closely as the steering wheel permitted, drawing his arm about her shoulders. "I hope you mean that, Nick."

"Then you mean it? You really do?"

"I really do."

"I'm glad," he said huskily. The girl thought she detected a strange dubious note in his voice. She glanced at his face; his eyes were gazing into the dim remoteness of the night horizon.

"Nick," she said, "why were you so—well, so reluctant about admitting this? You must have known I—like you. I showed you that deliberately in so many ways."

"I—I wasn't quite sure."

"You were! That isn't it. Nick, I had to practically browbeat you into confessing you cared for me. Why?"

He stepped on the starter; the motor ground into sudden life. The car backed into the road, turning toward Chicago that glared like a false dawn in the southern sky.

"I hope you never find out," he said.

CHAPTER TWO
Science of Mind

"She's out," said Pat as the massive form of Dr. Carl Horker loomed in the doorway.

"Your treatments must be successful; mother's out playing bridge."

The Doctor gave his deep, rumbling chuckle. "So much the better, Pat. I don't feel professional anyway." He moved into the living room, depositing his bulk on a groaning davenport. "And how's yourself?"

"Too well to be a patient of yours," retorted the girl. "Psychiatry! The new religion! Just between friends, it's all apple sauce, isn't it?"

"If I weren't trying to act in place of your father, I'd resent that, young lady," said the Doctor placidly. "Psychiatry is a definite science, and a pretty important one. Applied psychology, the science of the human mind."

"If said mind exists," added the girl swinging her slim legs over the arm of a chair.

"Correct," agreed the Doctor. "In my practice I find occasional evidence that it does. Or did; your generation seems to have found substitutes."

"Which appears to work just as well!" laughed Pat. "All our troubles are more or less inherited from your generation."

"Touché!" admitted Dr. Horker. "But my generation also bequeathed you some solid values which you don't know how to use."

"They've been weighed and found wanting," said Pat airily. "We're busy replacing them with our own values."

"Which are certainly no better."

"Maybe not, Doc, but at least they're ours."

"Yours and Tom Paine's. I can't see that you young moderns have brought any new ideas to the social scheme."

"New or not, we're the first ones to give 'em a try-out. Your crowd took it out in talk. ,.

"That's an insult," observed the Doctor cheerfully. "If I weren't acting *loco parentis*—"

"I know! You'd give me a few licks in the spot popularly supposed to do the most good! Well that's part of a parent s privilege, isn't it?"

"You've grown beyond the spanking age, my dear. Physically, if not mentally—though I don't say the process would hurt me as much as you. I'd doubtless enjoy it."

"Then you might try sending me to bed without my dinner," the girl laughed.

"That's a doctor's prerogative, Pat. I've even done that to your Mother."

"In other words, you're a complete flop as a parent. All the responsibilities, and none of the privileges."

"That expresses it."

"Well, you elected yourself, Doc. It's not my fault you happened to live next door."

"No. It's my misfortune."

"And I notice," remarked Pat wickedly, "that you're not too thoroughly in *loco* to neglect sending mother a bill for services rendered!"

"My dear girl, that's part of the treatment!"

"So? And how?"

"I furnish a bill just steep enough to keep your mother from in-dulging too frequently in medical services. Without that little prac-tical check on her inclinations, she'd be a confirmed neurotic. One of those sweet, resigned, professional invalids, you know."

"Then why not send her a bill tall enough to cure her altogether?"

"She might change to psychoanalysis or New Thought," chuck-led the Doctor. "Besides, your father wanted me to look after her, and besides that, I like having the run of the house."

"Well, I'm sure I don't mind," observed Pat. "We've a dog and a canary bird, too."

"You're in fine fettle this afternoon!" laughed her companion. "Must've been a successful date last night."

"It was." Her eyes turned suddenly dreamy.

"You're in love again, Pat!" he accused.

"Again? Why the 'again'?"

"Well, there was Billy, and that Paul—"

"Oh, those!" Her tone was contemptuous. "Merely passing fancies, Doc. Just whims, dreams of the moment—in other words, puppy love."

"And this? I suppose this is different—a grand passion?"

"I don't know," she said, frowning abruptly. "He's nice, but—odd. Attractive as–well, as the devil."

11

"Odd? How?"

"Oh, he's one of those minds you think we moderns lack."

"Intellectual, eh? New variety for you; out of the usual run of your dancing collegiates. I've often suspected that you picked your swains by the length and lowness of their cars."

"Maybe I did. That was one of the chief differences between them."

"How'd you meet this mental paragon?"

"Billy Fields dragged him around to one of those literary evenings he affects—where they read Oscar Wilde and Eugene O'Neil aloud. Bill met him at the library."

"And he outshone all the local lights, I perceive."

"He surely did!" retorted Pat. "And he hardly said a word the whole evening."

"He wouldn't have to, if they're all like Billy! What's this prodigy's specialty?"

"He writes, I think—laugh if you want to—I think perhaps he's a genius."

"Well," said Doctor Horker, "even that's possible. It's been known to occur, but rarely, to my knowledge, in your generation."

"Oh, we're just dimmed by the glare of brilliance from yours." She swung her legs to the floor, facing the Doctor. "Do you psychiatrists actually know anything about love?" she queried.

"We're supposed to."

"What is it, then?"

"Just a device of Nature's for perpetuating the species. Some organisms manage without it, and do pretty well."

"Yes. I've heard references to the poor fish!"

"Then they're inaccurate; fish have primitive symptoms of eroticism. But below the vertebrates, notably in the amoeba, I don't recall any amorous habits."

"Then your definition doesn't explain a thing, does it?"

"Not to one of the victims, perhaps."

"Anyway," said Pat decisively, "I've, heard of the old biological urge before your kind analysis. It doesn't begin to explain why one should be attracted to this person and repelled by that one, does it?"

"No, but Freud does. The famous Oedipus Complex."

"That's the love of son for mother, or daughter for father, isn't it? And I don't see how that clears up anything; for example, I can just barely remember my father."

"That's plenty. It could be some little trait in these swains of yours, some unimportant mannerism that recalls that memory. Or there's that portrait of him in the hall—the one under the mellow red light. It might happen that you'd see one of these chaps under a similar light in some attitude that brings the picture to mind—or a hundred other possibilities."

"Doesn't sound entirely convincing," objected Pat with a thoughtful frown.

"Well, submit to the proper treatments, and I'll tell you exactly what caused each and every one of your little passing fancies. You can't expect me to hit it first guess."

"Thanks, no! That's one of those courses where you tell the doctor all your secrets, and I prefer to keep what few I have."

"Good judgment, Pat. By the way, you said this chap was odd. Does that mean merely that he writes? I've known perfectly normal people who wrote."

"No," she said, "it isn't that. It's—he's so sweet and gentle and manageable most of the time, but sometimes he has such a thrilling spark of mastery that it almost scares me. It's puzzling but fascinating, if you grasp my import."

"Huh! He's probably a naturally selfish fellow who's putting on a show of gentleness for your benefit. Those flashes of tyranny are probably his real character in moments of forgetfulness."

"You doctors can explain anything, can't you?"

"That's our business. It's what we're paid for."

"Well, you're wrong this time. I know Nick well enough to know if he's acting. His personality is just what I said—gentle, sensitive, and yet—it's perplexing, and that's a good part of his charm."

"Then it's not such a serious case you've got," mocked the doctor.

"When you're cool enough to analyze your own feelings, and dissect the elements of the chap's attraction, you're not in any danger."

"Danger! I can look out for myself, thanks. That's one thing we mindless moderns learn young, and don't let me catch you puttering around in my romances! In *loco parentis* or just plain loco, you'll get the licking instead of me!"

"Believe me, Pat, if I wanted to experiment with affairs of the heart, I'd not pick a spitfire like you as the subject."

"Well, Doctor Carl, you're warned!"

"This Nick," observed the Doctor, "must be quite a fellow to get the princess of the North Side so het up. What's the rest of his cognomen?"

"Nicholas Devine. Romantic, isn't it?"

"Devine," muttered Horker. "I don't know any Devines. Who are his people?"

"Hasn't any."

"How does he live? By his writing?"

"Don't know. I gathered that he lives on some income left by his parents. What's the difference, anyway?"

"None. None at all." The other wrinkled his brows thoughtfully. "There was a colleague of mine, a Dr. Devine; died a good many years ago. Reputation wasn't anything to brag about; was a little off balance mentally."

"Well, Nick isn't!" snapped Pat with some asperity.

"I'd like to meet him."

"He's coming over tonight."

"So'm I. I want to see your mother." He rose ponderously. "If she's not playing bridge again!"

"Well, look him over," retorted Pat. "And I think your knowledge of love is a decided flop. I think you're woefully ignorant on the subject."

"Why's that?"

"If you'd known anything about it, you could have married mother some time during the last seventeen years. Lord knows you've tried, and all you've attained is the state of *in loco parentis* instead of *parens.*"

CHAPTER THREE
Psychiatrics of Genius

"How do you charge—by the hour?" Asked Pat, as Doctor Horker returned from the hall. The sound of her mother's departing footsteps pattered on the porch.

"Of course, Young One; like a plumber."

"Then your rates per minute must be colossal! The only time you ever see mother is a moment or so between bridge games."

"I add on the time I waste with you, my dear. Such as now, waiting to look over that odd swain of yours. Didn't you say he'd be over this evening?"

"Yes, but it's not worth your rates to have him psychoanalyzed. I can do as well myself."

"All right, Pat. I'll give you a sample analysis free," chuckled the Doctor, distributing his bulk comfortably on the davenport.

"I don't like free trials," she retorted. "I sent for a beauty-culture book once, on free trial. I was twelve years old, and returned it in seven days, but I'm still getting sales letters in the mails. I must be on every sucker list in the country."

"So that's the secret of your charm."

"What is?"

"You must have read the book, I mean. If you remember the title, I might try it myself. Think it'd help?"

"Dr. Carl," laughed the girl, "you don't need a book on beauty culture—you need one on bridge! It's that atrocious game you play that's bothering Mother."

"Indeed? I shouldn't be surprised if you were right."

"Save your surprise for when I'm wrong, Doc. You'll suffer much less from shock."

"Confident little brat! You're apt to get that knocked out of you someday, though I hope you never do."

"I can take it," grinned Pat.

"No doubt you can, but you're an adept at handing it out. Where's this chap of yours?"

"He'll be along. No one's ever stood me up on a date yet."

"I can understand that, you imp! Is that the famous Nick?" he queried as a car purred to a stop beyond the windows.

"No one else!" said the girl, glancing out. "The Big Thrill in person."

She darted to the door. Horker turned casually to watch her as she opened it, surveying Nicholas Devine with professional nonchalance. He entered, tall, slender, with his thin sensitive features sharply outlined in the light of the hall. He cast a quick glance toward the Doctor; the latter noted the curious amber-green eyes of the lad, set wide in the lean face, deep, speculative, the eyes' of a dreamer.

"'Evening, Nick," Pat was bubbling. The newcomer gave her a hasty smile, with another glance at the Doctor. "Don't mind Dr. Carl," she continued. "Aren't you going to kiss me? It irks the medico, and I never miss a chance."

Nicholas flushed in embarrassment; he gestured hesitantly, then placed a hasty peck of a kiss on the girl's forehead. He reddened again at the Doctor's rumble of "Young imp of Satan!"

"Not very good," said Pat reflectively, obviously enjoying the situation. I've known you to do better." She pulled him toward the area of the living room. "Come meet Dr. Horker. Dr. Carl, this is the aforesaid Nicholas Devine."

"Dr. Horker," repeated the lad, smiling diffidently. "You're the psychiatrist and brain specialist, aren't you, Sir?"

"So my patients believe," rumbled the massive Doctor rising at the introduction, and grasping the youth's hand. "And you're the genius Patricia has been raving about. I'm glad to have the chance of looking you over."

Nick gave the girl a harassed glance, shifting uncomfortably and patently at a loss for a reply. She grinned mischievously.

"Sit down, both of you," she suggested helpfully. She seized his hat from the reluctant hands of Nick, sailing it carelessly to a chair.

"So!" boomed the Doctor, lowering his great bulk again to the davenport. He eyed the youth sitting nervously before him. "Devine, did you say?"

"Yes, sir."

"I knew a Devine once. Colleague of mine."

"A doctor? My father was a doctor."

"Dr. Stuart Devine?"

"Yes, sir." He paused. "Did you say you knew him, Dr. Horker?"

"Slightly," rumbled the other. "Only slightly."

"I don't remember him at all, of course. I was very young when he—and my mother too—died."

"You must have been. Patricia claims you write."

"I try."

"What sort of material?"

"Why—any sort. Prose or poetry; what I feel like writing."

"Whatever inspires you, I suppose?"

"Yes, sir." The lad flushed again.

"Ever have anything published?"

"Yes, sir. In Nation's Poetry."

"Never heard of it."

"It has a large circulation," said Nick apologetically.

"Humph! Well, that's something. Whom do you like?"

"Whom do I like?" The youth's tone was puzzled.

"What authors—writers?"

"Oh.' He cast another uncomfortable glance at Pat. "Why—I like Baudelaire, and Poe, and Swinburne, and Villon, and—"

"Decadents, all of them!" sniffed the Doctor. "What prose writers?"

"Well—" He hesitated. "Poe again, and Stern, and Rabelais—"

"Rabelais!" Horker's voice boomed. "Well! Your taste can't be as bad as I thought, then. There's one we agree on, anyway. And I notice you name no moderns, which is another good point."

"I haven't read many moderns, sir."

"That's in your favor."

"Cut it!" put in Pat with assumed sharpness. "You've taken enough whacks at my generation for one day."

"I'm glad to find one of your generation who agrees with me," chuckled the Doctor. "At least to the extent of not reading its works."

"I'll teach him," grinned Pat. "I'll have him writing *vess libre*, and maybe even Dadaism, in a week."

"Maybe it won't be much loss," grunted Horker. "I haven't seen any of his work yet."

"We'll bring some around sooner or later. We will, won't we, Nick?"

"Of course, if you want to. But—"

"He's going to say something modest," interrupted the girl. "He's in the retiring mood now, but he's apt to change any moment, and snap your surly head off."

"Humph! I'd like to see it."

"So'd I," retorted Pat. "You've had it coming all day; maybe I'll do it myself."

"You have, my dear, innumerable times. But I'm like the Hydra, except that I grow only one head to replace the one you snap off." He turned again to Nicholas. "Do you work?"

"Yes, sir. At my writing."

"I mean how do you live?"

"Why," said the youth, reddening again in embarrassment, "my parents—"

"Listen!" said Pat. "That's enough of Dr. Carl's cross examination. You'd think he was a Victorian father who had just been approached for his daughter's hand. We haven't whispered any news of an engagement to you, have we, Doc?"

"No, but I'm acting—"

"Sure. *In loco parentis. We* know that."

"You're incorrigible, Pat! I wash my hands of you. Run along, if you're going out."

"You'll be telling me never to darken my own door again in the next breath!" She stretched forth a diminutive foot at the extremity of a superlatively attractive ankle, caught Nick's hat on her toe, and kicked it expertly to his lap. "Come on, Nick. There's a moon."

"There is not!" objected the Doctor huffily. "It rises at four, as you ought to know. You didn't see it last night, did you?"

"I didn't notice," said the girl. "Come on, Nick, and we'll watch it rise tonight. We'll check up on the Doctor's astronomy, or is it chronology?"

"You do and I'll know it! I can hear you come home, you imp!"

"Nice neighbor," observed Pat airily, as she stepped to the door. "I'll bet you peek out of the window, too."

She ignored the Doctor's irritated rumble as she passed into the hall where Nick, after a diffident murmur of farewell to Horker, followed. She caught up a light cape, which he draped about her shoulders.

"Nick," she said, "suppose you run out to the car and wait. I think I've stepped too hard on Dr. Carl's corns, and I want to give him a little cheering up. Will you?"

"Of course, Pat."

She darted back into the living room, perching on the arm of the davenport beside the Doctor.

"Well?" she said, running her hand through his grizzled hair. "What's the verdict?"

"Seems like a nice kid," grumbled Horker reluctantly. "Nice enough, but introverted, repressed, and I shouldn't be surprised to find him antisocial. Doesn't adjust easily to his environment; takes refuge in a dream world of his own."

"That's what he accuses me of doing," grinned Pat. "That all you've got against him?"

"That's all, but where's that streak of mastery you mentioned? You lead him around on a leash!"

"It didn't show up tonight. That's the thrill—the unexpectedness of it."

"Bah! You must've dreamed it. There's no more aggressiveness in that lad than in KoKo, your canary."

"Don't you believe it, Dr. Carl! The trouble is that he's a genius, and that's where your psychology falls flat."

"Genius," said the Doctor oracularly, "is a sublimation of qualities—"

"I'll tell you tomorrow how sublime the qualities are," called Pat as she skipped out of the door.

CHAPTER FOUR
The Transfiguration

The car slid smoothly along a straight white road that stretched ahead into the darkness like an earth-bound Milky Way. In the dim distance before them, red as Antares, glowed the tail-light of some automobile; except for this lone evidence of humanity, reflected

Pat, they might have been flashing through the cosmic depths of interstellar space, instead of following a highway in the very shadow of Chicago. The colossal city of the lake-shore was invisible behind them, and the clustering suburbs with it.

"Queer, isn't it?" said Pat, after a silence, "how contented we can be with none of the purchased amusement people crave—shows, movies, dancing, and all that."

"It doesn't seem queer to me," answered Nick. "Not when I look at you here beside me."

"Nice of you!" retorted Pat. "But it's never happened to me before." She paused, then continued, "How do you like the Doctor?"

"How does he like me? That's considerably more to the point, isn't it?"

"He thinks you're nice, but—let's see—introverted, repressed, and ill-adjusted to your environment, I think those were the points."

"Well, I liked *him*, in spite of your maneuvers, and in spite of his being a doctor."

"What's wrong with being a doctor?"

"Did you ever read *Tristram Shandy?*" was Nick's irrelevant response.

"No, but I read the newspapers!"

"What's the connection, Pat?"

"Just as much connection as there is between the evils of being a doctor and reading *Tristram Shandy*. *I* know that much about the book, at least."

"You're nearly right," laughed Nick. "I was just referring to one of Tristram's remarks on doctors and lawyers. It fits my attitude."

"What's the remark?"

"Well, he had the choice of professions, and it occurred to him that medicine and law were the vulture professions, since lawyers live by men's quarrels and doctors by men's misfortunes. So—he became a writer."

"And what do writers live by?" queried Pat mischievously. "By men's stupidity!"

"You're precious, Pat!" Nick chuckled delightedly. "If I'd created you to order, I couldn't have planned you more to taste—pepper, Tabasco sauce, vinegar, spice, and honey.

"And to be taken with a grain of salt," retorted the girl, puckering her piquant, impish features. She edged closer to him, locking her arm through his where it rested on the steering wheel.

"Nick," she said, her tones suddenly gentle, "I think I'm pretty crazy about you. Heaven knows why I should be, but it's a fact."

"Pat, dear!"

"I'm crazy about you in this meek, sensitive pose of yours, and I'm fascinated by those masterful moments you flash occasionally. Really, Nick, I almost wish you flamed out oftener."

"Don't!" he said sharply.

"Why not?"

"Let's not talk about me, Pat. It—embarrasses me."

"All right, Mr. Modesty! Let's talk about me, then. I'll promise we won't succeed in embarrassing me."

"And it's quite the most interesting subject in the world, Pat."

"Well, then?"

"What?"

"Why don't you start talking? The topic is all attention."

He chuckled. "How many men have told you that you were beautiful, Pat?"

"I never kept account."

"And in many different ways?"

"Why? Have you, perchance, discovered a new way, Nick?"

"Not at all. The oldest way of any the way of Shappho and Pindar."

"O-ooh!" She clapped her hands in mock delight. "Poetry!"

"The only medium that could possibly express how lovely you are," said Nick.

"Nicholas, have you gone and composed a poem to me?"

"Composed? No. It isn't necessary, with you here beside me."

"What's that? Some very subtle compliment?"

"Not subtle, Pat. You're the poem yourself; all I need do is look at you, listen to you, and translate."

"Neat!" applauded the girl. "Do I hear the translation?"

"You certainly do." He turned his odd amber-green eyes on her, and then bent forward to the road. He began to speak in a low voice.

"In no far country's silent ways
Shall I forget one little thing—
The soft intentness of your gaze,
The sweetness of your murmuring
Your generously tender praise.
The words just hinted by a breath—
In no far country's silent way.
Unless that country's name be Death—"

He paused abruptly, and drove silently onward.

"Oh," breathed Pat. "Why don't you go on, Nick? Please."

"No. It isn't the mood for this night, dear. Not this night, alone with you."

"What is, then?"

"Nothing sentimental. Something lighter, something—oh, Elizabethan. That's it."

"And what's stopping you?"

"Lack of an available idea. Or—wait. Listen a moment." He began, this time in a tone of banter.

"When mornings, you attire yourself
For riding in the city,
You're such a lovely little elf,
Extravagantly pretty!
And when at noon, you decide to wear
The habit of the town,
I cannot call to mind as fair
A symphony in brown.
Then evenings, you blithely don
A daintiness of white,
To flash a very paragon
Of lightsomeness—and light!
But when the sounds of pleasure cease,
And you retire at night,
The godling on your mantelpiece
Must know a fairer sight!"

THE DARK OTHER

"Sweet!" laughed Pat. "But personal. And anyway, how do you know I've a godling on my mantel? Don't you credit me with any modesty?"

"If you haven't, you should have! The vision I mentioned ought to enliven even a statue."

"Well," said the girl, "I have one—a jade Buddha, and with all the charms I flash before him nightly, he's never batted an eyelash. Explain that!"

"Easily. He's green with envy, and frozen with admiration, and struck dumb by wonder."

"Heavens! I suppose I ought to be thankful you didn't say he was petrified with fright!" Pat laughed. "Oh Nick," she continued, in a voice gone suddenly dreamy, "this is marvelous, isn't it? I mean our enjoying ourselves so completely, and our being satisfied to be so alone. Why, we've never even danced together."

"So we haven't. That's a subterfuge we haven't needed. Isn't it?"

"It is," replied the girl, dropping her glossy gleaming black head against his shoulder. "And besides, it's much more satisfactory to be held in your arms in private, instead of in the midst of a crowd, and sitting down, instead of standing up. But I should like to dance with you, Nick," she concluded.

"We'll go dancing, then, whenever you like."

"You're delightfully complaisant, Nick. But—you're puzzling." She glanced up at him. "You're so—so reluctant. Here we've been driving an hour, and you haven't tried to kiss me a single time, and yet I'm quite positive you care for me."

"Lord, Pat!" he muttered. "You never need doubt that."

"Then what is it? Are you so spiritual and ethereal, or is my attraction for you just sort of intellectual? Or—are you afraid?" As he made no reply, she continued, "Or are those poems you spout about my physical charms just—poetic license?"

"They're not, and you know it!" he snapped. "You've a mirror, haven't you? And other fellows than I have taken you around, haven't they?"

"Oh, I've been taken around! That's what perplexes me about you, Nick. I'd think you were actually afraid of kissing me if it weren't—" Her voice trailed into silence and she stared speculatively ahead at the ribbon of road that rolled steadily into the head-lights' glare.

She broke the interval of wordlessness. "What is it, Nick?" she resumed almost pleadingly. "You've hinted at something now and then. Please—you don't have to hesitate to tell me; I'm modern enough to forgive things past, entanglements, affairs, disgraces, or anything like that. Don't you think I should know?"

"You'd know," he said huskily, "if I could tell you."

"Then there is something, Nick!" She pressed his arm against her. "Tell me, isn't there?"

"I don't know," There was the hint of a groan in his voice.

"You don't know! I can't understand."

"I can't either. Please, Pat, let's not spoil tonight; if I could tell you, I would. Why, Pat, I love you—I'm terribly, deeply, solemnly in love with you."

"And I with you, Nick," She gazed ahead, where the road rose over the arch of a narrow bridge. The speeding car lifted to the rise like a zooming plane.

And suddenly, squarely in the center of the road, another car, until now concealed by the arch of the bridge, appeared almost upon them. There was a heart-stopping moment when a collision seemed inevitable, and Pat felt the arm against her tighten convulsively into a bar of steel. She heard her own sobbing gasp, and then, somehow, they had slipped unscathed between the other car and the rail of the bridge.

"Oh!" she gasped faintly, then with a return of breath, "That was nice, Nick!"

Beyond the bridge, the road widened once more; she felt the car slowing, edging toward the broad shoulder of the road.

"There was danger," said her companion in tones as emotionless as the rasping of metal. "I came to save it."

"Save what?" queried Pat as the car slid to a halt on the turf.

"Your body," The tones were still cold, like grinding wheels. "The beauty of your body!"

He reached a thin hand toward her, suddenly seized her skirt and snatched it above the silken roundness of her knees. "There," he snapped. "That is what I mean."

"Nick!" Pat half-screamed in appalled astonishment. "How—" She paused, shocked into abrupt silence, for the face turned toward her was but a remote, evil caricature of Nicholas Devine's. It leered at her out of bloodshot eyes, as if behind the mask of Nick's face peered a red-eyed demon.

CHAPTER FIVE
A Fantasy of Fear

The satyr beside Pat was leaning toward her; the arm about her was tightening with a brutal ruthlessness, and while still starring in fascination at the incredible eyes, she realized that another arm and a white hand was moving relentlessly, exploratively, toward her body.

It was the cold touch of this hand as it slipped over her silk-sheathed legs that broke the chilling spell of her fascination.

"Nick!" she screamed. "Nick!" She had a curious sensation of calling him back from far distances, the while she strove with both hands and all her strength to press him back from her. But the ruthless force of his arms was overcoming her resistance; she saw the red eyes a hand's breadth from her own.

"Nick!" she sobbed in terror.

There was a change. Abruptly, she was looking into Nick's eyes, bloodshot, frightened, puzzled, but indubitably Nick's eyes. The flaming orbs of the demon were no more; it was as if they had receded into Nick's head. The arm about her body relaxed, and they were staring at each other in a medley of consternation, amazement and unbelief. The youth drew back, huddled in his corner of the car, and Pat, breathing in sobs, smoothed out her rumpled apparel with a convulsive movement.

"Pat!" he gasped. "Oh, my God! He couldn't have—" He paused abruptly. The girl gazed at him without reply.

"Pat, dear," he spoke in a low, tense murmur, "I'm—sorry. I don't know—I don't understand how—"

"Never mind," she said, regaining a vestige of her customary composure. "It's—all right, Nick."

"But—oh, Pat—!"

"It was that near accident.' she said. "That upset you—both of us. I mean."

"Yes!" he said eagerly. "That's what it was. Pat. It must have been that, but dear, can you forgive? Do you want to forgive me?"

"It's all right," she repeated. "After all, you just complimented my legs, and I guess I can stand that. It's happened before, only not quite so—convincingly!"

"You're sweet, Pat!"

"No; I just love you Nick," She felt a sudden pity for the misery in his face. "Kiss me, Nick—only gently."

He pressed his lips to hers, very lightly, almost timidly. She lay back against the seat for a moment, her eyes closed.

"That's you again," she murmured. "This other—wasn't."

"Please, Pat! Don't refer to it—not ever."

"But it wasn't you, Nick. It was just the strain of that narrow escape. I don't hold it against you."

"You're—Lord, Pat, I don't deserve you. But you know that I—I myself—could never touch you except in tenderness, even in reverence. You're too dainty, too lovely, too spirited, to be hurt, or to be held roughly, against your will. You know I feel that way about you, don't you?"

"Of course. It was nothing, Nick. Forget it."

"If I can," he said somberly. He switched on the engine, backed out upon the pavement, and turned the car toward the glow that marked Chicago. Neither of them spoke as the machine hummed over the arching bridge and down the slope, where, so few minutes before, the threat of accident had thrust itself at them.

"We won't see a moon tonight," said Pat in a small voice, after an interval. "We'll never check up on Dr. Carl's astronomy."

"You don't want to tonight, Pat, do you?"

"I guess perhaps we'd better not," she replied. "We're both upset, and there'll be other nights."

Again they were silent. Pat felt strained, shaken; there was something uncanny about the occurrence that puzzled her. The red eyes that had glared out of Nick's face perplexed her, and the curious rasping voice he had used still sounded inhumanly in her memory. Out of recollection rose still another mystery.

"Nick," she said, "what did you mean—then—when you said there was danger and you came to save me?"

"Nothing," he said sharply.

"And then, afterwards, you started to say something about 'He couldn't have...' Who's 'he'?"

"It meant nothing, I tell you. I was frantic to think you might have been hurt. That's all."

"I believe you, honey," she said, wondering whether she really did. The thing was beginning to grow hazy; already it was assuming merely the proportions of an upheaval of youthful fervor. Such occurrences were not unheard of, though never before had it happened to Patricia Lane! Still, even that was conceivable, far more conceivable than the dark, unformed, inchoate suspicions she had been harboring. They hadn't even been definite enough to be called suspicions; indefinite apprehensions came closer.

And yet—that strange, wild face that had formed itself of Nick's fine features, and the terrible red eyes! Were they elements in a picture conjured out of her own imagination? They must be, of course. She had been frightened by that hair-breadth escape, and had seen things that didn't exist. And the rest of it—well, that might be natural enough. Still, there was something—she knew that; Nick had admitted it.

Horker's words concerning Nick's father rose in her mind. Suspected of being crazy! Was that it? Was that the cause of Nick's curious reluctance where she was concerned? Was the face that had glared at her the visage of a maniac? It couldn't be. It couldn't be, she told herself fiercely. Not her fine, tender, sensitive Nick! And besides, that face, if she hadn't imagined it, had been the face, not of a lunatic, but of a devil. She shook her head, as if to deny her thoughts, and placed her hand impulsively on Nick's.

"I don't care," she said. "I love you, Nick."

"And I you," he murmured. "Pat, I'm sorry about spoiling this evening. I'm sorry and ashamed."

"Never mind, honey. There'll be others."

"Tomorrow?"

"No," she said. "Mother and I are going out to dinner. And Friday we're having company."

"Really, Pat? You're not just trying to turn me off gently?"

"Really, Nick. Try asking me for Saturday evening and see!"

"You're asked, then."

"And it's a date," Then, with a return of her usual insouciance, she added, "If you're on good behavior."

"I will be. I promise."

"I hope so," said Pat. An inexplicable sense of foreboding had come over her; despite her self-given assurances, something unnamable troubled her. She gave a mental shrug, and deliberately relegated the unpleasant cogitations to oblivion.

The car turned into Dempster Road; the lights of the teeming roadhouses, dance halls, road-side hamburger and barbecue stands flashed by. There were many cars here; there was no longer any impression of solitude now, in the overflow from the vast city in whose shadow they moved. The incessant flow of traffic gave the girl a feeling of security; these were tangible things about her, and once more the memory of that disturbing occurrence became dim and dreamlike. This was Nick beside her, gentle, intelligent, kind; had he ever been otherwise? It seemed highly unreasonable, a fantasy of fear and the hysteria of the moment.

"Hungry?" asked Nick unexpectedly.

"I could use a barbecue, I guess. Beef."

The car veered to the graveled area before a brightly lit stand. Nick gave the order to an attendant. He chuckled as Pat, with the digestive disregard of youth attacked the greasy combination.

"That's like a humming bird eating hay!" he said.

"Or better, like a leprechaun eating that horse-meat they can for dogs."

"You might as well discover that I don't live on honey and rose petals," said Pat. "Not even on caviar and terrapin—at least, not exclusively. I leave the dainty palate for Mother to indulge."

"Which is just as well. Hamburger and barbecue are more easily budgeted."

"Nicholas," said the girl, tossing the paper napkin out of the car window, "is that an indirect and very evasive proposal of marriage?"

"You know it could be, if you wished it!"

"And do I?" she said, assuming a pensive air. "I wonder. Suppose we say I'll let you know later."

"And meanwhile?"

"Oh, meanwhile we can be sort of engaged. Just the way we've been."

"You're sweet, Pat," he murmured, as the car edged into the line of traffic. "I don't know just how to convey my appreciation, but it's there!"

The buildings drew more closely together; the road was suddenly a lighted street, and then, almost without realizing it, they were before Pat's home. Nick walked beside her to the door; he stood facing her hesitantly.

"Good night, Pat," he said huskily. He leaned down, kissing her very gently, turned, and departed.

The girl watched him from the open doorway, following the lights of his car until they vanished down the street. Dear, sweet Nick! Then the disturbing memory of that occurrence of the evening returned; she frowned in perplexity as the thought rose. That was all of a piece with the puzzling character of him, and the curious veiled references he'd made. References to what? She didn't know, couldn't imagine. Nick had said he didn't know either, which added still another quirk to the maze.

She thought of Dr. Horker's words. With the thought, she glanced at his house, adjacent to her own home. A light gleamed in the library; he was still awake. She closed the door behind her, and darted across the narrow strip of lawn to his porch. She rang the bell.

"Good evening, Dr. Carl," she said as the massive form of Horker appeared. She puckered her lips impudently at him as she slipped by him into the house.

CHAPTER SIX
A Question of Science

"Not that I'm displeased at this visit, Pat," rumbled the Doctor, seating himself in one of the great chairs by the fireplace, "but I'm curious, I thought you were dating your ideal tonight, yet here you are, back alone a little after eleven. How come?"

"Oh," said the girl nonchalantly, dropping crosswise in the other chair, "we decided we needed our beauty sleep."

"Then why are you here, you young imp?"

"Thought you might be lonesome."

"I'll bet you did! But seriously, Pat, what is it? Any trouble?"

"No-o," she said dubiously. "No trouble. I just wanted to ask you a few hypothetical questions. About science."

"Go to it, then, and quickly. I was ready to turn in."

"Well," said Pat, "about Nick's father. He was a doctor, you said, and supposed to be cracked. Was he really?"

"Humph! That's curious. I just looked up a brochure of his to-night in the American Medical Journal, after our conversation of this afternoon. Why do you ask that?"

"Because I'm interested, of course."

"Well, here's what I remember about him, Pat. He was an M.D. all right, but I see by his paper there—the one I was reading—that he was on the staff of Northern U. He did some work at the Cook County Asylum, some research work, and there was a bit of talk about his maltreating the patients. Then, on top of that, he published a paper that medical men considered crazy, and that started talk of his sanity. That's all I know."

"Then Nick—"

"I thought so! So it's conic to the point where you're investigating his antecedents, eh? With an eye to marriage or what?"

"Or what!" snapped Pat. "I was curious to know, naturally."

"Naturally," The Doctor gave her a keen glance from his shrewd eyes. "Did you think you detected incipient dementia in your ideal?"

"No," said the girl thoughtfully. "Dr. Carl, is there any sort of craziness that could take an ordinarily shy person and make a passionate devil of him? I don't mean passionate, either," she added. "Rather cold, ruthless, domineering."

"None that I know of," said Horker, watching her closely. "Did this Nick of yours have one of his masterful moments?"

"Worse than that," admitted Pat reluctantly. "We had a near accident, and it startled both of us, and then suddenly, he was looking at me like a devil, and then—" She paused. "It frightened me a little."

"What's he do?" demanded Horker sharply.

"Nothing." She lied with no hesitation.

"Were there any signs of Satyromania?"

"I don't know. I never heard of that."

"I mean, in plain Americanese, did he make a pass at you?"

"He—no, he didn't."

"Well, what did he do?"

"He just looked at me." Somehow a feeling of disloyalty was rising in her; she felt a reluctance to betray Nick further.

"What did he say, then? And don't lie this time."

"He just said— He just looked at my legs and said something about their being beautiful, and that was all. After that, the look on his face faded into the old Nick."

"Old Nick is right—the impudent scoundrel!" Horker's voice rumbled angrily.

"Well, they're nice legs," said Pat defiantly, swinging them as evidence. "You've said it yourself. Why shouldn't he say it? What's to keep him from it?"

"The code of a gentleman, for one thing!"

"Oh, who cares for your Victorian codes! Anyway, I came here for information, not to be cross-examined. I want to ask the questions myself."

"Pat, you're a reckless little spit-fire, and you're going to get burned some day, and deserve it," the Doctor rumbled ominously. "Ask your fool questions, and then I'll ask mine."

"All right," said the girl, still defiant. "I don't guarantee to answer yours, however."

"Well, ask yours, you imp!"

"First, then—is that Satyro-stuff you mentioned intermittent or continuous?"

"It's necessarily intermittent, you numb-skull! The male organism can't function continuously!"

"I mean, does the mania lie dormant for weeks or months, and then flare up?"

"Not at all. It's a permanent mania, like any other psychopathic sex condition."

"Oh," said Pat thoughtfully, with a sense of relief.

"Well, go on. What next?"

31

"What are these dual personalities you read about in the papers?"

"They're aphasias. An individual forgets his name, and he picks, or is given, another, if he happens to wander among strangers. He forgets much of his past experience; the second personality is merely what's left of the first—sort of a vestige of his normal character. There isn't any such thing as a dual personality in the sense of two distinct characters living in one body."

"Isn't there?" queried the girl musingly. "Could the second personality have qualities that the first one lacked?"

"Not any more than it could have an extra finger! The second is merely a split off the first, a forgetfulness, a loss of memory. It couldn't have more qualities than the whole, or normal, character; it must have fewer."

"Isn't that just too interesting!" said Pat in a bantering tone. "All right, Dr. Carl. It's your turn."

"Then what's the reason for all this curiosity about perversions and aphasias? What's happened to your genius now?"

"Oh, I'm thinking of taking up the study of psychiatry," replied the girl cheerfully.

"Aren't you going to answer me seriously?"

"No."

"Then what's the use of my asking questions?"

"I know the right answer to that one. None!"

"Pat," said Horker in a low voice, "you're an impudent little hoyden, and too clever for your own good, but you and your mother are very precious to me. You know that."

"Of course I do, Dr. Carl," said the girl, relenting. "You're a dear, and I'm crazy about you and you know that too."

"What I'm trying to say," proceeded the other, "is simply that I'm trying to help you. I want to help you, if you need help. Do you?"

"I guess I don't, Dr. Carl, but you're sweet."

"Are you in love with this Nicholas Devine?"

"I think perhaps I am," she admitted softly.

"And is he in love with you?"

"Frankly, could he help being?"

"Then there's something about him that worries you. That's it, isn't it?"

"I thought there was, Dr. Carl. I was a little startled by the change in him right after we had that narrow escape, but I'm sure it was nothing—just imagination. Honestly, that's all that troubled me."

"I believe you, Pat," said the Doctor, his eyes fixed on hers. "But guard yourself my dear. Be sure he's what you think he is; be sure you know him rightly."

"He's clean and fine," murmured the girl. "I am sure."

"But this puzzling yourself about his character, Pat—I don't like it. Make doubly sure before you permit your feelings to become too deeply involved. That's only common sense, child, not psychiatry or magic."

"I'm sure," repeated Pat. "I'm not puzzled or troubled any more. And thanks, Dr. Carl. You run along to bed and I'll do likewise."

He rose, accompanying her to the door, his face unusually grave.

"Patricia," he said, "I want you to think over what I've said. Be sure, be doubly sure, before you expose yourself to the possibility of suffering. Remember that, won't you?"

"I'll try to. Don't fret yourself about it, Dr. Carl; I'm a hard-boiled young modern, and it takes a diamond to even scratch me."

"I hope so," he said soberly. "Run along. I'll watch until you're inside."

Pat darted across the strip of grass, turned at her door to blow a goodnight kiss to the Doctor, and slipped in. She tiptoed quietly to her room, slipped off her dress, and surveyed her long, slim legs in the mirror.

"Why shouldn't he say they were beautiful?" she queried of the image. "I can't see any reason to get excited over a simple compliment like that."

She made a face over her shoulder at the green Buddha above the fireplace.

"And as for you, fat boy," she murmured, "I expect to see you wink at me tonight. And every night hereafter!"

She prepared herself for slumber, slipped into the great bed. She had hardly closed her lids before the image of a leering face with terrible bloody eyes flamed out of memory and set her trembling and shuddering.

CHAPTER SEVEN
The Red Eyes Return

"I suppose I really ought to meet your friends, Patricia," said Mrs. Lane, peering out of the window, "but they all seem to call when I'm not at home."

"I'll have some of them call in February," said Pat. "You're not out as often in February."

"Why do you say I'm not out as often in February?" demanded her mother. "I don't see what earthly difference the month makes."

"There are fewer days in February," retorted Pat airily.

"Facetious brat!"

"So I've been told. You needn't worry, though, mother; I'm sober, steady, and reliable, and if I weren't, Dr. Carl would see to it that my associates were."

"Yes; Carl is a gem," observed her mother. "By the way, who's this Nicholas you're so enthusiastic about?"

"He's a boy I met."

"What's he like?"

"Well, he speaks English and wears a hat."

"Imp! Is he nice?"

"That means is his family acceptable, doesn't it? He hasn't any family."

Mrs. Lane shrugged her attractive shoulders. "You're a self-reliant sort, Patricia, and cool as iced lettuce, like your father. I don't doubt that you can manage your own affairs, and here comes Claude with the car." She gave the girl a hasty kiss. "Goodbye, and have a good time, as I'm sure I shan't with Bret Cutter in the game."

Pat watched her mother's trim, amazingly youthful figure as she entered the car. More like a companion than a parent, she mused; she liked the independence her mother's attitude permitted her.

"Better than being watched like a prize-winning puppy," she thought. "Maybe Dr. Carl as a father would have a detriment or two along with the advantages. He's a dear, and I'm mad about him, but he does lean to the nineteenth century as far as parental duties are concerned."

She saw Nick's car draw to the curb; as he emerged she waved from the window and skipped into the hall. She caught up her wrap and bounded out to meet him just ascending the steps.

"Let's go!" she greeted him. She cast an apprehensive glance at his features, but there was nothing disturbing about him. He gave her a diffident smile, the shy, gentle smile that had taken her in that first moment of meeting. This was certainly no one but her own Nick, with no trace of the unsettling personality of their last encounter.

He helped her into the car, seating himself at her side. He leaned over her, kissing her very tenderly; suddenly she was clinging to him, her face against the thrilling warmth of his cheek.

"Nick," she murmured, "Nick. You're just safely you, aren't you? I've been imagining things that I knew couldn't be so!"

He slipped his arm caressingly about her, and the pressure of it was like the security of encircling battlements. The world was outside the circle of his arms; she was within, safe, inviolable. It was some moments before she stirred, lifting her pert face with tear-bright eyes from the obscurity of his shoulder.

"So!" she exclaimed, patting the black glow of her hair into composure. "I feel better, Nick, and I hope you didn't mind."

"Mind!" he ejaculated. "If you mean that as a joke, honey, it's far too subtle for me."

"Well, I didn't think you'd mind," said Pat demurely, settling herself beside him. "Let's be moving, then; Dr. Carl is nearly popping his eyes out in the window there."

The car hummed into motion; she waved a derisive arm at the Doctor's window by way of indicating her knowledge of his surveillance. *Ought to teach him a lesson sometime*, she thought. *One of these fine evenings I'll give him a real shock.*

"Where'll we go?" queried Nick, veering skillfully into the swift traffic of Sheridan Road.

"Anywhere!" she said blithely. "Who cares as long as we go together?"

"Dancing?"

"Why not? Know a good place?"

"No." He frowned in thought. "I haven't indulged much."

"The Picador?" she suggested. "The music's good, and it's not too expensive. But it's almost across town, and besides, Saturday nights we'd be sure to run into some of the crowd."

"What of it?"

"I want to dance with you, Nick—all evening. I want to be without distractions."

"Pat, dear! I could kiss you for that."

"You will," she murmured softly.

They moved aimlessly south with the traffic, pausing momentarily at the light-controlled intersections, then whirring again to rapid motion. The girl leaned against his arm silently, contentedly; block after block dropped behind.

"Why so pensive, honey?" he asked after an interval. "I've never known you so quiet before."

"I'm enjoying my happiness, Nick."

"Aren't you usually happy?"

"Of course, only these last two or three days, ever since our last date, I've been making myself miserable. I've been telling myself foolish things, impossible things, and it's only now that I've thrown off the blues. I'm happy, dear!"

"I'm glad you are," he said. His voice was strangely husky, and he stared fixedly at the street rushing toward them. "I'm glad you are," he repeated, a curious tensity in his tones.

"So'm I."

"I'll never do anything to make you unhappy, Pat—never. Not—if I can help it."

"You can help it, Nick. You're the one making me happy; please keep doing it."

"I—hope to," There was a queer catch in his voice. It was almost as if he feared something.

"Selah!" said Pat conclusively. She was thinking. "Wrong of me to refer to that accident. After all it was harmless—just a natural burst of passion. Might happen to anyone."

"Where'll we go?" asked Nick as they swung into the tree-shadowed road of Lincoln Park. "We haven't decided that."

"Anywhere," said the girl dreamily. "Just drive; we'll find a place."

"You must know lots of them."

"We'll find a new place; we'll discover it for ourselves. It'll mean more, doing that, than if we just go to one of the old places where I've been with every boy that ever dated me. You don't want me dancing with a crowd of memories, do you?"

"I shouldn't mind as long as they stayed merely memories."

"Well, I should! This evening's to be ours—exclusively ours."

"As if it could ever be otherwise!"

"Indeed?" said Pat. "And how do you know what memories might choose to carry along? Are you capable of inspecting my mental baggage?"

"We'll check it at the door. You're traveling light tonight, aren't you?"

"Pest!" she said, giving his cheek an impudent vicious pinch. "Nice, pleasurable pest!"

He made no answer. The car was idling rather slowly along Michigan Boulevard; half a block ahead glowed the green of a traffic light. Faster traffic flowed around them, passing them like water eddying about a slow floating branch.

Suddenly the car lurched forward. The amber flame of the warning light had flared out; they flashed across the intersection a split second before the metallic click of the red light, and a scant few feet before the converging lines of traffic from the side street swept in with protesting horns.

"Nick!" the girl gasped. "You'll rate yourself a traffic ticket! Why'd you cut the light like that?"

"To lose your guardian angel," he muttered in tones so low she barely understood his words.

Pat glanced back; the lights of a dozen cars showed beyond the barrier of the red signal.

"Do you mean one of those cars was following us? What on earth makes you think that, and why should it, anyway?"

The other made no answer; he swerved the car abruptly off the avenue, into one of the nondescript side streets. He drove swiftly to the corner, turned south again, and turned again on some street Pat failed to identify—South Superior or Grand, she thought. They were scarcely a block from the magnificence of Michigan Avenue and its skyscrapers, its brilliant lights, and its teeming night traffic, yet here they moved down a deserted dark thoroughfare, a street lined with ramshackle wooden houses intermingled with mean little shops.

"Nick!" Pat exclaimed. "Where are we going?"

The low voice sounded. "Dancing," he said.

He brought the car to the curb; in the silence as the motor died, the faint strains of a mechanical piano sounded. He opened the car door, stepped around to the sidewalk.

"We're here," he said.

Something metallic in his tone drew Pat's eyes to his eyes. The eyes that returned her stare were the bloody orbs of the demon of last Wednesday night!

CHAPTER EIGHT
Gateway to Evil

Pat stared curiously at the apparition but made no move to alight from the vehicle. She was conscious of no fear, only a sense of wonder and perplexity. After all, this was merely Nick, her own harmless, adoring Nick, in some sort of mysterious masquerade, and she felt full confidence in her ability to handle him under any circumstances.

"Where's here?" she said, remaining motionless in her place.

"A place to dance," came the toneless reply. Pat eyed him; a street car rumbled past, and the brief glow from its lighted windows swept over his face. Suddenly the visage was that of Nick; the crimson glare of the eyes was imperceptible, and the features were the well-known appurtenances of Nicholas Devine, but queerly tensed and strained.

A trick of the light, she thought, as the street car lumbered away, and again a faint gleam of crimson appeared. She gazed curiously at the youth, who stood impassively returning her survey as he held the door of the car. But the face was the face of Nick, she perceived, probably in one of his grim moods.

She transferred her glance to the building opposite which they had stopped. The strains of the mechanical piano had ceased; blank, shaded windows faced them, around whose edges glowed a subdued light from within. A drab, battered, paintless shack, she thought, dismal and unpleasant; while she gazed, the sound of the discordant music recommenced, adding, it seemed, the last unprepossessing item.

"It doesn't look very attractive, Nick," she observed dubiously.

"I find it so, however."

"Then you've been here?"

"Yes."

"But I thought you said you didn't know any place to go."

"This one hadn't occurred to me—then."

"Well," she said crisply, "I could have done as well as this with my eyes closed. It doesn't appeal to me at all, Nick."

"Nevertheless, here's where we'll go. You're apt to find it—interesting."

"Look here, Nicholas Devine!" Pat snapped. "What makes you think you can bully me? No one has ever succeeded yet!"

"I said you'd find it interesting," His voice was unchanged; she stared at him in complete bafflement.

"Oh, Nick!" she exclaimed in suddenly softer tones. "What difference does it make? Didn't I say anywhere would do, so long as we went together?" She smiled at him. "This will do if you wish, though really, honey, I'd prefer not."

"I do wish it," the other said.

"All right honey," said Pat the faintest trace of reluctance in her voice as she slipped from the car. "I stick to my bargains."

She winced at the intensity of his grip as he took her arm to assist her. His fingers were like taunt wires biting into her flesh.

"Nick," she cried, "you're hurting me! You're bruising my arm!" He released her; she rubbed the spot ruefully, then followed him to the door of the mysterious establishment. The unharmonious jangle of the piano dinned abruptly louder as he swung the door open. Pat entered and glanced around her at the room revealed.

Dull, smoky, dismal—not the least exciting or interesting as yet, she thought. A short bar paralleled one wall, behind which lounged a little, thin, nondescript individual with a small mustache. Half a dozen tables filled the remainder of the room; four or five occupied by the clientele of the place, as unsavory a group as the girl could recall having encountered on the hither side of the motion picture screen. Two women tittered as Nick entered; then with one accord, the eyes of the entire group fixed on Pat, where she stood drawing her wrap more closely about her, standing uncomfortably behind her escort. And the piano tinkled its discords in the far corner.

"Same place," said Nick shortly to the bartender, ignoring the glances of the others. Pat followed him across the room to a door, into a hall, thence into a smaller room furnished merely with a table and four chairs. The nondescript man stood waiting in the doorway as Nick took her wrap and seated her in one of the chairs.

"Quart," he said laconically, and the bartender disappeared.

Pat stared intently, studiously, into the face of her companion. Nick's face, certainly; here in full light there was no trace of the red-eyed horror she had fancied out there in the semi-darkness of the street. Or was there? Now—when he turned, when the light struck his eyes at an angle, was that a glint of crimson? Still, the features were Nick's, only a certain grim intensity foreign to him lurked about the set of his mouth, the narrowed eye-lids.

"Well!" she said. "So this is Paris! What are you trying to do— teach me capital L—life? And where do we dance?"

"In here."

"And what kind of quart was that you ordered? You know how little I drink, and I'm darned particular about even that little."

"You'll like this."

"I doubt it."

"I said you'll like it," he reiterated in flat tones.

"I heard you say it." She regarded him with a puzzled frown. "Nick," she said suddenly, "I've decided I like you better in your gentle pose; this masterful attitude isn't becoming, and you can for-get what I said about wishing you'd display it oftener."

"You'll like that, too."

"Again I doubt it. Nick, dear, don't spoil another evening like that last one!"

"This one won't be like the last one!"

"But honey—" she paused at the entrance of the bartender bearing a tray, an opened bottle of ginger ale, two glasses of ice, and a flask of oily amber liquid. He deposited the assortment on the red-checked table cloth.

"Two dollars," he said, pocketed the money and silently retired.

"Nicholas," said the girl tartly, "there's enough of that poison for a regiment."

"I don't think so."

"Well, I won't drink it and I won't let you drink it! So now what?"

"I think you'll do both."

"I don't!" she snapped. "And I don't like this Nick—the place, or the liquor, or your attitude, or anything. We're going to leave!"

Instead of answering, he pulled the cork from the bottle, pouring a quantity of the amber fluid into each of the tumblers. To one he added an equal quantity of ginger ale, and set it deliberately squarely in front of Pat. She frowned at it distastefully, and shook her head.

"No," she said. "Not I. I'm leaving."

She made no move, however; her eyes met those of her companion, gazing at her with a cold intentness in their curious amber depths. And again—was that a flash of red? Impulsively she reached out her hand, touched his.

"Oh, Nick!" she said in soft, almost pleading tones. "Please, honey—I don't understand you. Don't you know I love you, Nick? You can hear me say it: I love you. Don't you believe that?"

He continued his cold, intense stare; the grim set of his mouth was as unrelaxing as marble. Pat felt a shiver of apprehension run through her, and an almost hypnotic desire to yield herself to the demands of the inexplicable eyes. She tore her glance away, looking down at the red checks of the table cloth.

"Nick, dear," she said, "I can't understand this. Will you tell me what you—will you tell me why we're here?"

"It is out of your grasp."

"But—I know it has something to do with Wednesday night, something to do with that reluctance of yours, the thing you said you didn't understand. Hasn't it?"

"Do you think so?"

"Yes," she said. "I do! And Nick, honey—didn't I tell you I could forgive you anything? I don't care what's happened in the past; all I care for is now, now and the future. Don't you understand me? I've told you I loved you, honey! Don't you love me?"

"Yes," said the other, staring at her with no change in the fixity of his gaze.

"Then how can you—act like this to me?"

"This is my conception of love."

"I don't understand!" the girl said helplessly. "I'm completely puzzled—it's all topsy-turvy."

"Yes," he said in impassive agreement.

"But what is this, Nick? Please, please—what is this? Are you mad?" She had almost added. "Like your father."

"No," he said, still in those cold tones. "This is an experiment."

"An experiment!"

"Yes. An experiment in evil."

"I don't understand," she repeated.

"I said you wouldn't."

"Do you mean," she asked, struck by a sudden thought, "that discussion of ours about pure horror? What you said that night last week?"

"That!" His voice was icy and contemptuous. "That was the drivel of a weakling. No; I mean evil, not horror—the living evil that can be so beautiful that one walks deliberately, with open eyes, into Hell only to prevent its loss. That is the experiment."

"Oh," said Pat, her own voice suddenly cool. "Is that what you wish to do—experiment on me?"

"Yes."

"And what am I supposed to do?"

"First you are to drink with me."

"I see," she said slowly. "I see—dimly. I am a subject, a reagent, a guinea pig, to provide you material for your writing. You propose to use me in this experiment of yours—this experiment in evil. All right!" She picked up the tumbler; impulsively she drained it. The liquor, diluted as it was, was raw and strong enough to bring tears smarting to her eyes. Or was it the liquor?

"All right!" she cried. "I'll drink it all—the whole bottle!" She seized the flask, filling her tumbler to the brim, while her companion watched her with impassive gaze. "You'll have your experiment! And then, Nicholas Devine, we're through! Do you hear me? Through!"

She caught up the tumbler, raised it to her lips, and drained the searing liquid until she could see her companion's cold eyes regarding her through the glass of its bottom.

CHAPTER NINE
Descent into Avernus

Pat slammed the empty tumbler down on the checked table cloth and buried her face in her hands, choking and gasping from the effects of the fiery liquor. Her throat burned, her mouth was parched by the acrid taste, and a conflagration seemed to be raging somewhere within her. Then she steadied, raised her eyes, and stared straight into the strange eyes of Nicholas Devine.

"Well?" she said fiercely. "Is that enough?"

He was watching her coldly as an image or a painting; the intensity of his gaze was more cat-like than human. She moved her head aside; his eyes, without apparent shift, were still on hers, like the eyes of a pictured face. A resurgence of anger shook her at his immobility; his aloofness seemed to imply that nothing she could do would disturb him.

"Wasn't it enough?" she screamed. "Wasn't it? Then look!"

She seized the bottle, poured another stream of the oily liquid into her glass, and raised it to her lips. Again the burning fluid excoriated her tongue and throat, and then suddenly, the tumbler was struck from her hand, spilling the rest of its contents on the table.

"That is enough," said the icy voice of her companion.

"Oh, it is? We'll see!" She snatched at the bottle, still more than half full. The thin hand of Nicholas Devine wrenched it violently away.

"Give me that!" she cried. "You wanted what you're getting!" The warmth within her had reached the surface now: she felt flushed, excited, reckless, and desperately angry.

The other set the bottle deliberately on the floor; he rose, circled the table, and stood glaring down at her with that same inexplicable expression. Suddenly he raised his hand; twisting her black hair in his fist, he dealt her a stinging blow across the lips half-opened to scream, then flung her away so violently that she nearly sprawled from her chair.

The scream died in her throat; dazed by the blow, she dropped her head to the table, while sobs of pain and fear shook her. Coherent thought had departed, and she knew only that her lips stung, that her clear, active little mind was caught in a mesh of befuddlement. She couldn't think; she could only sob in the haze of dizziness that encompassed her. After a long interval, she raised her head, opened her eyes upon a swaying, unsteady world, and faced her companion, who had silently resumed his seat.

"Nicholas Devine," she said slowly, speaking as if each word were an effort, "I hate you!"

"Ah!" he said and was again silent.

She forced her eyes to focus on his face, while his features danced vaguely as if smoke flowed between the two of them. It was as if there was smoke in her mind as well; she made a great effort to rise above the clouds that bemused her thoughts.

"Take me home," she said. "Nicholas, I want to go home."

"Why should I?" he asked impassively. "The experiment is hardly begun."

"Experiment?" she echoed dully. "Oh, yes—experiment. I'm an experiment."

"An experiment in evil," he said.

"Yes—in evil. And I hate you! That's evil enough, isn't it?"

He reached down, lifted the bottle to the table, and methodically poured himself a drink of the liquor. He raised it, watching the oily swirls in the light, then tipped the fluid to his lips while the girl gazed at him with a sullen set to her own lips. A tiny crimson spot had appeared in the corner of her mouth; at its sting, she raised her hand and brushed it away. She stared as if in unbelief at the small red smear it left on her fingers.

"Nicholas," she said pleadingly, "won't you take me home? Please, Nicholas, I want to leave here."

"Do you hate me?" he asked, a queer twisting smile appearing on his lips.

"If you'll take me home I won't," said Pat, snatching through the rising clouds of dizziness at a straw of logic. "You're going to take me home, aren't you?"

"Let me hear you say you hate me!" he demanded, rising again. The girl cringed away with a little whimper as he approached. "You hate me don't you?"

He twisted his hand again in her ebony hair, drawing her face back so that he stared down at it.

"There's blood on your lips," he said as if gloating. "Blood on your lips!"

He clutched her hair more tightly; abruptly he bent over her, pressing his mouth to hers. Her bruised lips burned with pain at the fierce pressure of his; she felt a sharp anguish at the impingement of his teeth. Yet the cloudy pall of dizziness about her was unbroken; she was too frightened and bewildered for resistance.

"Blood on your lips!" he repeated exultingly. "Now is the beauty of evil!"

"Nicholas," she said wearily, clinging desperately to a remnant of logic, "what do you want of me? Tell me what you want and then let me go home."

"I want to show you the face of evil," he said. "I want you to know the glory of evil, the loveliness of supreme evil!"

He dragged his chair around the table, placing it beside her.

Seated, he drew her into his arms, where she lay passive, too limp and befuddled to resist. With a sudden movement, he turned her so that her back rested across his knees, her face gazing up into his. He stared intently down at her, and the light, shining at an angle into his eyes, suddenly struck out the red glow that lingered in them.

"I want you to know the power of evil," he murmured. "The irresistible, incomprehensible fascination of it, and the unspeakable pleasures of indulgence in it."

Pat scarcely heard him; she was struggling now in vain against the overwhelming fumes of the alcohol she had consumed. The room was wavering around her, and behind her despair and terror, a curious elation was thrusting itself into her consciousness.

"Evil," she echoed vaguely.

"Blood on your lips!" he muttered, peering down at her. "Taste the unutterable pleasure of kisses on bloody lips; drain the sweet anguish of pain, the fierce delight of suffering!"

He bent down; again his lips pressed upon hers, but this time she felt herself responding. Some still sane portion of her brain rebelled, but the intoxication of sense and alcohol was dominant. Suddenly she was clinging to him, returning his kisses, glorying in the pain of her lacerated lips. A red mist suffused her; she had no consciousness of anything save the exquisite pain of the kiss, which somehow contrived to transform itself into an ecstasy of delight. She lay gasping as the other withdrew his lips.

"You see!" he gloated. "You understand! Evil is open to us, and all the unutterable pleasures of the damned, who cry out in transports of joy at the bite of the flames of Hell. Do you see?"

The girl made no answer, sobbing in a chaotic mingling of pain and excruciating pleasure. She was incapable of speech or connected thought; the alcohol beat against her brain with a persistence that defied resistance. After a moment, she stirred, struggling erect to a sitting posture.

"Evil!" she said dizzily. "Evil and good—what's difference? All in a lifetime!"

She felt a surge of tipsy elation, and then the muffled music of the mechanical piano, drifting through the closed door, penetrated her befuddled consciousness.

"I want to dance!" she cried. "I'm drunk and I want to dance! Am I drunk?" she appealed to her companion.

"Yes," he said.

"I am not! I just want to dance; only it's hot in here. Dance with me, Nicholas—show me an evil dance! I want to dance with the Devil, and I will! You're the Devil, name and all! I want to dance with Old Nick himself!"

She rose unsteadily from her chair; instantly the room reeled crazily about her and she fell sprawling. She felt the grasp of arms beneath her shoulders, raising her erect; she leaned against the wall and heard herself laughing wildly.

"Funny room!" she said. "Evil room—on pivots!"

"You're still to learn," came the toneless voice of Nicholas Devine. "Do you want to see the face of evil?"

"Sure!" she said. "Got a good memory for faces!"

She realized that he was fumbling with the catch of her dress on her left shoulder; again some remnant, some vestige of sanity deep in her brain warned her.

"Mustn't," she said vaguely.

Then suddenly the catch was open; the dress dropped away around her, crumpling to a shapeless blob of cloth about her diminutive feet. She covered her face with her hands, fighting to hold that last, vanishing vestige of sobriety, while she stood swaying drunkenly against the wall.

Then Nicholas Devine's arms were about her again; she felt the sharp sting of his kisses on her throat. He swung her about, bent her backwards across the low table; she was conscious of a bewildered sensation of helplessness and of little else.

"Now the supreme glory of evil!' he was muttering in her ear. She felt his hands on her bare shoulders as he pressed her backward.

Then, abruptly, he paused, releasing her. She sat dizzily erect, following the direction of his gaze. In the half open door stood the nondescript bartender leering in at them.

CHAPTER TEN
Rescue from Abaddon

Pat slid dizzily from her perch on the table and sank heavily to a chair. The interruption of the mustached keeper of this den of contradictions struck her as extremely humorous; she giggled hysterically as her wavering gaze perceived the consternation in his sharp little face. Some forlorn shred of modesty asserted itself, and she dragged a corner of the red-checked table cloth across her knees.

"Get out!" said Nicholas Devine in that voice of rasping metal. "Get out!" he repeated in unchanging tones.

The other made no move to leave. "Yeah?" he said. "Listen, Bud—this place is respectable, see? You want to pull something like this, you go upstairs, see? And pay for your room."

"Get out!" There was no variation in the voice.

"*You* get out! The both of you, see?"

Nicholas Devine stepped slowly toward him; his back, as he advanced upon the bartender, was toward Pat, yet through the haze of intoxication, she had an impression of evil red eyes in a chill, impassive face. "Get out!"

The other had no stomach for such an adversary. He backed out of the door, closing it as he vanished. His voice floated in from the hall.

"I'm telling you!" he called. "Clear out!"

Nicholas Devine turned back toward the girl. He surveyed her sitting in her chair; she had dropped her chin to her hand to steady the whirling of her head.

"We'll go," he said. "Come on."

"I just want to sit here," she said. "Just let me sit here. I'm tired."

"Come on," he repeated.

"Why?" she muttered petulantly. "I'm tired."

"I want no interruptions. We'll go elsewhere."

"Must dress!" she murmured dazedly. "Can't go on street without dress."

Nicholas Devine swept her frock from its place in the corner, gathered her wrap from the chair, and flung them over his arm. He grasped her wrist, tugging her to an unsteady standing position. "Come on," he said.

"Dress!"

He snatched the red checked table cloth from its place, precipitating bottles, ash-tray, and glasses into an indiscriminate pile, and threw the stained and odorous fabric across her shoulders. She gathered it about her like a toga; it hung at most points barely below her waist, but it satisfied the urge of her muddled mind for a covering of some sort.

"We'll go through the rear," her companion said. "Into the alley. I want no trouble with that rat in the bar—yet!"

He still held Pat's wrist; she stumbled after him as he dragged her into the darkness of the hall. They moved through it blindly to a door at the far end; Nicholas swung it open upon a dim corridor flanked by buildings on either side, with a strip of star-sprinkled sky above.

Pat's legs were somehow incapable of their usual lithe grace; she failed to negotiate the single step, and crashed heavily to the concrete paving. The shock and the cooler air of the open steadied her momentarily; she felt no pain from her bruised knees, but a temporary rift in the fog that bound her mind. She gathered the red-checked cloth more closely about her shoulders as her companion, still clutching her wrist, jerked her violently to her feet.

They moved into the gulch of the alley, and here she found difficulty in following. Her tiny high-heeled pumps slipped at every step on the uneven cobbles of the paving, and the unsteady footing made her lurch and stumble until the dusty stretch of the alley was a writhing panorama of shadows and lighted windows and stars. Nicholas Devine turned an impatient glare on her, and here in the semi-darkness, his face was again the face of the red-eyed demon. She dragged him to a halt, laughing strangely.

"There it is!" she cried, pointing at him with her free hand. He turned again, staring at her with grim features.

"What?"

"There! Your face—the face of evil!" Again she laughed hysterically.

The other stepped to her side; the disturbing eyes were inches from her own. He raised his hand as she laughed, slapped her sharply, so that her head reeled. He seized her shoulders, shaking her until the checkered cloth billowed like a flag in a wind.

"Now come!" he muttered.

But the girl, laughing no longer, leaned pale and weak against a low board fence. Her limbs seemed paralyzed, and movement was quite impossible. She was conscious of neither the blow nor the shaking, but only of a devastating nausea and an all-encompassing weakening. She bent over the fence; she was violently ill.

Then the nausea had vanished, and weariness, a strange lassitude, was all that remained. Nicholas Devine stood over her; suddenly he pressed her body to him in a convulsive embrace, so that her head dropped back, and his face loomed above her, obliterating the stars.

"Ah!" he said. He seemed about to kiss her when a sound— voices—filtered out of somewhere in the maze of dark courts and littered yards along the alley. He released her, seized her wrist, and once more she was stumbling wretchedly behind him over the uneven surface of the cobblestones.

A numbness had come over her; consciousness burned very low as she wavered doggedly along through the darkness. She perceived dimly that they were approaching the end of the alley; the brighter glow of the street loomed before them, and a passing motor car cut momentary parallel shafts of luminescence across the opening.

Nicholas Devine slowed his pace, still clutching her wrist in a cold grip; he paused, moving cautiously toward the corner of the building. He peered around the edge of the structure, surveying the now deserted street, while Pat stood dully behind him, incapable alike of thought or voluntary movement, clutching desperately at the dirty cloth that hung about her shoulders.

Her companion finished his survey; apparently satisfied that progress was safe, he dragged her after him, turning toward the corner beyond which his car was parked. The girl staggered behind him with diminishing vigor; consciousness was very nearly at the point of disappearance, and her steps were wavering unsteadily, and doggedly slow. She dragged heavily on his arm; he gave a gesture of impatience at her weakness.

"Come on!" he growled. "We're just going to the corner." His voice rose slightly in pitch, still sounding harsh as rasping metals. "There still remains the ultimate evil!" he said. "There is still a depth of beauty unplumbed, a pain whose exquisite pleasure is yet to find!"

They approached the corner; abruptly Nicholas Devine drew back as two figures came unexpectedly into view from beyond it. He turned back towards the alleyway, dragging the girl in a dizzy circle. He took a few rapid steps.

But Pat was through, exhausted. At his first step she stumbled and sprawled, dragging prone behind him. He released her hand and turned defiantly to face the approaching men, while the girl lying on the pavement struggled to a sitting posture with her back against the wall. She turned dull, indifferent eyes on the scene, then was roused to a somewhat higher pitch of interest by the sound of a familiar voice.

"There he is! I told you it was his car."

Dr. Horker! She struggled for clarity of thought; she realized dimly that she ought to feel relief, happiness—but all she could summon was a faint quickening of interest, or rather, a diminution of the lassitude that held her. She drew the rag of a table cloth about her and huddled against the wall, watching. The Doctor and some strange man, burly and massive in the darkness, dashed upon them, while Nicholas Devine waited, his red-orbed face a demoniac picture of cold contempt. Then the Doctor glanced at her huddled, bedraggled figure; she saw his face aghast, incredulous, as he perceived the condition of her clothing.

"Pat! My God, girl! What's happened? Where've you been?"

She found a hidden reserve somewhere within her. Her voice rose, shrill and hysterical.

"We've been in Hell!" she said. "You came to take me back didn't you? Orpheus and Eurydice!" She laughed, "Dr. Orpheus Horker!'

The Doctor flashed her another incredulous glance and a grim and very terrible expression flamed in his face. He turned toward Nicholas Devine, his hands clenching, his mouth twisting without utterance, with no sound save a half-audible snarl. Then he spoke, a low grating phrase flung at his thick-set companion.

"Bring the car," was all he said. The man lumbered away toward the corner, and he turned again toward Nicholas Devine who faced him impassively. Suddenly his fist shot out; he struck the youth or demon squarely between the red eyes, reeling him back against the building. Then the Doctor turned, bending over Pat; she felt the pressure of his arms beneath knees and shoulders. He was carrying her toward a car that drew up at the curb; he was placing her gently in the back seat. Then, without a glance at the figure still leaning against the building, he swept from the sidewalk the dark mass that was Pat's dress and her wrap, and re-entered the car beside her.

"Shall I turn him in?" asked the man in the front seat.

"We can't afford the publicity," said the Doctor, adding grimly. "I'll settle with him later."

Pat's head lurched as the car started; she was losing consciousness, and realized it vaguely, but she retained one impression as the vehicle swung into motion. She perceived that the face of the lone figure leaning against the building, a face staring at her with horror and unbelief, was no longer the visage of the demon of the evening, but that of her own Nick.

CHAPTER ELEVEN
Wreckage

Pat opened her eyes reluctantly, with the impression that something unpleasant awaited her return to full consciousness. Something, as yet she could not recall just what, had happened to her; she was not even sure where she was awakening.

However, her eyes surveyed her own familiar room; there opposite the bed grinned the jade Buddha on his stand on the mantel—the one that Nick had—Nick! A mass of troubled, terrible recollections thrust themselves suddenly into consciousness. She visioned a medley of disturbing pictures, as yet disconnected, unassorted, but waiting only the return of complete wakefulness. And she realized abruptly that her head ached miserably, that her mouth was parched, that twinges of pain were making themselves evident in various portions of her anatomy. She turned her head and caught a glimpse of a figure at the bedside; her startled glance revealed Dr. Horker, sitting quietly watching her.

"Hello, Doctor," she said, wincing as her smile brought a sharp pain from her lips. "Or should I say. Good morning, Judge?"

"Pat!" he rumbled, his growling tones oddly gentle. "Little Pat! How do you feel, child?"

"Fair," she said. "Just fair. Dr. Carl, what happened to me last night? I can't seem to remember— Oh!"

A flash of recollection pierced the obscure muddle. She remembered now—not all of the events of that ghastly evening, but enough. Too much!

"Oh!" she murmured faintly. "Oh, Dr. Carl!"

"Yes," he nodded. " 'Oh!' —and would you mind very much telling me what that 'Oh' of yours implies?"

"Why—" She paused shuddering, as one by one the events of that sequence of horrors reassembled themselves. "Yes, I'd mind very much," she continued. "It was nothing—" She turned to him abruptly. "Oh, it was, though, Dr. Carl! It was horrible, unspeakable, incomprehensible!—But I can't talk about it! I can't!"

"Perhaps you're right," said the Doctor mildly. "Don't you really want to discuss it?"

"I do want to," admitted the girl after a moment's reflection. "I want to—but I can't. I'm afraid to think of all of it."

"But what in Heaven's name did you do?"

"We just started out to go dancing," she said hesitatingly. "Then, on the way to town, Nick—changed. He said someone was following us."

"Someone was," said Horker. "I was, with Mueller. That Nick of yours has the Devil's own cleverness!"

"Yes," the girl echoed soberly. "The Devil's own! Who's Mueller, Dr. Carl?"

"He's a plain-clothes man, friend of mine. I treated him once. What do you mean by changed?"

"His eyes," she said. "And his mouth. His eyes got reddish and terrible, and his mouth got straight and grim. And his voice turned sort of—harsh."

"Ever happen before, that you know of?"

"Once. When—" She paused.

"Yes. Last Wednesday night, when you came over to ask those questions about pure science. What happened then?"

"We went to a place to dance."

"And that's the reason, I suppose," rumbled the Doctor sardonically, "that I found you wandering about the streets in a table cloth, step-ins, and a pair of hose! That's why I found you on the verge of passing out from rotten liquor, and looking like the loser of a battle with an airplane propeller! What happened to your face?"

"My face? What's wrong with it?"

The Doctor rose from his chair and seized the hand-mirror from her dressing table.

"Look at it!" he commanded, passing her the glass.

Pat gazed incredulously at the reflection the surface presented; a dark bruise colored her cheek, her lips were swollen and discolored, and her chin bore a jagged scratch. She stared at the injuries in horror.

"Your knees are skinned, too," said Horker. "Both of them." Pat slipped one pajamaed limb from the covers, drawing the pants-leg up for inspection. She gasped in startled fright at the great red stain on her knee.

"That's mercurochrome," said the Doctor. "I put it there."

"You put it there. How did I get home last night, Dr. Carl? How did I get to bed?"

"I'm responsible for that, too. I put you to bed." He leaned forward. "Listen, child—your mother knows nothing about this as yet. She wasn't home when I brought you in, and she's not awake yet this morning. We'll tell her you had an automobile accident; explain away those bruises— And now, how did you get them?"

"I fell, I guess. Two or three times."

"That bruise on your cheek isn't from falling."

The girl shuddered. Now in the calm light of morning, the events of last night seemed doubly horrible; she doubted her ability to believe them, so incredible did they seem. She was at a loss to explain even her own actions, and those of Nicholas Devine were simply beyond comprehension, a chapter from some dark and blasphemous book of ancient times—the Kabala or the Necronomicon.

"What happened, Pat?" queried the Doctor gently. "Tell me," he urged her.

"I—can't explain it," she said doubtfully. "He took me to that place, but drinking the liquor was my own fault. I did it out of spite because I saw he didn't—care for me. And then—" She fell silent.

"Yes? And then?"

"Well—he began to talk about the beauty of evil, the delights of evil, and his eyes glared at me, and—I don't understand it at all, Dr. Carl, but all of a sudden I was—yielding. Do you see?"

"I see," he said gently, soberly.

"Suddenly I seemed to comprehend what he meant—all that about the supreme pleasure of evil. And I was sort of—swept away. The dress—was his fault, but I—somehow I'd lost the power to resist. I guess I was drunk."

"And the bruises? And your cut lips?" queried the Doctor grimly.

"Yes," she said in a low voice. "He—struck me. After a while I didn't care. He could have—would have done other things, only we were interrupted, and had to leave. And that's all, Dr. Carl."

"Isn't that enough?" he groaned. "Pat, I should have killed the fiend there!"

"I'm glad you didn't."

"Do you mean to say you'd care?"

"I—don't know."

"Are you intimating that you still love him?"

"No," she said thoughtfully. "No, I don't love him, but—Dr. Carl, there's something inexplicable about this. There's something I don't understand, but I'm certain of one thing!"

"What's that?"

"That it wasn't Nick—not my Nick—who did those things to me last night. It wasn't, Dr. Carl!"

"Pat, you're being a fool!"

"I know it. But I'm sure of it, Dr. Carl. I know Nick; I loved him, and I know he couldn't have done—that. Not the same gentle Nick that I had to beg to kiss me!"

"Pat," said the Doctor gently, "I'm a psychiatrist; it's my business to know all the rottenness that can hide in a human being. My office is the scene of a parade of misfits, failures, potential criminals, lunatics, and mental incompetents. It's a nasty, bitter side I see of life, but I know that side—and I tell you this fellow is dangerous!"

"Do you understand this, Dr. Carl?"

He reached over, taking her hand in his great palm with its long, curious delicate fingers. "I have my theory, Pat. The man's a sadist, a lover of cruelty, and there's enough masochism in any woman to make him terribly dangerous. I want your promise."

"About what?"

"I want you to promise never to see him again."

The girl turned serious eyes on his face; he noted with a shock of sympathy that they were filled with tears.

"You warned me I'd get burned playing with fire," she said. "You did, didn't you?"

"I'm an old fool, honey. If I'd believed my own advice, I'd have seen that this never happened to you." He patted her hand. "Have I your promise?"

She averted her eyes. "Yes," she murmured. He winced as he perceived that the tears were on her cheeks.

"So," he said, rising, "the patient can get out of bed when she feels like it—and don't forget that little fib we've arranged for your mother's peace of mind."

She stared up at him, still clinging to his hand.

"Dr. Carl," she said, "are you sure—quite sure—you're right about him? Couldn't there be a chance that you're mistaken—that it's something your psychiatry has overlooked or never heard of?"

"Small chance, Pat dear."

"But a chance?"

"Well, neither I nor any reputable medic claims to know everything, and the human mind's a subtle sort of thing."

CHAPTER TWELVE
Letter from Lucifer

"I'm glad!" Pat told herself, "I'm glad it's over, and I'm glad I promised Dr. Carl—I guess I was mighty close to the brink of disaster that time." She examined the injuries on her face, carefully powdered to conceal the worst effects from her mother. The trick had worked, too; Mrs. Lane had delivered herself of an excited lecture on the dangers of the gasoline age, and then thanked Heaven it was no worse. Well, Pat reflected, she had good old Dr. Carl to thank for the success of the subterfuge; he had broken the news very skillfully, set the stage for her appearance, and calmed her mother's apprehensions of scars. And Pat, surveying her image in the glass above her dressing table, could see for herself the minor nature of the hurts.

"Scars—pooh!" she observed. "A bruised cheek, a split lip, a skinned chin. All I need is a black eye, and I guess I'd have had that in five minutes more, and perhaps a cauliflower ear into the bargain."

But her mood was anything but flippant; she was fighting off the time when her thoughts had of necessity to face the unpleasant, disturbing facts of the affair. She didn't want to think of the thing at all; wanted to laugh it off and forget it, yet she knew that for an impossibility. The very desire to forget she recognized as a coward's wish, and she resented the idea that she was cowardly.

"Forget the wise-cracks," she advised her image. "Face the thing and argue it out; that's the only way to be satisfied."

She rose with a little grimace of pain at the twinge from her bruised knees, and crossed to the chaise lounge beside the far window. She settled herself in it and resumed her cogitations. She was feeling more or less herself again; the headache of the morning had nearly vanished, and aside from the various aches and a listless fagged-out sensation, she approximated her normal self physically, that is; the shadow of that other catastrophe, the one she hesitated to face, was another matter.

"I'm lucky to get off this easily," she assured herself, "after going on a bust like that one, like a lumberjack with his pay in his pocket." She shook her head in mournful amazement. "And I'm Patricia Lane, the girl whom Billy dubbed 'Pat the Impeccable!' Impeccable! Wandering through alleys in step-ins and a table cloth—getting beaten up in a drunken brawl—passing out on rot-gut liquor—being carried home and put to bed! Not impeccable, incapable is the word! I belong to Dr. Carl's parade of incompetents."

She continued her rueful reflections. "Well, item one is, I don't love Nick anymore. I couldn't now!" she flung at the smiling green Buddha on the mantel. "That's over; I've promised."

Somehow there was not satisfaction in the memory of that promise. It was logical, of course; there wasn't anything else to do now, but still—

"That *wasn't* Nick!" she told herself. "That wasn't *my* Nick. I guess Dr. Carl is right, and he's a depressed whatever-it-was; but if he's crazy, so am I! He had me convinced last night; I understood what he meant, and I felt what he wanted me to feel. If he's crazy, I am too; a fine couple we are!"

She continued, "But it wasn't Nick! I saw his face when we drove off, and it had changed again, and that was Nick's face, not the other. And he was sorry; I could see he was sorry, and the other could never have regretted it—not ever! The other isn't—quite human, but Nick is."

She paused, considering the idea. "Of course," she resumed, "I might have imagined that change at the end. I was hazy and quivery, and it's the last thing I *do* remember; that must have been just before I passed out."

And then, replying to her own objection, "But I *didn't* imagine it! I saw it happen once before, that other night when— Well, what difference does it make, anyway? It's over, and I've given my promise."

But she was unable to dismiss the matter as easily as that. There was some uncanny, elusive element in it that fascinated her. Cruel, terrible, demoniac, he might have been; he had also been kind, lovable, and gentle. Yet Dr. Carl had told her that split personalities could contain no characteristics that were not present in the original, normal character. Was cruelty, then, a part of kindness? Was cruelty merely the lack of kindness, or, cynical thought, was kindness but the lack of cruelty? Which qualities were positive in the antagonistic phases of Nicholas Devine's individuality, and which negative? Was the gentle, lovable, but indubitably weaker character the split, and the demon of last evening his normal self? Or vice versa? Or were both of these fragmentary entities, portions of some greater personality as yet unapparent to her?

The whole matter was a mystery; she shrugged in helpless perplexity.

"I don't think Dr. Carl knows as much about it as he says," she mused. "I don't think psychiatry or any other science knows that much about the human soul. Dr. Carl doesn't even believe in a soul; how could he know anything about it, then?" She frowned in puzzlement and gave up the attempt to solve the mystery.

The hours she had spent in her room, at her mother's insistence, began to pall; she didn't feel particularly ill—it was more of a languor, a depressed, worn-out feeling. Her mother, of course, was out somewhere; she felt a desire for human companionship, and wondered if the Doctor might by some chance drop in. It seemed improbable; he had his regular Sunday afternoon routine of golf at the Club, and it took a real catastrophe to keep him away from that. She sighed, stretched her legs, rose from her position on the chase lounge, and wandered toward the kitchen where Magda was doubtless to be found.

It was in the dusk of the rear hall that the first sense of her loss came over her. Heretofore her renunciation of Nicholas Devine was a rational thing, a promise given but not felt; but now it was suddenly a poignant reality. Nick was gone, she realized; he was out of her world, irrevocably sundered from her. She paused at the top of the rear flight of stairs, considering the matter.

"He's gone! I won't see him ever again." The thought was appalling; she felt already a premonition of loneliness to come, of an emptiness in her world, a lack that nothing could replace.

"I shouldn't have promised Dr. Carl," she mused, knowing that even without that promise her course must still have been the same. "I shouldn't have, not until I'd talked to Nick—my own Nick."

And still, she reflected forlornly, what difference did it make? She had to give him up; she couldn't continue to see him not knowing at what instant that terrible caricature of him might appear to torment her. But he might have explained, she argued miserably, answering her own objection at once—he's said he couldn't explain, didn't understand. The thing was at an impasse.

She shook her shining black head despondently, and descended the dusky well of the stairs to the kitchen. Magda was there clattering among her pots and pans; Pat entered quietly and perched on the high stool by the long table. Old Magda, who had warmed her babyhood milk and measured out her formula, gave her a single glance and continued her work.

"Sorry about the accident, I was," she said without looking up.

"Thanks," responded the girl. "I'm all right again."

"You don't look it."

"I feel all right."

She watched the mysterious, alchemistic mixing of a pastry and thought of the vast array of them that had come from Magda's hands. As far back as she could remember she had perched on this stool observing the same mystic culinary rites.

Suddenly another memory rose out of the grave of forgetfulness and went gibbering across her world. She remembered the stories Magda used to tell her, frightening stories of witchcraft and the evil eye, tales out of an older region and a more credulous age.

"Magda," she asked, "did you ever see a devil?"

"Not I, but I've talked with them that had."

"Didn't you ever see one?"

"No." The woman slid a pan into the oven. "I saw a man once, when I was a tot, possessed by a devil."

"You did? How did he look?"

"He screamed terrible, and then he said queer things. Then he fell down and foam came out of his mouth."

"Like a fit?"

"The Priest, he said it was a devil. He came and prayed over him, and after a while he was real quiet, and then he was all right."

"Possessed by a devil," said Pat thoughtfully. "What happened to him?"

"Dunno."

"What queer things did he say?"

"Wicked things, the Priest said. I couldn't tell! I was a tot."

"Possessed by a devil!" Pat repeated musingly. She sat in thought on the high stool while Magda clattered busily about. The woman paused finally, turning her face to the girl.

"What you so quiet about, Miss Pat?"

"I was just thinking."

"You get your letter?"

"Letter? What letter? Today's Sunday."

"Special delivery. The girl, she put it in the hall."

"I didn't know anything about it. Who'd write me a special?"

She slipped off the high stool and proceeded to the front hall.

The letter was there, solitary on the salver that always held the mail. She picked it up, examining the envelope in sudden startled amazement and more than a trace of illogical exultation.

For the letter, postmarked that same morning, was addressed in the irregular script of Nicholas Devine!

CHAPTER THIRTEEN
Indecision

Pat turned the envelope dubiously in her hands, while a maze of chaotic thoughts assailed her. She felt almost a sensation of guilt as if she were in some manner violating the promise given to Dr. Horker; she felt a tinge of indignation that Nicholas Devine should dare communicate with her at all, and she felt too that queer exultation, an inexplicable pleasure, a feeling of secret triumph. She slipped the letter in the pocket of her robe and padded quietly up the stairs to her own room. Strangely, her loneliness had vanished. The great house, empty now save for herself and Magda in the distant kitchen, was no longer a place of solitude; the discovery of the letter, whatever its contents, had changed the deserted rooms into chambers teeming with her own excitements, trepidations, doubts, and hopes. Even hopes, she admitted to herself though hopes of what nature she was quite unable to say.

What *could* Nick write that had the power to change things? Apologies? Pleas? Promises? None of these could alter the naked, horrible facts of the predicament. Nevertheless, she was almost a-tremble with expectation as she skipped hastily into her own room, carefully closed the door, and settled herself by the west windows. She drew the letter from her pocket, and then, with a tightening of her throat, tore open the envelope, slipping out the several pages of scrawled paper. Avidly she began to read,

I don't know whether you'll ever see this and I'll not blame you, Pat dear, if you do return it unopened. There's nothing you can do that wouldn't be justified, nor can you think worse of me than I do of myself. And that's a statement so meaningless that even as I wrote it, I could anticipate its effect on you.

Pat-How am I going to convince you that I'm sincere? Will you believe me when I write that I love you? Can you believe that I love you tenderly, worshipfully—reverently?

You can't; I know you can't after that catastrophe of last night. But it's true, Pat, though the logic of a Spinoza might fail to convince you of it.

I don't know how to write you this. I don't know whether you want to hear what I could say, but I know that I must try to say it. Not apologies, Pat—I shouldn't dare approach you for so poor a reason as that—but a sort of explanation, if you want to hear it.

I can't write it to you, Pat; it's something I can only make you believe by telling you—something dark and rather terrible. But please, dear, believe that I mean you no harm, and that I plan no subterfuge, when I suggest that you see me. It will be, I think, for the last time.

Tonight, and tomorrow night, and as many nights to follow as I can, I'll sit on a bench in the park near the place where I kissed you that first time. There will be people passing there, and cars driving by; you need fear nothing from me. I choose the place to bridle my own actions, Pat; nothing can happen while we sit there in the view of the world.

To write you more than this is futile. If you come, I'll be there; if you don't I'll understand.

I love you.

The letter was signed merely "'Nick." She stared at the signature with feelings so confused that she forebore any attempt to analyze them.

"But I can't go," she mused soberly. "I've promised Dr. Carl. Or at least I can't go without telling him."

That last thought, she realized, was a concession. Heretofore she hadn't let herself consider the possibility of seeing Nicholas Devine again, and now suddenly she was weakening, arguing with herself about the ethics of seeing him. She shook her head decisively.

"Won't do, Patricia Lane!" she told herself. "Next thing, you'll be slipping away without a word to anybody, and coming home with two black eyes and a broken nose. Won't do at all!"

She dropped her eyes to the letter. "Explanations", she reflected. "I guess Dr. Carl would give up a hole-in-one to hear that explanation. And I'd give more than that." She shook her head regretfully. "Nothing to do about it, though. I promised."

The sun was slanting through the west windows; she sat watching the shadows lengthen in the room, and tried to turn her thoughts into more profitable channels. This was the first Sunday in many months that she had spent alone in the house; it was a custom for herself and her mother to spend the afternoon at the club. The evening too, as a rule; there was invariably bridge for Mrs. Lane, and Pat was always the center of a circle of the younger members. She wondered dreamily what the crowd thought of her non-appearance, reflecting that her mother had doubtless enlarged on Dr. Carl's story of an accident. Dr. Carl wouldn't say much, simply that he'd ordered her to stay at home. But sooner or later, Nick would hear the accident story; she wondered what he'd think of it.

She caught herself up sharply. "My ideas wander in circles," she thought petulantly. "No matter where I start, they curve around back to Nick. It won't do; I've got to stop it."

Nearly time for the evening meal, she mused, watching the sun as it dropped behind Dr. Horker's house. She didn't feel much like eating; there was still a remnant of the exhausted, dragged-out sensation, though the headache that had accompanied her awakening this morning had disappeared.

"I know what the morning after feels like, anyway," she reflected with a wry little smile. "Everybody ought to experience it once, I suppose. I wonder how Nick—"

She broke off abruptly, with a shrug of disgust. She slipped the letter back into its envelope, rose and deposited it in the drawer of the night-table. She glanced at the clock ticking on its shiny top.

"Six o'clock," she murmured. Nick would be sitting in the park in another two hours or so. She had a twinge of sympathy at the thought of his lone vigil; she could visualize the harried expression on his face when the hours passed without her arrival.

"Can't be helped," she thought. "He's no right to ask for anything of me after last night. He knows that; he said so in his letter."

She suppressed an impulse to re-read that letter, and trotted deliberately out of the room and down the stairs. Magda had set the table in the breakfast room; it was far cozier than the great dining room, especially without her mother's company. And the maid was away; the breakfast room simplified serving, as well.

She tried valorously to eat what Magda supplied, but the food failed to tempt her. It wasn't so much her physical condition, either; it was— She clenched her jaws firmly; was the memory of Nicholas Devine to haunt her forever?

"Pat Lane," she said in admonition, "you're a crack-brained fool! Just because a man kicks you all over the place is no reason to let him become an obsession."

She drank her coffee, feeling the sting of its heat on her injured lips. She left the table, tramped firmly to her room, and began defiantly to read. The effort was useless; half a dozen times she forced her attention to the page only to find herself staring vaguely into space a moment or two later. She closed the book finally with an irritable bang, and vented her restlessness in pacing back and forth.

"This house is unbearable!" she snapped. "I'm not going to stay shut up here like a jail-bird in solitary confinement. A walk in the open is what I need, and that's what I'll have."

She glanced at the clock; seven-thirty. She tore off her robe pettishly, flung out of her pajamas, and began to dress with angry determination. She refused to think of a lonely figure that might even now be sitting disconsolately on a bench in the nearby park.

She disguised her bruised cheek as best she could, dabbed a little powder on the abrasion on her chin, and tramped militantly down the stairs. She caught up her wrap, still lying where the Doctor had tossed it last night, and moved toward the door, opening it and nearly colliding with the massive figure of Dr. Horker!

"Well!" boomed the Doctor as she started back in surprise. "You're pretty spry for a patient. Think you were going out?"

"Yes," said Pat defiantly.

"Not tonight, child! I left the Club early to take a look at you."

"I am perfectly all right. I want to go for a walk."

"No walk. Doctor's orders."

"I'm of legal age!" she snapped. "I want to go for a walk. Do I go?"

"You do not." The Doctor placed his great form squarely in the doorway. "Not unless you can lick me, my girl, and I'm pretty tough. I put you to bed last night, and I can do as much tonight. Shall I?"

Pat backed into the hall. "You don't have to," she said sullenly. "I'm going there myself." She flung her wrap angrily to a chair and stalked up the stairs.

"Goodnight, spit-fire," he called after her. "I'll read down here until your mother comes home."

The girl stormed into her room in anger that she knew to be illogical.

"I won't be watched like a problem child!" she told herself viciously. "I know damn well what he thought—and I wasn't going to meet Nick! I wasn't at all!"

She calmed suddenly, sat on the edge of her bed and kicked off her pumps. It had occurred to her that Nick had written his intention to wait for her in the park tomorrow night as well, and Dr. Horker's interference had confirmed her in a determination to meet him.

CHAPTER FOURTEEN
Bizarre Explanation

"I won't be bullied!" Pat told herself, examining her features in the mirror. The two day interval had faded the discoloration of her cheek to negligible proportions, and all that remained as evidence of the violence of Saturday night was the diminishing mark on her chin. Of course, her knees—but they were covered; most of the time, at least. She gave herself a final inspection, and somewhere below a clock boomed.

"Eight o'clock," she remarked to her image. "Time to be leaving, and it serves Dr. Carl right for his highhanded actions last night. I won't be bullied by anybody." She checked herself as her mind had almost added, "Except Nick." True or not, she didn't relish the thought; the recent recollections it roused were too disturbing.

She tossed a stray wisp of black hair from her forehead and turned to the door. She heard her mother's voice as she descended the stairs.

"Are you going out, Patricia? Do you think it wise?"

"I am perfectly all right. I want to go for a walk."

"I know, dear; it was largely your appearance I meant." She surveyed the girl with a critical eye. "Nice enough, except for that little spot on your chin, and will you never learn to keep your hair away from that side of your forehead? One can never do a bob right; why don't you let it grow out like the other girls?"

"Makes me individual," replied Pat, moving toward the outer door. "I won't be late at all," she added.

On the porch she cast a cautious glance at Dr. Horker's windows, but his great figure was nowhere evident. Only a light burning in the library evinced his presence. She gave a sigh of relief, and tiptoed down the steps to the sidewalk, and moved hastily away from the range of his watchful eyes.

No sooner had she sighted the park than doubts began to torment her. Suppose this were some trick of Nicholas Devine's, to trap her into some such situation as that of Saturday night. Even suppose that she found him the sweet personality that she had loved, might that also be a trick? Mightn't he be trusting to his ability to win her over, to the charm she had confessed to him that he held for her? Couldn't he be putting his faith in his own amorous skill, planning some specious explanation to win her forgiveness only to use her once more as the material for some horrible experiment? And if he were, would she be able to prevent herself from yielding?

"Forewarned is fore-armed," she told herself. "I'll not put up such a feeble resistance this time, knowing what I now know. And it's only fair of me to listen to his explanation, if he really has one."

She was reassured by the sight of the crowded park; groups strolled along the walks, and an endless procession of car-headlights marked the course of the roadway. Nothing could happen in such an environment; they'd be fortunate even to have an opportunity for confidential talk. She waited for the traffic lights, straining her eyes to locate Nicholas Devine; at the click of the signal she darted across the street.

She moved toward the lake; here was the spot, she was sure. She glanced about with eagerness unexpected even to herself, peering through the shadow-shot dusk. He wasn't there, she concluded, with a curious sense of disappointment; her failure to appear last night had disheartened him; he had abandoned his attempt.

Then she saw him. He sat on a bench isolated from the rest in a treeless area overlooking the lake. She saw his disconsolate figure, his chin on his hand, staring moodily over the waters. A tremor ran through her, she halted deliberately, waiting until every trace of emotion had vanished, then she advanced, standing coolly beside him.

For a moment he was unaware of her presence; he sat maintaining his dejected attitude without glancing at her. Suddenly some slight movement, the flutter of her skirt, drew his attention; he turned sharply, gazing directly into her face.

"Pat!" He sprang to his feet. "Pat! Is it you—truly you? Or are you one of these visions that have been plaguing me for hours?"

"I'm real," she said, returning his gaze with a studied coolness in her face. She made no other move; her cold composure disconcerted him, and he winced, flushed, and moved nervously aside as she seated herself. He dropped beside her; he made no attempt to touch her, but sat watching her in silence for so long a time that she felt her composure ebbing. There was a hungry, defeated look about him; there was a wistfulness, a frustration, in his eyes that seemed about to tug tears from her own eyes. Abruptly she dropped her gaze from his face.

"Well?" she said finally in a small voice, and as he made no reply. "I'm here."

"Are you really, Pat? Are you truly here?" he murmured, still watching her avidly. "I—I still don't believe it. I waited here for hours and hours last night, and I'd given up hope for tonight, or any night. But I would have come again and again."

She started as he bent suddenly toward her, but he was merely examining her face. She saw the gleam of horror in his expression as his eyes surveyed the faintly visible bruise on her cheek, the red mark on her chin.

"Oh my God, Pat!" His words were barely audible. "Oh my God!" he repeated, drawing away from her and resuming the attitude of desolation in which her arrival had found him. "I've hoped it wasn't true!"

"What wasn't?" She was keeping her voice carefully casual; this miserable contrition of Nick's was tugging at her rather too powerfully for complete safety.

"What I remembered. What I saw just now."

"You hoped it wasn't true?" she queried in surprise. "But you did it."

"*I* did it, Pat? Do you think I could have done it?"

"But you did!" Her voice had taken on a chill inflection; the memory of those indignities came to steel her against him.

"Pat, do you think I could assault your daintiness, or maltreat the beauty I worship? Didn't anything occur to you? Didn't anything seem queer about—about that ghastly evening?"

"Queer! That's certainly a mild word to use, isn't it?"

"But I mean—hadn't you any idea of what had happened? Didn't you think anything of it except that I had suddenly gone mad? Or that I'd grown to hate you?"

"What was I to think?" she countered, trying to control the tremor that had crept into her voice.

"But did you think that?"

"No," the girl confessed after a pause. "At first, when you started with that drink, I thought you were looking for material for your work. That's what you said—an experiment. Didn't you?"

"I guess so," he groaned.

"But after that, after I'd swallowed that horrible stuff, but before everything went hazy, I—thought differently."

"But what, Pat? What did you think?"

"Why, then I realized that it wasn't you—not the real you. I could feel the—well, the presence of the person I knew; this presence that was tormenting me was another person, a terrible, cold, inhuman stranger."

"Pat!" There was a note almost of relief in his voice. "Did you really feel that?"

"Yes. Does it help matters, my sensing that? I can't see how."

His eyes, which had been fixed on hers, dropped suddenly. "No," he muttered, all the relief gone out of his tones, "no, it doesn't help, does it? Except that it's a meager consolation to me to know that you felt it."

Pat struggled to suppress an impulse to reach out her hand, to stroke his hair. She caught herself sharply; this was the very danger against which she had warned herself—this was the very attitude she had anticipated in Nicholas Devine, the lure which might bait a trap. Yet he looked so forlorn, so wistful! It was an effort to forbear from touching him; her fingers fairly ached to brush his cheek.

"Only a fool walks twice into the same trap," she told herself. Aloud she said, "You promised me an explanation. If you've any excuse, I'd like to hear it." Her voice had resumed its coolness.

"I haven't any excuse," he responded gloomily, "and the explanation is perhaps too bizarre, too fantastic for belief. I don't believe it entirely; I suppose you couldn't believe it at all."

"You promised," she repeated. The carefully assumed composure of her voice threatened to crack; this wistfulness of his was a powerful weapon against her defense.

"Oh, I'll give you the explanation," he said miserably. "I just wanted to warn you you'd not believe me," He gave her a despondent glance. "Pat, as I love you I swear that what I tell you is the truth. Do you think you can believe me?"

"Yes," she murmured. The tremor had reappeared in her voice despite her efforts.

Nicholas Devine turned his eyes toward the lake and began to speak.

CHAPTER FIFTEEN
A Modern Mr. Hyde

"I don't remember when I first noticed it," began Nick in a low voice, "but I'm two people. I'm me, the person who's talking to you now, and I'm—another."

Pat, looking very pale and serious in the dusky light, said nothing at all. She simply gazed at him silently, without the slightest trace of surprise in her wide dark eyes.

"This is the real me," proceeded Nick miserably. "The other is an outsider that has somehow contrived to grow into me. He is different; cold, cruel, utterly selfish, and not exactly—human. Do you understand?"

"Y—Yes," said the girl, fighting to control her voice. "Sort of."

"This is a struggle that has continued for a long time," he pursued. "There were times in childhood when I remember punishments for offenses I never committed, for nasty little meanness's he perpetrated. My mother, and after her death, my tutoress, thought I was lying when I tried to explain; they thought I was trying to evade responsibility. After a while I learned not to explain; I learned to accept my punishments doggedly, and to fight this other when he sought dominance."

"And could you?" asked Pat, her voice frankly quivery. "Could you fight him?"

"I was the stronger; I could win—usually. He slipped into consciousness as willful, mean little impulses, nasty moods, unreasoning hates and such unpleasant things. But I was always the stronger. I learned to drive him into the background."

"You said you were the stronger," she mused. "What does that mean, Nick?"

"I've always been the stronger; I am now. But recently, Pat—I think it's since I fell in love with you—the struggle has been on evener terms. I've weakened or he's gained. I have to guard against him constantly; in any moment of weakness he may slip in, as on our ride last week, when we had that near accident. And again Saturday." He turned appealing eyes on the girl. "Pat, do you believe me?"

"I guess I'll have to," she said unhappily. "It—makes things rather hopeless, doesn't it?"

He nodded dejectedly. "Yes. I've always felt that sooner or later I'd win, and drive him away permanently. I've felt on the verge of complete victory more than once, but now—" He shook his head doubtfully. "He had never dominated me so entirely until Saturday night— Pat, you don't know what Hell is like until you're forced as I was to watch the violation of the being you worship, to stand helpless while a desecration is committed. I'd rather die than suffer it again!"

"Oh!" said the girl faintly. She was thinking of the sorry picture she must have presented as she reeled half-clothed through the alley. "Can you see what—he sees?"

"Of course, and think his thoughts. But only when he's dominant. I don't know what evil he's planning now, else I could forestall him. I would have warned you if I could have known."

"Where is he now?"

"Here," said Nick somberly. "Here listening to us, knowing what I'm thinking and feeling, laughing at my unhappiness."

"Oh!" gasped Pat again. She watched her companion doubtfully. Then the memory of Dr. Horker's diagnosis came to her, and set her wondering. Was this story the figment of an unsettled mind? Was this irrational tale of a fiendish intruder merely evidence that the Doctor was right in his opinion? She was in a maze of uncertainty.

"Nick," she said, "did you ever try medical help? Did you ever go to a doctor about it?"

"Of course, Pat! Two years ago I went to a famous psychiatrist in New York—you'd know the name if I mentioned it—and told him about the—the case. And he studied me, and he treated me, and psychoanalyzed me, and the net result was just nothing. And finally he dismissed me with the opinion that the whole thing is just a fixed delusion, fortunately harmless! Harmless! Bah! But it wasn't I that did those things, Pat; I had to stand by in horror and watch. It was enough to drive me crazy, but it didn't—quite."

"But—Oh. Nick, what is it? What is this—this outsider? Can't we fight it somehow?"

"How can anyone except me fight it?"

"Oh, I don't know!" she wailed miserably. "There must be a way. Doctors claim to know pretty nearly everything; there must be something to do."

"But there isn't," he retorted gloomily. "I don't know any more than you what that thing is, but it's beyond your doctors. I've got to fight it out alone."

"Nick—" Her voice was suddenly tense. "Are you sure it isn't some kind of madness? Something tangible like that could perhaps be treated."

"It's no kind your doctors can treat, Pat. Did you ever hear of a madman who stood aside and rationally watched the working of his own insanity? And that's what I'm forced to do. And yet—this other isn't insane either. Were its actions insane?"

Pat shuddered. "I—don't know," she said in low tones. "I guess not."

"No. Horrible, cruel, bestial, devilishly cunning, evil—but not insane. I don't know what it is, Pat, I know that the fight has to be made by me alone. There's nothing, nobody in the world, that can help."

"Nick!" she wailed.

"I'm sorry, Pat dear. You understand now why I was so reluctant to fall in love with you. I was afraid to love you; now I know I was right."

"Nick!" she cried, then paused hopelessly. After a moment she continued, "Yesterday I was determined to forget you, and now—now I don't care if this whole tale of yours is a mesh of fantastic lies. I love you! I'd love you even if your real self were that—that other creature—and even if I knew that this was just a trap, I'd love you anyway.

"Pat," he said seriously, "don't you believe me? Why should I offer to give you up if this were—what you said? Wouldn't I be pleading for another chance, making promises, finding excuses?"

"Oh, I believe you, Nick! It isn't that; I was just thinking how strange it is that I could hate you so two nights past and love you so tonight."

"Oh God, Pat! Even you can't know how much I love you; and to win you and then be forced to give you up—" He groaned.

The girl reached out her hand and covered his; it was the first time during the evening that she had touched him, and the feel of his flesh sent a tingle through her. She was miserably distraught.

"Honey," she murmured brokenly. "Nick, honey."

He looked at her. "Do you suppose there's a chance to beat the thing?" he asked. "I'd not ask you to wait. Pat, but if I only glimpsed a chance—"

"I'll wait. I don't think I could do anything else but wait for you."

"If I only knew what I had to fight!" he whispered. "If I only knew that!"

A sudden memory leaped into Pat's mind. "Nick," she said huskily, "I think I know."

"What do you mean, Pat?"

"It's something Magda—the cook—said to me. It's foolish, superstitious, but Nick, what else can it be?"

"Tell me!"

"Well, she was talking to me yesterday, and she said that when she was a child in the old country, she had seen a man once—" She hesitated. "—a man who was possessed by a devil. Nick, I think you're possessed by a devil!"

He stared at her. "Pat," he said hoarsely, "that's—an impossibility!"

"I know, but what else can it be?"

"Out of the Dark Ages," he muttered. "An echo of the Black Mass and witchcraft, but—"

"What did they do," asked the girl, "to people they thought were possessed?"

"Exorcism!" he whispered.

"And how did they—exorcise?"

"I don't know," he said in a low voice. "Pat, that's an impossible idea, but—I don't know!" he ended.

"We'll try," she murmured, still covering his hand with her own. "What else can we do, Nick?"

"What's done I'll do alone, Pat."

"But I want to help!"

"I'll not let you, dear. I won't have you exposed to a repetition of those indignities, or perhaps worse!"

"I'm not afraid."

"Then I am, Pat! I won't have it!"

"But what'll you do?"

"I'll go away. I'll battle the thing through once for all and I'll either come back free of it or—" He paused and the girl did not question him further, but sat staring at him with troubled eyes.

"I won't write you, Pat," he continued. "If you should receive a letter from me, burn it—don't read it. It might be from—the other, a trap or a lure of some sort. Promise me! You'll promise that, won't you?"

She nodded; there was a glint of tears in her eyes.

"And I don't want you to wait, Pat," he proceeded. "I don't want you to feel that you have any obligations to me. God knows you've nothing to thank me for! When— If I come back and you haven't changed, then we'll try again."

"Nick," she said in a small voice, "how do you know the—the other won't come back here? How can you promise for—it?"

"I'm still master!" he said grimly. "I won't be dominated long enough at any time for that to happen. I'll fight it down."

"Then—it's goodbye?"

He nodded. "But not for always—I hope."

"Nick," she murmured, "will you kiss me?" She felt a tear on her cheek. "I'll stand losing you a little better if I can have a—last kiss—to remember." Her voice was faltering.

His arms were about her. She yielded herself completely to his caress; the park, the crowd passing a few yards away, the people on nearby benches, were all forgotten, and once more she felt herself alone with Nicholas Devine in a vast empty cosmos.

An insistent voice penetrated her consciousness; she realized that it had been calling her name for some seconds.

"Miss Lane," she heard, and again, "Miss Lane," A hand tapped her shoulder; with a sudden start, she tore her lips away, and looked up into a face unrecognized for a moment. Then she placed it. It was the visage of Mueller, Dr. Horker's companion on that disastrous Saturday night.

CHAPTER SIXTEEN
Possessed

Pat stared at the intruder in a mingling of embarrassment, perplexity, and indignation. She felt her cheeks reddening as the latter emotion gained the dominance of her mood. "Well!" she snapped. "What do you want?"

"I thought I'd walk home with you," Mueller said amiably.

"Walk home with me! Please explain that!" She grasped the arm of Nicholas Devine, who had risen angrily at the interruption. "Sit down, Nick. I know the fellow."

"So should he," said Mueller. "Sure; I'll explain. I'm on a job for Dr. Horker."

"Spying on me for him, I suppose!" taunted the girl.

"No. Not on you."

"He means on me," said Nick soberly. "You can't blame him, Pat. And perhaps you had better go home; we've finished here. There's nothing more we can do or say."

"Very well," she said, her voice suddenly softer. "In a moment, Nick." She turned to Mueller. "Would you mind telling me why you waited until now to interfere? We've been here two hours, you know."

"Sure I'll tell you. I got no orders to interfere, that's why."

"Then why did you?" queried Pat tartly.

"I didn't until I saw him there..." He nodded at Nick. "...put his arms around you. Then I figured, having no orders, it was time to use my own judgment."

"If any!" sniffed the girl. She turned again to Nick; her face softened, became very tender. "Honey," she murmured huskily, "I guess it's goodbye now. I'll be fighting with you; you know that."

"I know that," he echoed looking down into her eyes. "I'm almost happy, Pat."

"When'll you go?" she whispered in tones inaudible to Mueller.

"I don't know," he answered, his voice unchanged. "I'll have to make some sort of preparations—and I don't want you to know."

She nodded. She gazed at him a moment longer with tear-bright eyes. "Goodbye, Nick," she whispered.

She rose on tiptoe, and kissed him very lightly on his lips, then turned and walked quickly away, with Mueller following behind. She walked on, ignoring him until he halted beside her at the crossing of the Drive. Then she gave him a cold glance.

"Why is Dr. Carl having him watched?" she asked.

Mueller shrugged. "The ins and outs of this case are too much for me," he said. "I do what I'm paid to do."

"You're not watching him now."

"Nope. Seemed like the Doctor would think it was more important to get you home."

"You're wasting your time," she said irritably as the lights changed and they stepped into the street. "I was going home anyway."

"Well, now you got company all the way." Mueller's voice was placid.

The girl sniffed contemptuously, and strode silently along. The other's presence irritated her; she wanted time and solitude to consider the amazing story Nicholas Devine had given her. She wanted to analyze her own feelings, and most of all she wanted just a place of privacy to cry out her misery. For now the loss of Nicholas Devine had changed from a fortunate escape to a tragedy, and liar, madman, or devil, she wanted him terribly, with all the power of her tense little heart. So she moved as swiftly as she could, ignoring the silent companionship of Mueller.

They reached her home; the light in the living room window was evidence that the bridge game was still in progress. She mounted the steps, Mueller watching her silently from the walk; she fumbled for her key.

Suddenly she snapped her hand-bag shut; she couldn't face her mother and the two spinster Brocks and elderly, inquisitive Carter Henderson. They'd suggest that she cut into the game, and they'd argue if she refused, and she couldn't play bridge now! She glanced at the impassive Mueller, turned and crossed the strip of lawn to Dr. Horker's residence, where the light still glowed in the library, and rang the bell. She saw the figure on the sidewalk move away as the shadow of the Doctor appeared on the lighted square of the door.

"Hello," boomed the Doctor amiably. "Come in." Pat stalked into the library and threw herself angrily into Dr. Horker's particular chair. The other grinned, and chose another place. "Well," he said, "what touched off the fuse this time?"

"Why are you spying on my friends?" snapped the girl. "By what right?"

"So he's spotted Mueller, eh? That lad's diabolically clever."

"That's no answer!"

"So it isn't," agreed the Doctor. "Say it's because I'm acting in *loco parentis.*"

"And in loco is as far as you'll get, Dr. Carl, if you're going to spy on me!"

"On you?" he said mildly. "Who's spying on you?"

"On us, then!"

"Or on us?" queried the Doctor. "I set Mueller to watch the Devine lad. Have you by some mischance broken your promise to me?"

Pat flushed. She had forgotten that broken promise; the recollection of it suddenly took the wind from her sails, placed her on the defensive.

"All right," she said defiantly. "I did; I admit it. Does that excuse you?"

"Perhaps it helps to explain my actions. Pat. Don't you understand that I'm trying to protect you? Do you think I hired Mueller out of morbid curiosity, or professional interest in the case? Times aren't so good that I can throw money away on such whims."

"I don't need any protection. I can take care of myself!"

"So I noticed," said the Doctor dryly. "You gave convincing evidence of it night before last."

"Oh!" said the girl in exasperation. "You would say that!"

"It's true, isn't it?"

"Suppose it is! I don't have to learn the same lesson twice."

"Well, apparently once wasn't enough," observed the other amiably. "You walked into the same danger tonight."

"I wasn't in any danger tonight!" Suddenly her mood changed as she recalled the circumstances of her parting with Nicholas Devine. "Dr. Carl," she said, her voice dropping, "I'm terribly unhappy."

"Lord!" he exclaimed staring at her. "Pat, your moods are as changeable as my golf game! You're as mercurial as your Devine lad! A moment ago you were snapping at me, and now I'm suddenly acceptable again." He perceived the misery in her face. "All right, child; I'm listening."

"He's going away," she said mournfully.

"Don't you think that's best for everybody concerned? I commend his judgment."

"But I don't want him to!"

"You do, Pat. You can't continue seeing him, and his absence will make it easier for you."

"It'll never be easier for me, Dr. Carl," She felt her eyes fill. "I guess I'm—just a fool about him."

"You still feel that way, after the experience you went through?"

77

"Yes. Yes, I do."

"Then you are a fool about him, Pat. He's not worth such devotion."

"How do you know what he's worth? I'm the only one to judge that."

"I have eyes," said the Doctor. "What happened tonight to change your attitude so suddenly? You were amenable to reason yesterday."

"I didn't know yesterday what I know now."

"So he told a story, eh?" The Doctor watched her serious, troubled features. "Would you mind telling me, honey? I'm interested in the defense mechanisms these psychopathic cases erect to explain their own impulses to themselves."

"No, I won't tell you!" snapped Pat indignantly. "Psychopathic cases! We're all just cases to you. I'm a case and he's another, and all you want is our symptoms!"

Doctor Horker smiled placatingly into her face. "Pat dear," he said earnestly, "don't you see I'd give my eyes to help you? Don't take my flippancies too seriously, honey; look once in a while at the intentions behind them." He continued his earnest gaze.

The girl returned his look; her face softened. "I'm sorry," she said contritely. "I never doubted it, Dr. Carl—it's only that I'm so—so torn to pieces by all this that I get snappy and irritable." She paused. "Of course I'll tell you."

"I'd like to hear it."

"Well," she began hesitantly, "he said he was two personalities— one the character I knew, and one the character that we saw Saturday night. And the first one is—well, dominant, and fights the other one. He says the other has been growing stronger; until lately he could suppress it. And he says— Oh, it sounds ridiculous, the way I tell it, but it's true! I'm sure it's true!" She leaned toward the Doctor. "Did you ever hear of anything like it? Did you, Dr. Carl?"

"No," He shook his head, still watching her seriously. "Not exactly like that, honey. Don't you think he might possibly have lied to you, Pat? To excuse himself for the responsibility of Saturday night, for instance?"

"No, I don't," she said defiantly.

"Then you have an idea yourself what the trouble is? I judge you have."

"Yes," she said in low tones. "I have an idea."

"What is it?"

"I think he's possessed by a devil!" said the girl flatly.

A quizzical expression came into the Doctor's face. "Well, of all the queer ideas that harum-scarum mind of yours has ever produced, that's the queerest!" He broke into a chuckle.

"Queer, is it?" flared Pat. "I don't think you and your mind-doctors know as much as a Swahili medicine man with a mask!"

She leaped angrily to her feet, stamped viciously into the hall. "Devil and all," she repeated, "I love him!"

"Pat!" called the Doctor anxiously. "Where are you going, child?"

"Where do devils live?" Her voice floated tauntingly back from the front door. "Hell, of course!"

CHAPTER SEVENTEEN
Witch-Doctor

Pat had no intentions, however, of following the famous highway that evening. She stamped angrily down the Doctor's steps, swished her way through the break in the hedge with small regard to the safety of her sheer hose, and mounted to her own porch. She found her key, opened the door and entered.

As she ascended the stairs, her fit of temper at the Doctor passed, and she felt lonely, weary, and unutterably miserable. She sank to a seat on the topmost step and gave herself over to bitter reflections.

Nick was gone! The realization came poignantly at last; there would be no more evening rides, no more conversations whose range was limited only by the scope of the universe, no more breath-taking kisses, the sweeter for his reluctance. She sat mournfully silent, and considered the miserable situation in which she found herself.

In love with a madman! Or worse—in love with a demon! With a being half of whose nature worshiped her while the other

half was bent on her destruction! Was anyone, she asked herself—
was anyone, anywhere, ever in a more hopeless predicament?

What could she do? Nothing, she realized, save sit helplessly
aside while Nick battled the thing to a finish. Or possibly—the
only alternative—take him as he was, chance the vicissitudes of his
unstable nature, lay herself open to the horrors she had glimpsed
so recently, and pray for her fortunes to point the way of salvation.
And in the mood in which she now found herself, that seemed
infinitely the preferable solution. Yet rationally she knew it was
impossible; she shook her head despondently, and leaned against
the wall in abject misery.

Then, thin and sharp sounded the shrill summons of the door
bell, and a moment later, the patter of the maid's footsteps in the
hall below. She listened idly to distract herself from the chain of
despondency that was her thoughts, and was mildly startled to
recognize the booming drums of Dr. Horker's voice. She heard his
greeting and the muffled reply from the group, and then a phrase
understandable because of his sonorous tones.

"Where's Pat?" The words drifted up the well of the stairs, followed by a scarcely audible reply from her mother. Heavy footfalls
on the carpeted steps, and then his figure bulked on the landing
above her. She cupped her chin in her hand and stared down at
him while he ascended to her side, sprawling his great figure beside
her.

"Pat, honey," he rumbled, "you're beginning to get me
worried!"

"Am I?" Her voice was weary, dull. "I've had myself like that
for a long time."

"Poor kid! Are you really so miserable over this Nick problem
of yours?"

"I love him."

"Yes," He looked at her with sympathy and calculation
mingling in his expression. "I believe you do. I'm sorry, honey; I
didn't realize until now what he means to you."

"You don't realize now," she murmured, still with the weary
intonation.

"Perhaps not, Pat, but I'm learning. If you're in this thing as
deeply as all that, I'm in too—to the finish. Want me?"

She reached out her hand, plucking at his coat-sleeve. Abruptly she leaned toward him, burying her face against the rough tweed of his suit; she sobbed a little, while he patted her gently with his great delicately fingered hand. "I'm sorry, honey," he rumbled. "I'm sorry."

The girl drew herself erect and leaned back against the wall, shaking her head to drive the tears from her eyes. She gave the Doctor a wan little smile.

"Well?" she asked.

"I'll return your compliment of the other night," said Horker briskly. "I'll ask a few questions—purely professional, of course."

"Fire away, Dr. Carl."

"Good. Now, when our friend has one of these—uh—attacks, is he rational? Do his utterances seem to follow a logical thought sequence?"

"I—think so."

"In what way does he differ from his normal self?"

"Oh, every way," she said with a tremor. "Nick's kind and gentle and sensitive and—and naive, and this—other—is cruel harsh, gross, crafty, and horrible. You can't imagine a greater difference."

"Um. Is the difference recognizable instantly? Could you ever be in doubt as to which phase you were encountering?"

"Oh, no! I can—well, sort of dominate Nick, but the other— Lord!" She shuddered again. "I felt like a terrified child in the presence of some powerful, evil god."

"Humph! Perhaps the god's name was Priapus. Well, we'll discount your feelings, Pat, because you weren't exactly in the best condition for—let's say sober judgment. Now about this story of his. What happens to his own personality when this other phase is dominant? Did he say?"

"Yes. He said his own self was compelled to sort of stand by while the—the intruder used his voice and body. He knew the thoughts of the other, but only when it was dominant. The rest of the time he couldn't tell its thoughts."

"And how long has he suffered from these—intrusions?"

"As long as he can remember. As a child he was blamed for the other's mischief, and when he tried to explain, people thought he was lying to escape punishment."

"Well," observed the Doctor, "I can see how they might think that."

"Don't you believe it?"

"I don't exactly disbelieve it, honey. The human mind plays queer tricks sometimes, and this may be one of its little jokes. It's a psychiatrist's business to investigate such things, and to painlessly remove the point of the joke."

"Oh, if you only can, Dr. Carl! If you only can!"

"We'll see." He patted her hand comfortingly.

"Now, you say the kind, gentle, and all that, phase is the normal one. Is that usually dominant?"

"Yes. Nick can master the other, or could until recently. He says this last—attack—is the worst he's ever had; the other has been gaining strength."

"Strange!" mused the Doctor. "Well," he said with a smile of encouragement, "I'll have a look at him."

"Do you think you can help?" Pat asked anxiously. "Have you any idea what it is?"

"It isn't a devil, at any rate," he smiled.

"But have you any idea?"

"Naturally I have, but I can't diagnose at second hand. I'll have to talk to him."

"But what do you think it is?" she persisted.

"I think it's a fixation of an idea gained in childhood, honey. I had a patient once—" He smiled at the reminiscence. "—who had a fixed delusion of that sort. He was perfectly rational on every point save one—he believed that a pig with a pink ribbon was following him everywhere! Down town, into elevators and offices, home to bed—everywhere he went this pink-ribboned prize porker pursued him!"

"And did you cure him?"

"Well, he recovered," said the Doctor noncommittally. "We got rid of the pig. And it might be something of that nature that's troubling your boyfriend. Your description doesn't sound like a praecox or a manic depressive, as I thought originally."

"Oh," said Pat abruptly, "I forgot. He went to a doctor in New York, a very great doctor."

"Muenster?"

"He didn't say whom. But this doctor studied him a long time, and finally came out with this fixed idea theory of yours. Only he couldn't cure him."

"Um." Horker grunted thoughtfully.

"Do fixed ideas do things like that to people?" queried the girl. "Things like the pig and what happened to Nick?"

"They might."

"Then they're devils!" she announced with an air of finality. "They're just your scientific jargon for exactly what Magda means when she says a person's possessed by a devil. So I'm right any-way!"

"That's good orthodox theology, Pat," chuckled the Doctor. "We'll try a little exorcism on your devil, then," He rose to his feet. "Bring your boyfriend around, will you?"

"Oh, Dr. Carl!" she cried, "he's leaving! I'll have to call him tonight!"

"Not tonight, honey, Mueller would let me know if anything of that sort were happening. Tomorrow's time enough."

The girl stood erect, mounting to the top step to bring her head level with the Doctor's. She threw her arms about him, burying her face in his massive shoulder.

"Dr. Carl," she murmured, "I'm a nasty, ill-tempered, vicious little shrew, and I'm sorry, and I apologize. You know I'm crazy about you, and," she whispered in his ear, "so's mother!"

CHAPTER EIGHTEEN
Vanished

He doesn't answer! I'm too late, thought Pat disconsolately as she replaced the telephone. The cheerfulness with which she had awakened vanished like a patch of spring sunshine. Now, with the failure of her third attempt in as many hours to communicate with Nicholas Devine, she was ready to confess defeat. She had waited too long. Despite Dr. Horker's confidence in Mueller, she should have called last night—at once.

"He's gone!" she murmured distractedly. She realized now the impossibility of finding him. His solitary habits, his dearth of friends, his lonely existence, left her without the least idea of how to commence a search. She knew, actually, so little about him—not even the source of the apparently sufficient income on which he subsisted. She felt herself completely at a loss, puzzled, lonesome, and disheartened. The futile buzzing of the telephone signal symbolized her frustration.

Perhaps, she thought, Dr. Horker might suggest something to do; perhaps, even, Mueller had reported Nick's whereabouts. She seized the hope eagerly. A glance at her wrist-watch revealed the time as ten-thirty; squarely in the midst of the Doctor's morning office hours, but no matter. If he were busy she could wait. She rose, bounding hastily down the stairs.

She glimpsed her mother opening mail in the library, and paused momentarily at the door. Mrs. Lane glanced up as she appeared.

"Hello," said the mother. "You've been on the telephone all morning, and what did Carl want of you last night?"

"Argument," responded Pat briefly.

"Carl's a gem! He's been of inestimable assistance in developing you into a very charming and clever daughter, and Heaven knows what I'd have raised without him!"

"Cain, probably," suggested Pat. She passed into the hall and out the door, blinking in the brilliant August sunshine. She crossed the strip of turf, picked her way through the break in the hedge, and approached the Doctor's door. It was open; it often was in summer time, especially during his brief office hours. She entered and went into the chamber used as waiting room.

His office door was closed; the faint hum of his voice sounded. She sat impatiently in a chair and forced herself to wait.

Fortunately, the delay was nominal; it was but a few minutes when the door opened and an opulent, middle-aged lady swept past her and away. Pat recognized her as Mrs. Lowry, some sort of cousin of the Brock pair.

"Good morning!" boomed the Doctor. "Professional call, I take it, since you're here during office hours." He settled his great form in a chair beside her.

"He's gone!" said Pat plaintively. "I can't reach him."

"Humph!" grunted Horker helpfully.

"I've tried all morning—he's always home in the morning."

"Listen, you little scatterbrain!" rumbled the Doctor. "Why didn't you tell me Mueller brought you home last night? I thought he was on the job."

"I didn't think of it," she wailed. "Nick said he'd have to make some preparations, and I never dreamed he'd skip away like this."

"He must have gone home directly after you left him, and skipped out immediately," said the Doctor ruminatively. "Mueller never caught up with him."

"But what'll we do?" she cried desperately.

"He can't have gone far with no more preparation than this," soothed Horker. "He'll write you in a day or two."

"He won't! He said he wouldn't. He doesn't want me to know where he is!" She was on the verge of tears.

"Now, now," said the Doctor still in his soothing tones. "It isn't as bad as all that."

"Take off your bedside manner!" she snapped, blinking to keep back the tears. "It's worse! Whatever can we do? Dr. Carl," she changed to a pleading tone, "can't you think of something?"

"Of course, Pat! I can think of several things to do if you'll quiet down for a moment or so."

"I'm sorry, Dr. Carl—but what can we do?"

"First, perhaps Mueller can trace him. That's his business, you know."

"But suppose he can't—what then?"

"Well, I'd suggest you write him a letter."

"But I don't know where to write!" she wailed. "I don't know his address!"

"Be still a moment, scatterbrain! Address it to his last residence; you know that, don't you? Of course you do. Now, don't you suppose he'll leave a forwarding address? He must receive some sort of mail about his income, or estate, or whatever he lives on. Your letter'll find him, honey; don't you doubt it."

"Oh, do you think so?" she asked, suddenly hopeful. "Do you really think so?"

"I really think so. You would too if you didn't fly into a panic every time some little difficulty confronts you. Sometimes even my psychiatry is puzzled to explain how you can be so clever and so stupid, so self-reliant and so dependent, so capable and so helpless—all at one and the same time. Your Nick can't be as much of a paradox as you are!"

"I wonder if a letter *will* reach him," she said eagerly, ignoring the Doctor's remarks. "I'll try. I'll try immediately."

"I sort of had a feeling you would," said Horker amiably. "I hope you succeed; and not only for your sake, Pat, because God knows how this thing will work out. But I'm anxious to examine this youngster of yours on my own account; he must be a remarkable specimen to account for all the perturbation he's managed to cause you. And this Jekyll and Hyde angle sounds interesting, too."

"Jekyll and Hyde!" echoed Pat. "Dr. Carl, is that possible?"

"Not literally," chuckled the other, "though in a sense, Stevenson anticipated Freud in his thesis that liberating the evil serves also to release the good."

"But it was a drug that caused that change in the story, wasn't it?"

"Well? Do you suspect your friend of being addicted to some mysterious drug? Is that the latest hypothesis?"

"Is there such a drug? One that could change a person's character?"

"All alkaloids do that, honey. Some of them stimulate, some depress, some breed frenzies, and some give visions of delight—but all of them influence one's mental and emotional organization, which you call character. So for that matter, does a square meal, or a cup of coffee, or even a rainy day."

"But isn't there a drug that can separate good qualities from evil, like the story?"

"Emphatically not, Pat! That's not the trouble with this pesky boyfriend of yours."

"Well," said the girl doubtfully, "I only wish I had as much faith in your psychologies as you have. If you brain-doctors know it all, why do you switch theories every year?"

"We don't know it all. On the other hand, there are a few things to be said in our favor."

"What are they?"

"For one," replied the Doctor, "we do cure people occasionally. You'll admit that."

"Sure," said Pat. "So did the Salem witches—occasionally." She gave him a suddenly worried look. "Oh, Dr. Carl, don't think I'm not grateful! You know how much I'm hoping for your help, but I'm miserably anxious over all this."

"Never mind, honey. You're not the first one to point out the shortcomings of the medical profession. That's a game played by plenty of physicians too." He paused at the sound of footsteps on the porch, followed by the buzz of the doorbell. "Run along and write your letter, dear—here comes that Tuesday hypochondriac of mine, and he's rich enough for my careful attention."

Pat flashed him a smile of farewell and slipped quietly into the hall. At the door she passed the Doctor's patient—a lean, elderly gentleman of woebegone visage—and returned to her own home.

Her spirits, mercurial to a degree, had risen again. She was suddenly positive that the Doctor's scheme would bring results, and she darted into the house almost buoyantly. Her mother had abandoned the desk, and she ensconced herself before it finding paper and pen, and staring thoughtfully at the blank sheet. Finally she wrote:

Dear Nick—

Something has happened, favorable, I think, to us. I believe I have found the help we need.

Will you come if you can, or if that's not possible, break that self-given promise of yours, and communicate with me?

I love you.

She signed it simply Pat, placed it in an envelope, addressed it hastily, and hurried out to post it. On her return she spied the Doctor's hypochondriac in the act of leaving, he walked past her with his lean, worry-smitten face like a study of Hogarth, and she heard him mumbling to himself. The elation went out of her; she mounted the steps very soberly, and went miserably inside.

CHAPTER NINETEEN
Man or Monster

Pat suffered Wednesday through somehow, knowing that any such early response to her letter was impossible. Still, that impossibility did not deter her from starting at the sound of the telephone, and sorting through the mail with an eagerness that drew a casual attention from her mother.

"Good Heavens, Patricia! You're like a child watching for an answer to his note to Santa Claus!"

"That's what I am, I guess," responded the girl ruefully. "Maybe I expect too much from Santa Claus."

Late in the afternoon she drifted over to Dr. Horker's residence, to be informed that he was out. For distraction, she went in anyway, and spent a while browsing among the books in the library. She blundered into Kraft-Ebing, and read a few pages in growing indignation.

"I'm ashamed to be human!" she muttered disgustedly to herself, slamming shut the *Psychopathia Sexualis*. "I wouldn't be a doctor, or have a child of mine become one, if I were positively certain he'd turn into Lord Lister himself! Nick was right when he said doctors live on people's troubles."

She wondered how Dr. Horker could remain so human, so kindly and understanding, when as he said himself his world was a parade of misfits, incompetents, and all the nastiness of mortals. He was nice; she felt no embarrassment in confiding in him even when she might hesitate to bare her feelings to her own mother. Or was it simply the natural thing to do to tell one's troubles to a doctor?

Not, of course, that the situation reflected any discredit on her mother. Mrs. Lane was a very precious sort of parent, she mused, young as Pat in spirit, appreciative and enthusiastically fond of her daughter. That she trusted Pat, that she permitted her to do entirely as she pleased, was exactly as the girl would have it; it argued no lack of affection that each of them had their separate interests, and if the girl occasionally found herself in unpleasantness such as this, that too was her own twit.

And yet, she reflected, it was a bitter thing to have no one to whom to turn. If it weren't for Dr. Carl and his jovial willingness to commit any sin up to malpractice to help her, she might have felt differently. But there always *was* Dr. Carl, and that, she concluded, was that.

She wandered back to her own side of the hedge, missing for the first time in many weeks the companionship of the old crowd.

There hadn't been many idle afternoons heretofore during the summer; there'd always been some of the collegiate vacationing in town, and Pat had never needed other lure than her own piquant vivacity to assure herself of ample attention. Now, of course, it was different; she had so definitely tagged herself with the same Nicholas Devine that even the most ardent of the group had taken the warning.

"And I don't regret it either!" she told herself as she entered the house. "Trouble, mystery, suffering and all—I don't regret it! I've had my compensations too."

She sighed and trudged upstairs to prepare for dinner.

Morning found Pat in a fair frenzy of trepidation. She kept repeating to herself that two days wasn't enough, that more time might be required, that even had Nicholas Devine received her letter, he might not have answered at once. Yet she was quivering as she darted into the hall to examine the mail.

It was there! She spied a fragment of the irregular handwriting and seized the envelope from beneath a clutter of notes, bills, and advertisements. She glanced at the postmark. Chicago! He hadn't left the city, trusting perhaps to the anonymity conferred by its colossal swarm of humanity. Indeed, she thought as she stared at the missive, he might have moved around the corner, and save for the chance of a fortuitous meeting she'd never know it.

She tore open the envelope and scanned the several scrawled lines,

No heading, no salutation, not even a signature, just "Thursday evening at our place in the park." No more; she studied the few words intently, as if she could read into their bald phrasing the moods and hidden emotions of the writer.

A single phrase, but sufficient. The day was suddenly brighter, and the hope which had glowed so dimly yesterday was abruptly almost more than a hope—a certainty. All her doubts of Dr. Horker's abilities were forgotten; already the solution of this uncanny mystery seemed assured, and the restoration of romance imminent.

She carried the letter to her own room and tucked it carefully by the other in the drawer of the night-table.

Thursday evening—this evening! Many hours intervened between now and a reasonable time for the meeting, but they loomed no longer drab, dull, and hopeless. She lay on her bed and dreamed.

She could meet Nick as early as possible; perhaps at eight-thirty, and bring him directly to the Doctor's residence. No use wasting a moment, she mused; the sooner some light could be thrown on the affliction, the sooner they could lay the devil—exorcise it. Demon, fixed idea, mental aberration, or whatever Dr. Carl chose to call it, it had to be met and vanquished once and forever. And it could be vanquished; in her present mood she didn't doubt it. Then—after that—there was the prospect of her own Nick regained, and the sweet vistas opened by that reflection.

She lunched in an abstracted manner. In the afternoon, when the phone rang, she jumped in a startled manner, then relaxed with a shrug.

But this time it was for her. She darted into the hall to take the call on the lower phone; she was hardly surprised but thoroughly excited to recognize the voice of Nicholas Devine.

"Pat?"

"Nick! Oh, Nick, honey! What is it?"

"My note to you." Even across the wire she sensed the strain in his tense tones. "You've read it?"

"Of course, Nick! I'll be there."

"No," His voice was trembling. "You won't come, Pat. Promise you won't!"

"But why? Why not, Nick? Oh, it's terribly important that I see you!"

"You're not to come, Pat!"

"But—" An idea was struggling to her consciousness. "Nick, was it—?"

"Yes. You know now."

"But, honey, what difference does it make? You come. You must, Nick!"

"I won't meet you, I tell you!" She could hear his voice rising excitedly in pitch; she could feel the intensity of the struggle across unknown miles of lifeless copper wire.

"Nick," she said. "I'm going to be there, and you're going to meet me."

There was silence at the other end.

"Nick!" she cried anxiously. "Do you hear me? I'll be there. Will you?"

His voice sounded again, now flat and toneless.

"Yes," he said. "I'll be there."

The receiver clicked at the far end of the wire; there was only a futile buzzing in Pat's ears. She replaced the instrument and sat staring dubiously at it.

Had that been Nick, really her Nick, or—? Suppose she went to that meeting and found—the other? Was she willing to face another evening of indignities and terrors like those still fresh in her memory?

Still, she argued, what harm could come to her on that bench, exposed as it was to the gaze of thousands who wandered through the park on summer evenings? Suppose it was the other who met her; there was no way to force her into a situation such as that of Saturday night. Nick himself had chosen that very spot for their other meeting, and for that very reason.

"There's no risk in it," she told herself. "Nothing can possibly happen. I'll simply go there and bring Nick back to Dr. Carl's, along a lighted, busy street, the whole two blocks. What's there to be afraid of?"

Nothing at all, she answered herself. But suppose— She shuddered and deliberately abandoned her chain of thought as she rose and rejoined her mother.

CHAPTER TWENTY
The Assignation

Pat was by no means as buoyant as she had been in the morning. She approached the appointed meeting place with a feeling of trepidation that all her arguments could not subdue.

She surveyed the crowded walks of the park with relief; she felt confirmed in her assumption that nothing unpleasant could occur with so many onlookers. So she approached the bench with somewhat greater self-assurance than when she had left the house.

She saw the seat with its lone occupant, and hastened her steps. Nicholas Devine was sitting exactly as he had on that other occasion, chin cupped on his hands, eyes turned moodily toward the vast lake that coruscated now with the reflection of stars and many lights. As before, she moved close to his side before he looked up, but here the similarity of the two occasions vanished. Her fears were realized; she was looking into the red-gleaming eyes and expressionless features of his other self—the demon of Saturday evening!

"Sit down!" he said as a sardonic half-smile twisted his lips. "Aren't you pleased? Aren't you thrilled to the very core of your being?"

Pat stood irresolute; she controlled an impulse to break into sudden, abandoned flight. The imminence of the crowded walks again reassured her, and she seated herself gingerly on the extreme edge of the bench, staring at her companion with coolly inimical eyes. He returned her gaze with features as immobile as carven stone; only his red eyes gave evidence of the obscene, uncanny life behind the mask.

"Well?" said Pat in as frigid a voice as she could muster.

"Yes," said the other surveying her. "You are quite as I recalled you. Very pretty, almost beautiful, save for a certain irregularity in your features. Not unpleasant, however." His eyes traveled over her body; automatically she drew back, shrinking away from him. "You have a seductive body," he continued. "A most seductive body; I regret that circumstances prevented our full enjoyment of it. But that will come. Yes, that will come!"

"Oh!" said Pat faintly. It took all her determination to remain seated by the side of the horror.

"You were extremely attractive as I attired you Saturday," the other proceeded. His lips took on a curious sensual leer. "I could have done better with more time; I would have stripped you somewhat more completely. Everything, I think, except your legs; I am pleased by the sight of long, straight, silk clad legs, and should perhaps have received some pleasure by running these hands along them—scratching at proper intervals for the aesthetic effect of blood. But that too will come."

The girl sprang erect gasping and speechless in outraged anger. She turned abruptly; nothing remained of her determination now. She felt only an urge to escape from the sneering tormentor who had lost in her mind all connection with her own Nicholas Devine. She took a sudden step.

"Sit down!" She heard the tones of the entity behind her, flat, unchanged. "Sit down, else I'll drag you here!"

She paused in sheer surprise, turning a startled face on the other. "You wouldn't dare!" she said, amazed at the bald effrontery of the threat. "You won't dare touch me here!"

The other laughed. "Won't I? What have I to risk? He'll suffer for any deed of mine! You'll call for aid against me and only loose the hounds on him."

Pat stared blankly at the evil face. She had no answer; for once her ready tongue found no retort.

"Sit down!" reiterated the other, and she dropped dazedly to her position on the bench. She turned dark questioning eyes on him.

"Do you see," he sneered, "how weakening an influence is this love of yours? To protect him you are obeying me; this is my authority over you—this body I share with him!"

She made no reply; she was making a desperate effort to lash her mind into activity, to formulate some means of combating the being who tortured her.

"It has weakened him, too," the other proceeded. "This disturbed love of his has taken away the mastery which birth gave him, and his enfeeblement has given that mastery to me. He knows now the reason for his weakness; I tell it to him too late to harm me."

Pat struggled for composure. The very presence of the cold demon tore at the roots of her self-control, and she suppressed a fierce desire to break into hysterical laughter. Ridiculous, hopeless, incomprehensible situation! She forced her quivering throat to husky speech.

"What—what are you?" she stammered.

"Synapse! I'm a question of synapses," jeered the other. "Simple! Very simple! Ask your friend the Doctor!"

"I think," said the girl, a measure of control returning to her voice, "that you're a devil. You're some sort of a fiend that has managed to attach itself to Nick, and you're not human. That's what I think!"

"Think what you please," said the other. "We're wasting time here," he said abruptly. "Come."

"Where?" Pat was startled; she felt a recurrence of fright.

"No matter where. Come."

"I won't! Why do you want me?"

"To complete the business of Saturday night," he said. "Your lips have healed; they bleed no longer, but that is easy to remedy. Come."

"I won't!" exclaimed the girl in sudden panic. "I won't!" She moved as if to rise.

"You forget," intoned the being beside her. "You forget the authority vested in me by virtue of this love of yours. Let me convince you," He stretched forth a thin hand. "Move and you condemn your sweetheart to the punishment you threaten me."

He seized her arm, pinching the flesh brutally, his nails breaking the smooth skin. Pat felt her face turn ashy pale; she closed her eyes and bit her nearly-healed lips at the excruciating pain, but she made neither the slightest sound nor the faintest movement. She simply sat and suffered.

"You see!" sneered the other, releasing her. "Thank my kindly nature that I marked your arm instead of your face. Shall we go?"

A scarcely audible whimper of pain came from the girl's lips. She sat palled and unmoving, with her eyes still closed.

"No," she murmured faintly at last. "No, I won't go with you."

"Shall I drag you?"

"Yes. Drag me if you dare."

His hand closed on her wrist; she felt herself jerked violently to her feet, so roughly that it wrenched her shoulder. A startled, frightened little cry broke from her lips, and then she closed them firmly at the sight of several by-passers turning curious eyes on them.

"I'll come," she murmured. The glimmering of an idea had risen in her chaotic mind.

She followed him in grim, bitter silence across the clipped turf to the limit of the park. She recognized Nick's modest automobile standing in the line of cars along the street; her companion, or captor, moved directly towards it, opened the door and clambered in without a single backward glance. He turned about and watched her as she paused with one diminutive foot on the running board, and rubbed her hand over her aching arm.

"Get in!" he ordered coldly.

She made no move. "I want to know where you intend to take me."

"It doesn't matter. To a place where we can complete that unfinished experiment of ours. Aren't you happy at the prospect?"

"Do you think," she said unsteadily, "that I'd consent to that even to save Nick from disgrace and punishment? Do you think I'm fool enough for that?"

"We'll soon see," He extended his hand. "Scream—fight—struggle!" he jeered. "Call them down on your sweetheart!"

He had closed his hand on her wrist; she jerked it convulsively from his grasp.

"I'll bargain with you!" she gasped. She needed a moment's respite to clarify a thought that had been growing in her mind.

"Bargain? What have you to offer?"

"As much as you!"

"Ah, but I have a threat—the threat to your sweetheart! And I'm offering, too, the lure of that evil whose face so charmed you recently. Have you forgotten how nearly I won you to the worship of that principle? Have you forgotten the ecstasy of that pain?"

His terrible, bloodshot eyes were approaching her face; and strangely, the girl felt a curious recurrence of that illogical desire to yield that had swept over her on that disastrous night of Saturday. There had been an ecstasy; there had been a wild, ungodly, unhallowed pleasure in his blows, in the searing pain of his kisses on her lacerated lips. She realized vaguely that she was staring blankly, dazedly, into the red eyes, and that somewhere within her, some insane brain-cells were urging her to clamber to the seat beside him.

She tore her eyes away. She rubbed her bruised shoulder, and the pain of her own touch restored her vanishing logical faculties.

She returned her gaze to the face of the other, meeting his gaze now coolly.

"Nick!" she said earnestly, as if calling him from afar. "Nick!"

There was, she fancied, the faintest gleam of concern apparent in the features opposite her. She continued.

"Nick!" she repeated. "You can hear me, honey. Come to the house as soon as you are able. Come tonight, or any time; I'll wait until you do. You'll come, honey; you must!"

She backed away from the car; the other made no move to halt her. She circled the vehicle and dashed recklessly across the street. From the safety of the opposite walk she glanced back; the red-eyed visage was regarding her steadily through the glass of the window.

CHAPTER TWENTY-ONE
A Question of Synapses

Pat almost ran the few blocks to her home. She hastened along in a near panic, regardless of the glances of pedestrians she chanced to pass. With the disappearance of the immediate urge, the composure for which she had struggled had deserted her, and she felt shaken, terrified, and weak. Her arm ached miserably, and her wrenched shoulder pained at each movement. It was not until she attained her own doorstep that she paused, panting and quivering, to consider the events of the evening.

"I can't stand any more of this!" she muttered wretchedly to herself. "I'll just have to give up, I guess; I can't pit myself another time against—that thing."

She leaned wearily against the railing of the porch, rubbing her injured arm.

"Dr. Carl was right," she thought. "Nick was right; it's dangerous. There was a moment there at the end when he—or it—almost had me. I'm frightened," she admitted. "Lord only knows what might have happened had I been a little weaker. If the Lord does know," she added.

She found her latch-key and entered the house. Only a dim light burned in the hall; her mother, of course, was at the Club, and the maid and Magda were far away in their chambers on the third floor. She tossed her wrap on a chair, switched on a brighter light, and examined the painful spot on her arm, a red mark already beginning to turn a nasty blue, with two tiny specks of drying blood. She shuddered, and trudged wearily up the stairs to her room.

The empty silence of the house oppressed her. She wanted human companionship—safe, trustworthy, friendly company, anyone to distract her thoughts from the eerie, disturbing direction they were taking. She was still in somewhat of a panic, and suppressed with difficulty a desire to peep fearfully under the bed.

"Coward!" she chided herself. "You knew what to expect."

Suddenly the recollection of her parting words recurred to her. She had told Nick—if Nick had indeed heard—to come to the house, to come at once, tonight, if he could. A tremor of apprehension ran through her. Suppose he came; suppose he came as her own Nick, and she admitted him, and then—or suppose that other came, and managed by some trick to enter, or suppose that unholy fascination of his prevailed on her—she shivered, and brushed her hand distractedly across her eyes.

"I can't stand it!" she moaned. "I'll have to give up, even if it means never seeing Nick again. I'll have to!" She shook her head miserably as if to deny the picture that had risen in her mind of herself and that horror alone in the house.

"I won't stay here!" she decided. She peeped out of the west windows at the Doctor's residence, and felt a surge of relief at the sight of his iron-gray hair framed in the library window below. He was reading; she could see the book on his knees. There was her refuge; she ran hastily down the stairs and out of the door.

With an apprehensive glance along the street she crossed to his door and rang the bell. She waited nervously for his coming, and, with a sudden impulse, pulled her vanity-case from her bag and dabbed a film of powder over the mark on her arm. Then his ponderous footsteps sounded and the door opened.

"Hello," he said genially. "These late evening visits of yours are becoming quite customary—and see if I care!"

"May I come in a while?" asked Pat meekly.

"Have I ever turned you away?" He followed her into the library, pushed a chair forward for her, and dropped quickly into his own with an air of having snatched it from her just in time.

"I didn't want your old armchair," she remarked, occupying the other.

"And what's the trouble tonight?" he queried.

"I—well, I was just nervous. I didn't want to stay in the house alone."

"You?" His tone was skeptical. "You were nervous? That hardly sounds reasonable, coming from an independent little spitfire like you."

"I was, though. I was scared."

"And of what—or whom?"

"Of haunts and devils."

"Oh." He nodded, "I see you've had results from your letter-writing."

"Well, sort of."

"I'm used to your circumlocutions, Pat. Suppose you come directly to the point for once. What happened?"

"Why, I wrote Nick to get in touch with me, and I got a reply. He said to meet him in the park at a place we knew. This evening."

"And you did, of course."

"Yes, but before that, this afternoon, he called up and told me not to, but I insisted and we did."

"Told you not to, eh? And was his warning justified?"

"Yes. Oh, yes! When I came to the place, it was—the other."

"So! Well, he could hardly manhandle you in a public park."

Pat thought of her wrenched shoulder and bruised arm. She shuddered.

"He's horrible!" she said. "Inhuman! He kept referring to Saturday night, and he threatened that if I moved or made a disturbance he'd let Nick suffer the consequences. So I kept still while he insulted me."

"You nitwit!" There was more than a trace of anger in the Doctor's voice. "I want to see that pup of yours! We'll soon find out what this thing is—a mania or simply lack of a good licking!"

"What it is?" echoed Pat. "Oh—it told me! Dr. Carl, what's a synopsis."

"A synopsis! You know perfectly well."

"I mean applied to physiology or psychology or something. It—he told me he was a question of synopsis."

"This devil of yours said that?"

"Yes."

"Hum!" The Doctor's voice was musing. He frowned perplexedly, and then looked up abruptly. "Was it—did he by any chance say synapses? Not synopsis—synapses?"

"That's it!" exclaimed the girl. "He said he was a question of synapses. Does that explain him? Do you know what he is?"

"Doesn't explain a damn thing!" snapped Horker. "A synapse is a juncture, or the meeting of two nerves. It's why you can develop automatic motions and habits, like playing piano, or dancing. When you form a habit, the synapses of the nerves involved are sort of worn thin, so the nerves themselves are, in a sense, short-circuited. You go through motions without the need of your brain intervening, which is all a habit amounts to. Understand?"

"Not very well," confessed Pat.

"Humph! It doesn't matter anyway. I can't see that it helps to analyze your devil."

"I don't care if it's never analyzed," said Pat with a return of despondency. "Dr. Carl, I can't face that evil thing again. I can't do it, not even if it means never seeing Nick!"

"Sensible," said the Doctor approvingly. "I'd like to have a chance at him, but not enough to keep you in this state of jitters. Although," he added, "a lot of this mystery is the product of your own harum-scarum mind. You can be sure of that, honey."

"You would say so," responded the girl wearily. "You've never seen that—change. If it's my imagination, then I'm the one that needs your treatments, not Nick."

"It isn't all imagination, most likely," said Horker defensively. "I know these introverted types with their hysterias, megalomanias, and defense mechanisms! They've paraded through my office there for a good many years, Pat; they've provided the lion's share of my practice. But this young psychopathic of yours seems to have it bad—abnormally so, and that's why I'm so interested, apart from helping you, of course."

"I don't care," said Pat, repressing a desire to rub her injured arm. "I'm through. I'm scared out of the affair. Another week like this last one and I would be one of your patients."

"Best drop it, then," said Horker, eyeing her seriously. "Nothing's worth upsetting yourself like this, Pat."

"Nick's worth it," she murmured. "He's worth it—only I just haven't the strength. I haven't the courage. I can't do it!"

"Never mind, honey," the Doctor muttered, regarding her with all expression of concern. "You're probably well out of the mess. I know damn well you haven't told me everything about this affair—notably, how you acquired that ugly mark on your arm that's so carefully powdered over. So, all in all, I guess you're well out of it."

"I suppose I am." Her voice was still weary. Suddenly the glare of headlights drew her attention to the window; a car was stopping before her home. "There's Mother," she said. "I'll go on back now, Dr. Carl, and thanks for entertaining a lonesome and depressed lady."

She rose with a casual glance through the window, then halted in frozen astonishment and a trace of terror.

"Oh!" she gasped. The car was the modest coupe of Nicholas Devine.

She peered through the window; the Doctor rose and stared over her shoulder. "I told him to come," she whispered. "I told him to come when he was able. He heard me, he or—the other."

A figure alighted from the vehicle. Even in the dusk she could perceive the exhaustion, the weariness in its movements. She pressed her face to the pane, surveying the form with fascinated intentness. It turned, supporting itself against the car and gazing steadily at her own door. With the movement the radiance of a street-light illuminated its features.

"It's Nick!" she cried with such eagerness that the Doctor was startled. "It's my Nick!"

CHAPTER TWENTY-TWO
Doctor and Devil

Pat rushed to the door, out upon the porch, and down to the street. Dr. Horker followed her to the entrance and stood watching her as she darted toward the dejected figure beside the car.

"Nick!" she cried. "I'm here, honey. You heard me, didn't you?"

She flung herself into his arms; he held her eagerly, pressing a hasty, tender kiss on her lips. "You heard me!" she murmured.

"Yes," His voice was husky, strained. "What is it, Pat? Tell me quickly— God knows how much time we have!"

"It's Dr. Carl. He'll help us, Nick."

"Help us! No one can help us, dear. No one!"

"He'll try. It can't do any harm, honey. Come in with me. Now!"

"It's useless, I tell you!"

"But come," she pleaded. "Come anyway!"

"Pat. I tell you this battle has to be fought out by me alone. I'm the only one who can do anything at all and," he lowered his voice. "Pat, I'm losing!"

"Nick!"

"That's why I came tonight. I was too cowardly to make our last meeting—Monday evening in the park—a definite farewell. I wanted to, but I weakened. So tonight, Pat, it's a final goodbye, and you thank Heaven for it!"

"Oh, Nick dear!"

"It was touch and go whether I came at all tonight. It was a struggle, Pat; he is as strong as I am now. Or stronger."

The girl gazed searchingly into his worn, weary face. He looked miserably ill, she thought; he seemed as exhausted as one who had been engaged in a physical battle.

"Nick," she said insistently, "I don't care what you say; you're coming in with me. Only for a little while."

She tugged at his hand, dragging him reluctantly after her. He followed her to the porch where the open door still framed the great figure of the Doctor.

"You know Dr. Carl," she said.

"Come inside," growled Horker. Pat noticed the gruffness of his voice, his lack of any cordiality, but she said nothing as she pulled her reluctant companion through the door and into the library.

The Doctor drew up another chair, and Pat, more accustomed to his devices, observed that he placed it in such position that the lamp cast a stream of radiance on Nick's face. She sank into her own chair and waited silently for developments.

"Well," said Horker, turning his shrewd old eyes on Nick's countenance, "let's get down to cases. Pat's told me what she knows; we can take that much for granted. Is there anything more you might want to tell?"

"No, sir," responded the youth wearily. "I've told Pat all I know."

"Humph! Maybe I can ask some leading questions, then. Will you answer them?"

"Of course, any that I can."

"All right. Now," the Doctor's voice took on a cool professional edge, "you've had these—uh—attacks as long as you can remember. Is that right?"

"Yes."

"But they've been more severe of late?"

"Much worse, sir!"

"Since when?"

"Since—about as long as I've known Pat. Four or five weeks."

"Mm," droned the Doctor. "You've no idea of the cause for this increase in the malignancy of the attacks?"

"No sir," said Nick, after a barely perceptible hesitation.

"You don't think the cause could be in any way connected with, let us say, the emotional disturbances attending your acquaintance with Pat here?"

"No, sir," said the youth flatly.

"All right," said Horker. "Let that angle go for the present. Are there any after effects from these spells?"

"Yes. There's always a splitting headache." He closed his eyes. "I have one of them now."

"Localized?"

"Sir?"

"Is the pain in any particular region? Forehead, temples, eyes, or so forth?"

"No. Just a nasty headache."

"But no other after-effects?"

"I can't think of any others. Except, perhaps, a feeling of exhaustion after I've gone through what I've just finished." He closed his eyes as if to shut out the recollection.

"Well," mused the Doctor, "we'll forget the physical symptoms. What happens to your individuality, your own consciousness, while you're suffering an attack?"

"Nothing happens to it," said Nick with a suppressed shudder. "I watch and hear, but what he does is beyond my control. It's terrifying—horrible!" he burst out suddenly.

"Doubtless," responded Horker smoothly. "What about the other? Does that one stand by while you're in the saddle?"

"I don't know," muttered Nick dully. "Of course he does!" he added abruptly. "I can feel his presence at all times—even now. He's always lurking, waiting to spring forth, as soon as I relax!"

"Humph!" ejaculated the Doctor. "How do you manage to sleep?"

"By waiting for exhaustion," said Nick wearily. "By waiting until I can stay awake no longer."

"And can you bring this other personality into dominance? Can you change controls, so to speak, at will?"

"Why—yes," the youth answered, hesitating as if puzzled. "Yes, I suppose I could."

"Let's see you, then."

"But—" Horror was in his voice.

"No, Dr. Carl!" Pat interjected in fright. "I won't let him!"

"I thought you declared yourself out of this," said Horker with a shrewd glance at the girl.

"Then I'm back in it! I won't let him do what you want—anyway, not that!"

"Pat," said the Doctor with an air of patience, "you want me to treat this affliction, don't you? Isn't that what both of you want?"

The girl murmured a scarcely audible assent.

"Very well, then," he proceeded. "Do you expect me to treat the thing blindly—in the dark? Do you think I can guess at the cause without observing the effect?"

"No," said Pat faintly.

"Now then," he turned to Nick. "Let's see this transformation."

"Must I?" asked the youth reluctantly.

"If you want my help."

"All right," he agreed with another tremor. He sat passively staring at the Doctor; a moment passed. Horker heard Pat's nervous breathing; other than that, the room was in silence. Nicholas Devine closed his eyes, brushed his hand across his forehead. A moment more and he opened them to gaze perplexedly at the Doctor.

"He won't!" he muttered in astonishment. "He won't do it!"

"Humph!" snapped Horker, ignoring Pat's murmur of relief. "Finicky devil, isn't he? Likes to pick company he can bully!"

"I don't understand it!" Nick's face was blank. "He's been tormenting me until just now!" He looked at the Doctor. "You don't think I'm lying about it, do you, Dr. Horker?"

"Not consciously," replied the other coolly. "If I thought you were responsible for a few of the indignities perpetrated on Pat here, I'd waste no time in questions, young man, I'd be relieving myself of certain violent impulses instead."

"I couldn't harm Pat!"

"You gave a passable imitation of it, then! However, that's beside the point; as I say, I don't hold you responsible for aberrations which I believe are beyond your control. The main thing is a diagnosis."

"Do you know what it is?" cut in Pat eagerly.

"Not yet—at least, not for certain. There's only one real method available; these questions will get us nowhere. We'll have to psychoanalyze you, young man."

"I don't care what you do, if you can offer any hope!" he declared vehemently. "Let's get it over!"

"Not as easy as all that!" rumbled Horker. "It takes time; and besides. It can't be successful with the subject in a hectic mood such as yours," He glanced at his watch. "Moreover, it's after midnight."

He turned to Nicholas Devine. "We'll make it Saturday evening," he said. "Meanwhile, young man, you're not to see Pat. Not at all—understand? You can see her here when you come."

"That's infinitely more than I'd planned for myself," said the youth in a low voice. "I'd abandoned the hope of seeing her."

THE DARK OTHER

He rose and moved toward the door, and the others followed. At the entrance he paused; he leaned down to plant a brief tender kiss on the girl's lips, and moved wordlessly out of the door. Pat watched him enter his car, and followed the vehicle with her eyes until it disappeared. Then she turned to Horker.

"Do you really know anything about it?" she queried. "Have you any theory at all?"

"He's not lying," said the Doctor thoughtfully. "I watched him closely; he believes he's telling the truth."

"He is. I know what I saw!"

"He hasn't the signs of praecox or depressive," mused the Doctor. "It's puzzling; it's one of those functional aberrations, or a fixed delusion of some kind. We'll find out just what it is."

"It's the devil," declared Pat positively. "I don't care what sort of scientific tag you give it—that's what it is. You doctors can hide a lot of ignorance under a long name."

Horker paid no attention to her remarks. "We'll see what the psychoanalysis brings out," he said. "I shouldn't be surprised if the whole thing were the result of a defense mechanism erected by a timid child in an effort to evade responsibility. That's what it sounds like."

"It's a devil!" reiterated Pat.

"Well," said the Doctor, "if it is, it has one thing in common with every spook or devil I ever heard of."

"What's that?"

"It refuses to appear under any conditions where one has a chance to examine it. It's like one of these temperamental mediums trying to perform under a spotlight."

CHAPTER TWENTY-THREE
Werewolf

Pat awoke in rather better spirits. Somehow, the actual entrance of Dr. Horker into the case gave her a feeling of security, and her natural optimistic nature rode the pendulum back from despair to hope. Even the painful black-and-blue mark on her arm, as she examined it ruefully, failed to shake her buoyant mood.

Her mood held most of the day; it was only at evening that a recurrence of doubt assailed her. She sat in the dim living room awaiting the arrival of her mother's guests, and wondered whether, after all, the predicament was as easily solvable as she had assumed.

She watched the play of lights and shadows across the ceiling, patterns cast through the windows by moving headlights in the street, and wondered anew whether her faith in Dr. Carl's abilities was justified. Science! She had the faith of her generation in its omnipotence, but here in the dusk, the outworn superstitions of childhood became appalling realities, and some of Magda's stories, forgotten now for years, rose out of their graves and went squeaking and maundering like sheeted ghosts in a ghastly parade across the universe of her mind. The meaningless taunts she habitually flung at Dr. Carl's science became suddenly pregnant with truth; his patient, hard-learned science seemed intact no more than the frenzies of a witch-doctor dancing in the heart of a Rhodesian swamp.

What was it worth—this array of medical facts—if it failed to cure? Was medicine falling into the state of Chinese science—a vast collection of good rules for which the reasons were either unknown or long forgotten? She sighed; it was with a feeling of profound relief that she heard the voices of the Brocks outside; she played miserable bridge the whole evening, but it was less of an affliction than the solitude of her own thoughts.

Saturday morning, cloudy and threatening though it was found the pendulum once more at the other end of the arc. She found herself, if not buoyantly cheerful, at least no longer prey to the inchoate doubts and fears of the preceding evening. She couldn't even recall their nature; they had been apart from the cool, daytime logic that preached a common-sense reliance on accepted practices. They had been, she concluded, no more than childish nightmares induced by darkness and the play of shadows.

She dressed and ate a late breakfast; her mother was already *en route* to the Club for her bridge luncheon. Thereafter, she wandered into the kitchen for the company of Magda, whom she found with massive arms immersed in dish water. Pat perched on her particular stool beside the kitchen table and watched her at her work.

"Magda," she said finally.

"I'm listening, Miss Pat."

"Do you remember a story you told me a long time ago? Oh, years and years ago, about a man in your town who could change into something—some fierce animal. A wolf, or something like that."

"Oh, him!" said Magda, knitting her heavy brows. "You mean the werewolf."

"That's it! The werewolf. I remember it now—how frightened I was after I went to bed. I wasn't more than eight years old, was I?"

"I couldn't remember. It was years ago, though, for sure."

"What was the story?" queried Pat. "Do you remember that?"

"Why, it was the time the sheep were being missed," said the woman, punctuating her words with the clatter of dishes on the drain board. "Then there was a child gone, and another, and then tales of this great wolf about the country. I didn't see him; us little ones stayed under roof by darkness after that."

"That wasn't all of it," said Pat. "You told me more than that."

"Well," continued Magda, "there was my uncle, who was best hand with a rifle in the village. He and others went after the creature, and my uncle, he came back telling how he'd seen it plain against the sky, and how he'd fired at it. He couldn't miss, he was that close, but the wolf gave him a look and ran away."

"And then what?"

"Then the Priest came, and he said it wasn't a natural wolf. He melted up a silver coin and cast a bullet, and he gave it to my uncle, he being the best shot in the village. And the next night he went out once more."

"Did he get it?" asked Pat. "I don't remember."

"He did. He came upon it by the pasture, and he aimed his gun. The creature looked straight at him with its evil red eyes, and he shot it. When he came to it, there wasn't a wolf at all, but this man—his name I forget—with a hole in his head. And then the Priest, he said he was a werewolf, and only a silver bullet could kill him. But my uncle, he said those evil red eyes kept staring at him for many nights."

"Evil red eyes!" said Pat suddenly. "Magda," she asked in a faint voice, "could he change any time he wanted to?"

"Only by night, the Priest said. By sunrise he had to be back."

"Only by night!" mused the girl. Another idea was forming in her active little mind, another conception, disturbing, impossible to phrase. "Is that worse than being possessed by a devil, Magda?"

"Sure it's worse! The Priest, he could cast out the devil, but I never heard no cure for being a werewolf."

Pat said nothing further, but slid from her high perch to the floor and went soberly out of the kitchen. The fears of last night had come to life again, and now the overcast skies outside seemed a fitting symbol to her mood. She stared thoughtfully out of the living room windows, and the sudden splash of raindrops against the pane lent a final touch to the whole desolate ensemble.

"I'm just a superstitious little idiot!" she told herself. "I laugh at Mother because she always likes to play North and South, and here I'm letting myself worry over superstitions that were discarded before there was any such thing as a game called contract bridge."

But her arguments failed to carry conviction. The memory of the terrible eyes of that *other* had clicked too aptly to Magda's phrase. She couldn't subdue the picture that haunted her, and she couldn't cast off the apprehensiveness of her mood. She recalled gloomily that Dr. Horker was at the Club—wouldn't be home before evening, else she'd have gladly availed herself of his solid, matter-of-fact company.

She thought of Nick's appointment with the Doctor for that evening. Suppose his psychoanalysis brought to light some such horror as these fears of hers—that would forever destroy any possibility of happiness for her and Nick. Even though the Doctor refused to recognize it, called it by some polysyllabic scientific name, the thing would be there to sever them.

She wandered restlessly into the hall. The morning mail, unexamined, lay in its brazen receptacle, she moved over, fingering it idly. Abruptly she paused in astonishment—a letter in familiar script had flashed at her. She pulled it out; it was! It was a letter from Nicholas Devine!

She tore it open nervously, wondering whether he had reverted to his original refusal of Dr. Horker's aid, whether he was unable to

come, whether that had happened. But only a single unfolded
sheet slipped from the envelope, inscribed with a few brief lines of
poetry.

"The grief that is too faint for tears,
And scarcely breathes of pain,
May linger on a hundred years
Ere it creep forth again.
But I, who love you all too well,
To suffer your disdain,
Must try tonight that love to quell—
And try in vain!"

CHAPTER TWENTY-FOUR
The Dark Other

It was early in the evening, not yet eight o'clock, when Pat saw
the car of Nicholas Devine draw up before the house. She had already been watching half an hour, sitting cross-legged in the deep
window seat, like her jade Buddha. That equivocal poem of his
had disturbed her, lent an added strength to the moods and doubts
already implanted by Magda's mystical tale, and it was with a feeling
of trepidation that she watched him emerge wearily from his
vehicle and stare in indecision first at her window and then at the
Horker residence. The waning daylight was still sufficient to
delineate his worn features; she could see them, pale, harried, but
indubitably the mild features of her own Nick.

While he hesitated, she darted to the door and out upon the
porch. He gave her a wan smile of greeting, advanced to the foot
of the steps, and halted there.

"The Doctor's not home yet," she called to him. He stood motionless below her.

"Come up on the porch," she invited, as he made no move.

She uttered the words with a curious feeling of apprehension;
for even as she ached for his presence, the uncertain state of affairs
was frightening. She thought fearfully that what had happened
before might happen again. Still, there on the open porch, in
practically full daylight, and for so brief a time— Dr. Carl would be
coming very shortly, she reasoned.

"I can't," said Nick, staring wistfully at her. "You know I can't."

"Why not?"

"I promised. You remember—I promised Dr. Horker I'd not see you except in his presence."

"So you did," said Pat doubtfully. The promise offered escape from a distressing situation, she thought, and yet—somehow, seeing Nick standing pathetically there, she couldn't imagine anything harmful emanating from him. There had been many and many evenings in his company that had passed delightfully, enjoyably, safely. She felt a wave of pity for him; after all, the affliction was his, most of the suffering was his.

"We needn't take it so literally," she said almost reluctantly. "He'll be home very soon now."

"I know," said Nick soberly, "but it was a promise, and besides, I'm afraid."

"Never mind, honey," she said, after a momentary hesitation. "Come up and sit here on the steps, then—here beside me. We can talk just as well as there on the settee."

He climbed the steps and seated himself, watching Pat with longing eyes. He made no move to touch her, nor did she suggest a kiss.

"I read your poem, honey," she said finally. "It worried me."

"I'm sorry, Pat. I couldn't sleep. I kept wandering around the house, and at last I wrote it and took it out and mailed it. It was a vent, a relief from the things I'd been thinking."

"What things, honey?"

"A way, mostly," he answered gloomily, "of removing myself from your life. A permanent way."

"Nick!"

"I didn't, as you see, Pat. I was too cowardly, I suppose. Or perhaps it was because of this forlorn hope of ours. There's always hope, Pat; even the condemned man with his foot on the step to the gallows feels it."

"Nick dear!" she cried, her voice quavering in pity. "Nick, you mustn't think of those things! It might weaken you—make it easier for him!"

"It can't. If it frightens him, I'm glad."

"Honey," she said soothingly, "we'll give Dr. Carl a chance. Promise me you'll let him try, won't you?"

"Of course I will. Is there anything I'd refuse to promise you, Pat? Even," he added bitterly, "when reason tells me it's a futile promise."

"Don't say it!" she urged fiercely. "We've got to help him. We've got to believe— There he comes!" she finished with sudden relief.

The Doctor's car turned up the driveway beyond his residence. Pat saw his face regarding them as he disappeared behind the building.

"Come on, honey," she said, "let's get at the business."

They moved slowly over to the Doctor's door, waiting there until his ponderous footsteps sounded. A light flashed in the hall, and his broad shadow filled the door for a moment before it opened. "Come in," he rumbled jovially. "Fine evening we're spoiling, isn't it?"

"It could be," said Pat as they followed him into the library, "only it'll probably rain some more."

"Hah!" snorted the Doctor, frowning at the mention of rain. "The course was soft. Couldn't get any distance, and it added six strokes to my score. At least six!"

Pat chuckled commiserating. "You ought to lay out a course in Greenland," she suggested. "They say anyone can drive a ball a quarter of a mile on smooth ice."

"Humph!" The Doctor waved toward a great, low chair. "Suppose you sit over there, young man, and we'll get about our business. And don't look so woebegone about it."

Nick settled himself nervously in the designated chair; the Doctor seated himself at a little distance to the side, and Pat sat tensely in her usual place beside the hearth. She waited in strained impatience for the black magic of psychoanalysis to commence.

"Now," said Horker, "I want you to keep quiet, Pat—if possible. And you, young man, are to relax, compose yourself, get yourself into as passive a state as possible. Do you understand?"

"Yes, sir," The youth leaned back in the great chair, closing his eyes.

"So! Now, think back to your childhood, your earliest memories. Let your thoughts wander at random, and speak whatever comes to your mind."

Nick sat a moment in silence. "That's hard to do, sir," he said finally.

"Yes. It will take practice, weeks of it, perhaps. You'll have to acquire the knack of it, but to do that, we'll have to start."

"Yes, sir," He sat with closed eyes. "My mother," he murmured, "was kind. I remember her a little, just a little. She was very gentle, not apt to blame me. She could understand. Made excuses to my father. He was hard, not cruel—strict. Couldn't understand. Blamed me when I wasn't to blame. Other did it. I wasn't mischievous—but got the blame. Couldn't explain, he wouldn't believe me." He paused uncertainly.

"Go on," said Horker quietly, while Pat strained her ears to listen.

"Mrs. Stevens," he continued. "Governess after Mother died. Strict like Father, got punished when I wasn't to blame. Just as bad after Father died. Always blamed. Couldn't explain, nobody believed me. Other threw cat in window. I had to go to bed. Put salt in bird seed, broke leg of chair to make it fall. Punished—I couldn't explain." His voice droned into silence; he opened his eyes. "That all," he said nervously.

"Good enough for the first time," said the Doctor briskly. "Wait a few weeks; we'll have your life's history out of you. It takes practice."

"Is that all?" queried Pat in astonishment.

"All for the first time. Later we'll let him talk half an hour at a stretch, but it takes practice, as I've mentioned. You run along home now," he said to Nick.

"But it's early!" objected Pat.

"Early or not," said the Doctor, "I'm tired, and you two aren't to see each other except here. You remember that."

Nick rose from his seat in the depths of the great chair. "Thank you, sir," he said. "I don't know why, but I feel easier in your presence. The—the struggle disappears while I'm here."

"Well," said Horker with a smile, "I like patients with confidence in me. Goodnight."

At the door Nick paused, turning wistful eyes on Pat. "Good night," he said, leaning to give her a light kiss. A rush of some emotion twisted his features; he stared strangely at the girl. "I'd better go," he said abruptly, and vanished through the door.

"Well?" said Pat questioningly, turning to the Doctor. "Did you learn anything from that?"

"Not much," the other admitted, yawning. "However, the results bear out my theory."

"How?"

"Did you notice how he harped on the undeserved punishment theme? He was punished for another's mischief?"

"Yes. What of that?"

"Well, picture him as a timid, sensitive child, rather afraid of being punished. Afraid, say, of being locked up in a dark closet. Now, when he inadvertently commits a mischief as all children do, he tries desperately to divert the blame from himself. But there's no one else to blame! So what does he do?"

"What?"

"He invents this other, the mischievous one, and blames him. And now the other has grown to the proportions of a delusion, haunting him, driving him to commit acts apart from his normal inclinations. Understand? Because I'm off to bed whether you do or not."

"I understand all right," murmured Pat uncertainly as she moved to the door. "But somehow, it doesn't sound reasonable."

"It will," said the Doctor. "Goodnight."

Pat wandered slowly down the steps and through the break in the hedge, musing over Doctor Horker's expression of opinion. Then, according to him, the devil was nothing more than an invention of Nick's mind, the trick of a cowardly child to evade just punishment. She shook her head; it didn't sound like Nick at all. For all his gentleness and sensitivity, he wasn't the one to hide behind a fabrication. He wasn't a coward; she was certain of that. And she was as sure as she could ever be that he hated, feared, loathed this personality that afflicted him; he couldn't have created it.

She sighed, mounted the steps, and fumbled for her key. The sound of a movement behind her brought a faint gasp of astonishment. She turned to see a figure materializing from the shadows of the porch. The light from the hall fell across its features, and she drew back as she recognized Nicholas Devine—not the being she had just kissed good night, but in the guise of her tormentor, the red-eyed demon!

CHAPTER TWENTY-FIVE
The Demon Lover

Pat drew back, leaning against the door, and her key tinkled on the concrete of the porch. She was startled, shocked, but not as completely terrified as she might have expected. After all, she thought rapidly, they were standing in full view of a public street, and Dr. Carl's residence was but a few feet distant. She could summon his help by screaming.

"Well!" she exclaimed, eyeing the figure inimically. "Your appearances and disappearances are beginning to remind me of the Cheshire Cat."

"Except for the grin," said the other in his cold tones.

"What do you want?" snapped Pat.

"You know what I want."

"You'll not get it," said the girl angrily. "You—you're doomed to extinction, anyway! Go away!"

"Suppose," said the other with a strange, cold, twisted smile, "it were *he* that's doomed to extinction—what then?"

"It isn't!" cried Pat. "It isn't!" she repeated, while a quiver of uncertainty shook her. "He's the stronger," she said defiantly.

"Then where is he now?"

"Dr. Carl will help us!"

"Doctor!" sneered the other. "He and his clever theory! Am I an illusion?" he queried sardonically, thrusting his red-glinting eyes toward her. "Am I the product of his puerile, vacillating nature? Bah! I gave you the clue, and your Doctor hasn't the intelligence to follow it!"

"Go away!" murmured Pat faintly. The approach of his face had unnerved her, and she felt terror beginning to stir within her. "Go away!" she said again. "Why do you have to torment me? Anyone would serve your purpose—any woman!"

"You have an aesthetic appeal, as I've told you before," replied the other in that toneless voice of his. "There is a pleasure in the detachment of black hair and pale skin, and your body is seductive, most seductive. Another might afford me less enjoyment, and besides, you hate me. Don't you hate me?" He peered evilly at her.

"Oh, God—yes!" The girl was shuddering.

"Say it, then! Say you hate me!"

"I hate you!" the girl cried vehemently. "Will you go away now?"

"With you!"

"I'll scream if you come any closer. You don't dare touch me; I'll call Dr. Horker."

"You'll only damage *him*—your lover."

"Then I'll do it! He'll understand."

"Yes," said the other reflectively. "He's fool enough to forgive you. He'll forgive you anything—the weakling!"

"Go away! Get away from here!"

The other stared at her out of blood-shot eyes. "Very well," he said in his flat tones. "This time the victory is yours."

He backed slowly toward the steps. Pat watched him as he moved, feeling a surge of profound relief as his shadow shifted, her key gleamed silver at her feet, and she stooped to retrieve it.

There was a flash of motion as her eyes left the form of her antagonist. A hand was clamped violently over her mouth, an arm pressed with steel-like rigidity about her body. Nicholas Devine was dragging her toward the steps; she was half-way down before she recovered her wits enough to struggle.

She writhed and twisted in his grasp. She drove her elbow into his body with all her power, and kicked with the strength of desperation at his legs. She bit into the palm across her mouth—and suddenly, with a subdued grunt of pain, he released her so abruptly that her own struggles sent her spinning blindly into the bushes of the hedge.

She turned gasping, unable for the moment to summon sufficient breath to scream, the other stood facing her with his eyes gleaming terribly into her own; then they ranged slowly from her diminutive feet to the rumpled ebony of her hair that she was brushing back with her hands from her pallid, frightened face.

"Obstinate," he observed, rubbing his injured palm. "Obstinate and unbroken—but worth the trouble. Well worth it!" He reached out a swift hand, seizing her wrist as she backed against the bushes.

Pat twisted around, gazing frantically at Doctor Horker's house, where a light had only now flashed on in the upper windows. Her breath flowed back into her lungs with a strengthening rush.

"Dr. Carl!" she screamed. "Dr. Carl! Help me!"

The other spun her violently about. She had a momentary glimpse of a horribly evil countenance, then he drew back his arm and shot a clenched fist to her chin.

The world reeled into a blaze of spinning lights that faded quickly to darkness. She felt her knees buckling beneath her, and realized that she was crumpling forward toward the figure before her. Then for a moment she was aware of nothing.

She didn't quite lose consciousness, or at least for no more than a moment. She was suddenly aware that she was gazing down at a moving pavement, at her own arms dangling helplessly toward it. She perceived that she was lying limply across Nicholas Devine's shoulder with his arms clenched about her knees. And then, still unable to make the slightest resistance, she was bundled roughly into the seat of his coupe; he was beside her, and the car was purring into motion.

She summoned what remained of her strength. She drew herself erect, fumbling at the handle of the door with a frantic idea of casting herself out of the car to the street. The creature beside her jerked her violently back; as she reeled into the seat, he struck her again with the side of his fist. It was a random blow, delivered with scarcely a glance at her; it caught her on the forehead, snapping her head with an audible thump against the wall of the vehicle. She swayed for a moment with closing eyes, then collapsed limply against him, this time in complete unconsciousness.

That lapse too must have been brief. She opened dazed eyes on a vista of moving street lights; they were still in the car, passing now along some unrecognized thoroughfare lined with dark old homes. She lay for some moments uncomprehending; she was completely unaware of her situation.

It dawned on her slowly. She moaned, struggled away from the shoulder against which she had been leaning, and huddled miserably in the far corner of the seat. Nicholas Devine gave her a single glance with his unpleasant eyes, and turned them again on the street.

The girl was helpless, unable to put forth the strength even for another attempt to open the door. She was still only half aware of her position, and realized only that something appalling was occurring to her. She lay in passive misery against the cushions of the seat as the other turned suddenly up a dark driveway and into the open door of a small garage. He snapped off the engine, extinguished the headlights, and left them in a horrible, smothering, silent darkness.

She heard him open the door on his side; after an apparently interminable interval, she heard the creak of the hinges on her own side. She huddled terrified, voiceless, and immobile.

He reached in, fumbling against her in the darkness. He found her arm, and dragged her from the car. Again, as on that other occasion, she found herself reeling helplessly behind him through the dark as he tugged at her wrist. He paused at a door in the building adjacent to the garage, searching in his pocket with his free hand.

"I won't go in there!" she said dazedly. The other made no reply, but inserted a key in the lock, turned it, and swung open the door.

He stepped through it, dragging her after him. With a sudden access of desperate strength, she caught the frame of the door, jerked violently on her prisoned wrist, and was unexpectedly free. She reeled away, turned toward the street, and took a few faltering steps down the driveway.

Almost instantly her tormentor was upon her, and his hand closed again on her arm. Pat had no further strength; she sank to the pavement and crouched there, disregarding the insistent tugging on her arm.

"Come on," he growled. "You only delay the inevitable. Must I drag you?"

She made no reply. He tugged violently at her wrist, dragging her a few inches along the pavement. Then he stooped over her, raised her in his arms, and bore her toward the dark opening of the door. He crowded her roughly through it, disregarding the painful bumping of her shoulders and knees. She heard the slam of the door as he kicked it closed, and she realized that they were mounting a flight of stairs, moving somewhere into the oppressive threatening darkness.

Then they were moving along a level floor, and her arm was bruised against another door. There was a moment of stillness, and then she was released, dropped indifferently to the surface of a bed or couch. A moment later a light flashed on.

The girl was conscious at first only of the gaze of the red eyes. They held her own in a fascinating, unbreakable, trance-like spell. Then, in a wave of dizziness, she closed her own eyes.

"Where are we?" she murmured. "In Hell?"

"You should call it Heaven," came the sardonic voice. "It's the home of your sweetheart. His home—and mine!"

CHAPTER TWENTY-SIX
The Depths

"Heaven and hell always were the same place," said Nicholas Devine, his red eyes glaring down at the girl. "We'll demonstrate the fact."

Pat shifted wearily, and sat erect, passing her hand dazedly across her face. She brushed the tangled strands of black hair from before her eyes, and stared dully at the room in which she found herself.

It had some of the aspects of a study, and some of a laboratory, or perhaps a doctor's office. There was a case of dusty books on the wall opposite, and another crystal-fronted cabinet containing glassware, bottles, little round boxes suggestive of drugs or pharmaceuticals. There was a paper-littered table too; she gave a convulsive shudder at the sight of a bald, varnished death's head, its lower jaw articulated, that reposed on a pile of papers and grinned at her.

"Where—" she began faintly.

"This was the room of your sweetheart's father," said the other. "His and my mutual father. He was an experimenter, a researcher, and so, in another sense, am I!" He leered evilly at her. "He used this chamber to further his experiments, and I for mine—the carrying on of a noble family tradition!"

The girl scarcely heard his words; the expressionless tone carried no meaning to the chaos which was her mind. She felt only an inchoate horror and a vague but all-encompassing fear, and her head was aching from the blows he had dealt her.

"What do you want?" she asked dully.

"Why, there is an unfinished experiment. You must remember our interrupted proceedings of a week ago! Have you already forgotten the early steps of our experiment in evil?"

Pat cringed at the cold, sardonic tones of the other. "Let me go," she whimpered. "Please!" she appealed. "Let me go!"

"In due time," he responded. "You lack gratitude," he continued. "Last time, out of the kindness that is my soul, I permitted you to dull your senses with alcohol, but you failed, apparently, to appreciate my indulgence. But this time—" His eyes lit up queerly. "—this time you approach the consummation of our experiment with undimmed mind!"

He approached her. She drew her knees up, huddling back on the couch, and summoned the final vestiges of her strength.

"I'll kick you!" she muttered desperately. "Keep back from me!" He paused just beyond her reach. "I had hoped," he ironically, "if not for your cooperation, at least for no further active resistance. It's quite useless; I told you days ago that this time would come."

He advanced cautiously; Pat thrust out her foot, driving it with all her power. Instantly he drew back, catching her ankle in his hand. He jerked her leg sharply upwards, and she was precipitated violently to the couch. Again he advanced.

The girl writhed away from him. She slipped from the foot of the couch and darted in a circle around him, turning in an attempt to gain the room's single exit—the door by which they had entered. He moved quickly to intercept her; he closed the door as she backed despairingly away, retreating to the far end of the room. Once more he faced her, his malicious eyes gleaming, and moved deliberately toward her.

She drew back until the table halted her; she pressed herself against it as if to force her way still further. The other moved at unaltered pace. Suddenly her hand pressed over some smooth, round, hard object; she grasped it and flung the grinning skull at the more terrible face that approached her. He dodged; there was a crash of glass as the gruesome missile shattered the pane of the cabinet of drugs. And inexorably, Nicholas Devine approached once more.

She moved along the edge of the table, squeezed herself between it and the wall. Behind her was one of the room's two windows, curtainless, with drawn shades. She found the cord, jerked it, and let the blind coil upward with an abrupt snap.

"I'll throw myself through the window!" she announced with a son of desperate calm. "Don't dare move a step closer!"

The demon paused once more in his deliberate advance. "You will, of course," he said as if considering. "Given the opportunity. Your body torn and broken, spotted with blood—that might be a pleasure second only to that I plan."

"You'll suffer for it!" said the girl hysterically. "I'll be glad to do it, knowing you'll suffer!"

"Not I—your sweetheart."

"I don't care! I can't stand it!"

The other smiled his demoniac smile, and resumed his advance. She watched him in terror that had now reached the ultimate degree; her mind could bear no more. She turned suddenly, raised her arm, and beat her fist against the pane of the window.

With the surprising resistance glass sometimes displays, it shook at her blow but did not shatter. She drew back for a second attempt, and her udraised arm was caught in a rigid grip, and she was dragged backward to the center of the room, thrown heavily to the floor. She sat dazedly looking up at the form standing over her.

"Must I render you helpless again?" queried the flat voice of the other. "Are you not yet broken, convinced of the uselessness of this struggle?"

She made no answer, staring dully at his immobile features.

"Are you going to fight me further?" As she was still silent, he repeated, "Are you?"

She shook her head vaguely. "No," she muttered. She had reached the point of utter indifference; nothing at all was important enough now to struggle for.

"Stand up!" ordered the being above her.

She pulled herself wearily to her feet, leaning against the wall. She closed her eyes for a moment, then opened them dully as the other moved.

"What—are you—are you going to do?" she murmured.

"First," said the demon coldly, "I shall disrobe you somewhat more completely than on our other occasion. Thereafter we will proceed to the consummation of our experiment."

She watched him indifferently, uncomprehendingly, as he crooked a thin finger in the neck of her frock. She felt the pressure as he pulled, heard the rip of the fabric, and the pop of buttons, but she was conscious of no particular sensation as the garment cascaded into a black and red pool at her feet. She stood passive as he hooked his finger in the strap of her vest, and that too joined the little mound of cloth. She shivered slightly as she stood bared to the waist, but gave no other sign.

Again the thin hand moved toward her; from somewhere in her tormented spirit a final shred of resistance arose, and she pushed the questing member feebly to one side. She heard a low, sardonic laugh from her oppressor.

"Look at me!" he commanded.

She raised her eyes wearily; she drew her arm about her in a forlorn gesture of concealment. Her eyes met the strange orbs of the other, and a faint thrill of horror stirred; other than this, she felt nothing. Then his eyes were approaching her; she was conscious of the illusion that they were expanding, filling all the space in front of her. Their weird glow filled the world, dominated everything.

"Will you yield?" he queried.

The eyes commanded. "Yes," she said dully.

She felt his hands icy cold on her bare shoulders. They traveled like a shudder about her body, and suddenly she was pressed close to him.

"Are you mine?" he demanded. For the first time there was a tinge of expression in the toneless voice, a trace of eagerness. She made no answer; her eyes, held by his, stared like the eyes of a person in a trance, unwinking, fascinated.

"Are you mine?" he repeated, his breath hissing on her check.

"Yes," She heard her own voice in automatic reply.

"Mine—for the delights of evil?"

"Yours!" she murmured. The eyes had blotted out everything.

"And do you hate me?"

"No."

The arms about her tightened into crushing bands. The pressure stopped her breath; her very bones seemed to give under their fierce compression.

"Do you hate me?" he muttered.

"Yes!" she gasped. "Yes! I hate you!"

"Ah!" He twisted his hand in her black hair, wrenching it roughly back. "Are you ready now for the consummation? To look upon the face of evil?"

She made no reply. Her eyes, as glassy as those of a sleepwalker, stared into his.

"Are you ready?"

"Yes," she said.

He pressed his mouth to hers. The fierceness of the kiss bruised her lips, the pull of his hand in her hair was a searing pain, the pressure of his arm about her body was a suffocation. Yet—somehow—there was again the dawning of that unholy pleasure—the same degraded delight that had risen in her on that other occasion, in the room of the red-checked table cloth. Through some hellish alchemy the leaden pain was transmuting itself into the garish gold of a horrible, abnormal pleasure. She found her crushed lips attempting a feeble, painful response.

At her movement, she felt herself swung abruptly from her feet. With his lips still crushing hers, he raised her in his arms; she felt herself borne across the room. He paused; there was a sudden release, and she crashed to the hard surface of the couch, whose rough covering scratched the bare flesh of her back. Nicholas Devine bent over her; she saw his hand stretch toward her single remaining garment. And again, from somewhere in her harassed soul, a spark of resistance flashed.

"Nick!" she moaned. "Oh, Nick! Help me!"

"Call him!" said the other, a sneer on his face. "Call him! He hears; it adds to his torment!"

She covered her eyes with her hands. She felt his hand slip coldly between her skin and the elastic about her waist.

"Nick!" she moaned again. "Nick! Oh, my God! Nick!"

CHAPTER TWENTY-SEVEN
Two in Hell

The cold hand against Pat was still; she felt it rigid and stiff on her flesh. She lay passive with closed eyes; having voiced her final appeal, she was through. The words torn from her misery represented the final iota of spirit remaining to her; and her bruised body and battered mind had nothing further to give.

The hand quivered and withdrew. For a moment more she lay motionless with her arms clutched about her, then she opened her eyes, gazing dully, hopelessly at the demon standing over her. He was watching her with a curious abstracted frown; as she stirred the scowl intensified, and he drew back a step.

His face, contorted suddenly in a spasm of some unguessable emotion. His fists clenched; a low unintelligible mutter broke from his lips, "Strange!" she heard him say, and after a moment, "I'm still master here!"

He was master; in a moment the emotion vanished, and he was again standing over her, his face the same impassive demoniac mask. She watched him in a dull stupor of despair that was too deep for even a whimper of pain as he wrenched at the elastic about her waist and it cut into her flesh and parted. He tore the garment away, and the red eyes bored, down with a wild elation in their depths.

Mine!" the being muttered, a new hoarseness in his voice. "Are you mine?" Pat made no answer; his voice croaked in more insistent tones, "Are you mine?"

She could not reply. She felt his fingers bite into the flesh of her shoulder. She was shaken roughly, violently, and the question came again, fiercely. The eyes flamed in command, and she felt through her languor and weakness, the stirring of that strange and unholy fascination that he held over her.

"Answer!" he croaked. "Are you mine?"

The torture of his searing grip on her shoulder wrung an answer from her.

"Yes," she murmured faintly. "Yours." She closed her eyes again in helpless resignation. She felt the hand withdrawn, and she lay passive, waiting, on the verge of unconsciousness, numb, spirit-broken, and beaten.

Nothing happened. After a long interval she opened her eyes, and saw the other standing again with clenched fists and contorted countenance. His features were writhing in the intensity of his struggle; a strange low snarl came from his lips. He backed away from her, step by step; he leaned against the bookshelves, and beads of perspiration formed on his scowling face.

He was no longer master! She saw the change; imperceptibly the evil vanished from his features, and suddenly they were no longer his, but the weary, horror-stricken visage of her Nick! The red eyes were no longer Satanic, but only the blood-shot, troubled, gentle eyes of her sweetheart, and the lips had lost their grimness, and gasped and quivered and trembled. He reeled against the wall, staggered to the chair at the table, and sank weakly into it.

Pat was far too exhausted, far too dazed, to feel anything but the faintest sensation of relief. She realized only dimly that tears were welling from her eyes, and that sharp sobs were shaking her. She was for the moment unable to stir, but it was not long before the being at the table turned stricken eyes on her and she moved. Then she drew her knees up before her, as if to hide her body behind their slim, chiffon-clad grace.

Nick rose from the table, approaching her with weary, hesitant tread. He seized a cover of some sort that was folded over the foot of the couch, shook it out and cast it over her. She clutched it about her body, sat erect and leaned back against the wall in utter exhaustion. Many minutes passed with no word from either of the occupants of the unholy chamber. It was Nick who broke the long silence.

"Pat," he murmured in low tones. "Pat—Dear. Are you—all right?"

She stared at him dazedly without answer.

"Honey!" he said. "Honey! Tell me you're all right!"

"All right?" she repeated uncomprehendingly. "Yes. I guess I'm all right."

"Then go, Pat! Get away from here before he—before anything happens! Put your clothes on and hurry away!"

"I can't!" she faintly. "I—can't!"

"You must, Honey!"

"I'm just—not able to. I will soon, Nick—honest. When I—when I get my breath back."

"Pat!" There was anguish in the cry. "Oh, God—Pat! We mustn't ever be together again—not ever!"

"No," she said. A bit of sanity was returning to her; comprehension of her position sent a shudder through her. "No, we mustn't."

"I couldn't bear another night like this—watching! I'd go mad!"

"Oh!" she choked, tears starting. "If you hadn't come back, Nick!"

"I conquered him," he said. "I don't think I could do it again. It was your call that gave me the strength, Pat." He shook his head as if bewildered. "He thought it was being in love with you that weakened me, but in the end it was that which gave me the strength to subdue him."

"I'm scared!" said the girl suddenly. "Oh, Nick! I'm frightened!"

"You'd better go. You'd better dress and leave at once, Honey. Here…" He gathered her clothes from the floor, depositing them beside her on the couch. "There are pins in the tray on the table, Pat. Fix yourself up as well as you can, dear—and hurry out of here!"

He turned toward the door as if to leave, and a shock of terror shook her.

"Nick!" she cried. "Don't go away! I'm more afraid when I can't see you—afraid that he—" She broke off sobbing.

"All right, Honey, I'll turn my back."

She slipped out from under the blanket, found the pins, and repaired her ruined costume. The frock was torn, crushed and bedraggled; she pinned it together at the throat, though her trembling fingers made the task difficult. She pulled it on and took a tentative step toward the door.

"Nick!" she called as a wave of dizziness sent her swaying against the wall.

"What's the matter, Honey?" He turned anxiously at her cry.

"I'm dizzy," she moaned. "My head aches, and—I'm scared!"

"Pat, darling! You can't go out alone like this—and," he added miserably, "I can't take you!" He slipped his arm around her tenderly, supporting her to the couch. "Honey, what'll we do?"

"I'll be—all right," she murmured. "I'll go in a moment." The dizziness was leaving her; strength was returning.

"You must!" he said dolefully. "What a parting, Pat! Never to see you again, and then having this to remember as farewell!"

"I know, Nick. You see, I love you too." She turned her dark, troubled eyes on him. "Honey, kiss me goodbye! We'll have that to remember anyway!" Tears were again on her cheeks.

"Do I dare?" he asked despondently. "After the things these lips of mine have said, and what these arms have done to you?"

"But you didn't, Nick! Could I blame you for—that *other?*"

"God! You're kind, Pat! Honey, if ever I win out in this battle, if ever I know I'm the final victor, I'll—No," he said his tones dropping abruptly. "I'll never come back to you, Pat. It's far too dangerous, and—can I ever be certain? Can I?"

"I don't know, Nick. Can you?"

"I can't be, Pat! I'll never be sure that he isn't just dormant, as he was before, waiting for my weakness to betray me! I'll never be certain, Honey! It has to be goodbye!"

"Then kiss me!"

She clung to him; the room that had been so recently a chamber of horrors was transformed. As she held him, as her lips were pressed to his, she thought suddenly of the words of the demon, that Heaven and Hell were always the same place. They had taken on a new meaning, those words; she drew away from Nick and turned her tear-bright eyes tenderly on his.

"Honey," she murmured, "I don't want you to leave me. I don't want you to go!"

"Nor do I want to, Pat! But I must."

"You mustn't! You're to stay, and we'll fight it out together—be married, or any way that permits us to fight it through together."

"Pat! Do you think I'd consent to that?"

"Nick," she said. "Nick darling—it's worth it to me! I'm realizing it now; thought it wasn't—but it is! I can't lose you, Nick—anything, even that *other*, is better than losing you."

"You're sweet, Pat! You know I'd trade my very soul for that, but— No. I can't do it! And don't torture me by suggesting it again."

"But I will, Nick!" She was speaking softly, earnestly. "You're worth anything to me! If he should kill me, you'd still be worth it!" She gazed tenderly at him. "I'd want to die anyway without you!"

"No more than I without you," he muttered brokenly. "But I won't do it, Pat! I won't do that to you!"

"I love you, Nick!" she said in a low voice. "I don't want to live without you. Do you understand me, dear? I don't want to live without you!"

He stared at her somberly. "I've thought of that too," he said. "Pat—if I only believed that we'd be together after, together anywhere, I'd say yes. If only I believed there were an afterwards!"

"Doesn't he prove that by his very existence?"

"Your Doctor would deny that."

"Doctor Carl never saw him, Nick. And anyway, even oblivion together would be better than being separated, and far better than this!"

He gazed at her silently. She spoke again, "That doesn't frighten me, Nick. It's only losing you that frightens me, especially the fear of losing you to him."

He continued his silent gaze. Suddenly he drew her close to him, held her in a tight, tender embrace.

CHAPTER TWENTY-EIGHT
Lunar Omen

After a considerable interval, during which Nick held the girl tightly and silently in his arms, he released her, sat with his head resting on his cupped palms in an attitude of deep study. Pat, beside him, fell mechanically to re-pinning the throat of her frock, which had opened during the moments of the embrace. He rose to his feet, pacing nervously before her.

"It isn't a thing to do on the impulse of a moment, Pat," he muttered, pausing at her side. "You must see that."

"It isn't the impulse of a moment."

"But one doesn't abandon everything, the whole world, so easily, Honey. One doesn't cast away a last hope, however forlorn a hope it may be!"

"Is there a hope, Nick?" she asked gently. "Is there a chance left to us?"

"I don't know! Before God—I—don't know!"

"If there's a chance, the very slightest shadow of the specter of a chance, we'll take it, won't we? Because the other way is always open to us, Nick."

"Yes. It's always open."

"But we won't take that chance," she continued defiantly, "if it involves my losing you, Honey. I meant what I said, Nick. I don't want to live without you!"

"What chance have we?" he queried somberly. "Those are our alternatives—life apart, death together."

"Then you know my choice!" she cried desperately. "Nick, Honey—don't let's draw it out in futile talking! I can't stand it!"

He moved his hand in a gesture of bewilderment and frustration, and turned away, striding nervously toward the window whose blind she had raised. He leaned his hands on the table, peering dejectedly out upon the street below.

"What time," he asked irrelevantly in a queer voice, "did the Doctor say the moon rose? Do you remember?"

"No," she said tensely. "Oh, Honey! Please—don't stand there with your back to me now, when I'm half crazy!"

"I'm thinking," he responded. "It rises a little earlier each night—or is it later? No matter; come here, Pat."

She rose wearily and joined him; he slipped his arm about her, and drew her against him.

She looked out upon a dim-lit street or court, at the blind end of which the house was apparently situated. Far off at the open end, across a distant highway where even at this hour passed a constant stream of traffic, flashed a narrow strip of lake; and above it, rising gigantic from the coruscating moon-path, lifted the satellite. She watched the remote flickering of the waves as they tossed back the broken bits of the light strewn along the path. Then she turned puzzled eyes on her companion.

"That's Heaven," he said pointing a finger at the great flowing lunar disk. "There's a world that never caught the planet-cancer called Life, or if it ever suffered, it's cured. It's clean—burned clean by the sun and scoured clean by the airless zero of space. A dead world, and therefore not an unhappy one."

The girl stared at him without comprehension. She murmured, "I don't understand, Nick."

"Don't you, Pat?" He pointed again at the moon. "That's Heaven, the dead world, and this is Hell, the living one. Heaven and Hell swinging forever about their common center!" He gestured toward the sparkling moon-path on the water. "Look, Pat! The dead world strews flowers on the grave of the living one!"

Some of his bitter ecstasy caught the girl; she felt his somber mood of exaltation.

"I love you, Nick!" she whispered, pressing closely to him.

"What difference does it make—our actions?" he queried. "There's the omen, that lifeless globe in the sky. Where we go, all humanity now living will follow before a century, and in a million years, the human race as well! What if we go a year or a million years before the rest? Will it make any difference in the end?" He looked down at her. "All we've been valuing here is hope. To the devil with hope! Let's have peace instead!"

"I'm not afraid, Nick."

"Nor I. And if we go, he goes, and he's mortally afraid of death!"

"Can he—prevent you?"

"Not now! I'm the stronger now. For this time, I'm master." He turned again to stare at the glowing satellite as it rose imperceptibly from the horizon. "There's nothing to regret," he murmured, "except one thing—the loss of beauty. Beauty like that—and like you, Pat. That's bitterly hard to foreswear!" He leaned forward toward the remote disk of the moon; he spoke as if addressing it, in tones so low that the girl, pressed close to him, had to quiet the sound of her own breath to listen. He said:

"Long miles above cloud-bank and blast,

And many miles above the sea,
I watch you rise majestically
Feeling your chilly light at last—
Cold beauty in the way you cast
Split silver fragments on the waves,
As if this planet's life were past,
And all men peaceful in their graves."

Pat was silent for a moment as he paused, then she murmured a low phrase. "Oh, I love you, Nick!" she said.

"And I you, dear," he responded. "Have we decided anything? Are we—going through with it?"

"I've not faltered," she said soberly. "I meant it, Nick. Without you, life would be as empty as that airless void you speak of. I'm not afraid. What's there to be afraid of?"

"Only the transition, Pat. That and the unknown—but no situation could possibly be more terrible than our present one. It couldn't be! Oblivion, annihilation—they're preferable, aren't they?"

"Oh, yes! Nothing I can imagine could be other than a change for the better."

"Then let's face it!" His voice took on a note of determination. "I've thought to face it a dozen times before this, and each time I've hesitated. The hesitation of a coward, Pat."

"You're no coward, dear. It was that illusion of hope; that always weakens one. No one's strong who hasn't given up hope."

"Then," he repeated, "let's face it!"

"How, Nick?"

"My father has left us the means. There in the cabinet are a hundred deaths—swift ones, lingering ones, painful, and easy! I don't know one from the other; our choice must be blind." He strode over to the case, sending slivers of glass from the shattered front glistening along the floor. "I'd choose an easy one, dear, if I knew, for your sake. Euthanasia!"

He stared hesitantly at the files of mysterious drugs with their incomprehensible labels.

Suddenly the scene appeared humorous to the girl, queerly funny, in some unnatural horrible fashion. Her nerves, overstrained for hours, were on the verge of breaking; without realization of it, she had come to the border of hysteria.

"Shopping for death!" she choked, trying to suppress the wild laughter that beat in her throat. "Which one's most suitable? Which one's most becoming? Which one—" An hysterical laughing sob shook her. "—will wear the longest?"

He turned, gazing at her with an illogical concern in his face.

"What's the difference?" she cried wildly. "I don't care—painful or pleasant, it all ends in the same grave! Close your eyes and choose!"

Suddenly he was holding her in his arms again, and she was sobbing, clinging to him frantically. She was miserably unstrung; her body shook under the impact of her gasping breath. Then gradually, she quieted, and was silent against him.

"We've been mad!" he murmured. "It's been an insane idea for me to inflict this on you, Pat. Do you think I could consider the destruction of your beauty, dear? I've been lying to myself, stifling my judgment with poetic imagery, when all the while it was just that I'm afraid to face the thing alone!"

"No," she murmured, burying her face against his shoulder. "I'm the coward, Nick. I'm the one that's frightened, and I'm the one that broke down! It's just been—too much, this evening; I'm all right now."

"But we'll not go through with this, Pat!"

"But we will! It's better than life without you, dear. We've argued and argued, and at last forgotten the one truth, the one thing I'll never retract: I can't face living without you, Nick! I can't!"

He brushed his hand wearily before his eyes. "Back at the starting point," he muttered. "All right, Honey. So be it!"

He strode again to the cabinet. "Corrosive sublimate," he murmured. "Cyanide of Potassium. They're both deadly, but I think the second is rapid, and therefore less painful. Cyanide let it be!"

He extracted two small beakers from the glassware on the shelf. He filled them with water from a carafe on the table, and, while the girl watched him with fascinated eyes, he deliberately tilted a spoonful or so of white crystals into each of them. The mixture swirled a moment, then settled clear and colorless, and the crystals began to shrink as they passed swiftly into solution.

"There it is," he announced grimly. "There's peace oblivion forgetfulness, and annihilation for you, for me, and—for him! Beyond all doubt, the logical course for us, isn't it? Do we take it?"

"Please," she said daintily, "Kiss me first, Honey. Isn't that the proper course for lovers in this situation?" She felt a faint touch of astonishment at her own irony; the circumstances had ceased to have any reality to her, and had become merely a dramatic sequence like the happenings in a play.

He gathered her again into his arms and pressed his lips to hers.

It was a long, tender, wistful kiss; when at last it ended, Pat found her eyes again filled with tears, but not this time the tears of hysteria. "Nick," she murmured. "Nick, darling!" He gave her a deep, somber, but very tender smile, and reached for one of the deadly beakers. "To another meeting!" he said as his fingers closed on it.

Suddenly, amazingly, the strident ring of a doorbell sounded, the more surprising since they had all but forgotten the existence of a world about them. Interruption! It meant only the going through once more of all that they had just passed.

"Drink it!" exclaimed Pat impulsively, seizing the remaining beaker.

CHAPTER TWENTY-NINE
Scopolamine for Satan

The glass was struck from Pat's hand, and the water-clear contents streamed into pools and darkening blots over the table and its litter of papers. She stared unseeingly at the mess, without realizing that it was Nick who had dashed the draught from her very lips. She felt neither anger nor relief, but only a numbness, and a sense of anticlimax. Somewhere below the bell was ringing again, and a door was resounding to violent blows, but she only continued her bewildered, questioning gaze. "I can't let you, Pat!" he muttered, answering her unspoken query.

"But Nick-why?"

"There's somebody at the door, isn't there? Mustn't we find out who?"

132

"What difference can it make?" she asked wearily.

"I don't know. I want to find out."

"It's that illusion of hope again," she murmured. "That's all it is, Nick—and it means now that it's all to do over again! The whole thing, from the beginning—and we were so near—the end!"

"I know," he said miserably. "I know all that, but—" He paused as the insistent racket below was redoubled. "I'm going to answer that bell," he ended.

He moved away from her, vanishing through the room's single door. She watched his disappearance without moving, but no sooner had he passed from sight than a curious feeling of fear oppressed her. She cast off the numbness and languor, and darted after him into the darkness of the hall.

"Nick!" she called. Somewhere ahead a light flashed on; she saw the well of a staircase, and heard his footsteps descending. She followed in frantic haste, gaining the top step just as the pounding below ceased. She heard the click of the door, and paused suddenly at the sound of a familiar voice.

"Where's Pat?" The words drifted up in low, rumbling, ominous tones.

"Dr. Carl!" she shrieked. She ran swiftly down the stairs to Nick's side, where he stood facing the great figure of the Doctor. "Dr. Carl! How'd you find me?"

The newcomer gave her a long, narrow-eyed, speculative survey. "I spent nearly the whole night doing it," he growled at last. "It took me hours to locate Mueller and get this address from him." He stepped forward, taking the girl's arm. "Come on!" he said gruffly, without a glance at Nick standing silently beside her. "I'm taking you home!"

She held back. "But why?"

"Why? Because I don't like the company you keep. Is that reason enough?"

She still resisted his insistent tug. "Nick hasn't done anything," she said defiantly, with a side glance at the youth's flushed, unhappy features.

"He hasn't? Look at yourself girl! Look at your clothes, and your forehead! What's more, I saw enough from my window; I saw him bundle you into that car!" His eyes were flashing angrily and his grip on her arm tightened, while his free hand clenched into an enormous fist.

"That wasn't Nick!"

"No. It was your devil. I suppose!" said Horker sarcastically. "Anyway, Pat, you're coming with me before I do violence to what remains of your devil!"

Nick spoke for the first time since the Doctor's entrance, "Please do, Pat," he said softly. "Please go with him."

"I won't!" she snapped. The sudden shifts of situation during the long hours of that terrible evening were irritating her. She had alternated so rapidly between horror and hope and despair that her frayed nerves had seized now at the same reality of anger.

Her mind, so long overstrained, was now deliberately forgetting her swing from the pit of terror to the verge of death. "You come up like a hero to the rescue!" she taunted the doctor. "Hairbreadth Horker!"

"You little fool!" growled the Doctor. "A fine reception, after losing a night's sleep! I'll drag you home if I have to!" He moved ponderously toward the door; she gave a violent wrench and freed her arm from his grasp.

"If you can, you mean!" she jeered. She looked at his exasperated face, and suddenly, with one of her abrupt changes of mood, she softened. "Dr. Carl, Honey," she said in apologetic tones, "I'm sorry. You're very sweet, and I'm really grateful, but I can't leave Nick now," Her eyes turned troubled. "Not now."

"Why, Pat?" Mollified by the change in her mien, his voice rumbled in sympathetic notes.

"I can't," she repeated. "It's—it's getting worse."

"Bah!"

"So it's 'Bah'!" she flared. "Well, if you're so contemptuous of the thing, why don't you cure it? What good did your psychoanalysis do? You don't even know what it is!"

"What do you expect?" roared the Doctor. "Can I diagnose it by absent treatment? I haven't had a chance to see the condition active yet!"

"All right!" said Pat, her strained nerves driving her to impatience. "You're here and Nick's here! Go on with your diagnosis; get it over with, and let's see what you can do. You ought at least to be able to name the condition—the outstanding authority in the Middle West on neural and mental pathology!" Her tone was sardonic.

"Listen, Pat," said Horker with exaggerated patience, in the manner of one addressing a stupid child, "I've explained before that I can't get at the root of a mental aberration when the subject's as unstrung as your young man here seems to be. Psychoanalysis just won't work unless the subject is calm, composed, and not in a nervous state. Can you comprehend that?"

"Just dimly!" she snapped. "You ought to know another way—you, the outstanding authority—"

"Be still!" he interrupted gruffly. "Of course I know another way, if I wanted to drag all of us back to my office, where I have the equipment—which I won't do tonight," he finished grimly.

"Then do it here."

"I haven't what I need."

"There's everything upstairs," said Pat. "It's all there, all Nick's father's equipment."

"Not tonight! That's final."

The girl's manner changed again. She turned troubled, imploring eyes on Horker. "Dr. Carl," she said plaintively, "I can't leave Nick now." She seized the arm of the silent, dejected youth, who had been standing passively by. "I can't leave him, really. I'd not be sure of seeing him again, ever. Please, Dr. Carl!"

"If these frenzies of yours," rumbled Horker, "are so violent and malicious, you ought to be confined. Do you know that, young man?"

"Yes, sir," mumbled Nick wretchedly.

"And I've thought of it," continued the Doctor. "I've thought of it!"

"Please!" cried Pat imploringly. "Won't you try, Dr. Carl?"

"The devil!" he growled. "All right, then."

He followed the girl up the stairs, while Nick trailed disconsolately behind. She led him back into the chamber they had quitted, where a curious odor of peach pits seemed to scent the air. Horker sniffed suspiciously, then seized the remaining beaker, raising it cautiously to his nostrils.

"Damnation!" he exploded. "Prussic acid—or cyanide! What in—" He caught sight of Pat's tragic eyes, and suddenly replaced the container. "Pat!" he groaned. "Pat, Honey!" He drew her into the circle of his great arm. "I'll help you, dear! All I can, with all my heart, since it means that much to you!" He groaned again under his breath. "Oh, my God!"

He held her a moment, patting her tousled black head with his massive, delicate fingered hand. Then he released her, turning to Nick.

"This the stuff?" he asked, brusquely, indicating the cabinet of bottles, with its splintered front.

Nick nodded. Pat sank to the chair beside the table and watched Horker as he scanned the array of containers. He pulled out a tiny wooden case and snapped it open to reveal a number of steel needles that glinted brightly in the yellow light. He grunted in satisfaction and continued his inspection.

"Atropine," he muttered, reading the labeled boxes. "Cocaine, daturine, hyoscine, hyoscyamine—won't do!"

"What do you need?" the girl queried faintly.

"A mild hypnotic," said the Doctor abstractedly, still searching. "Pretty good substitutes for psychoanalysis—certain drugs. Dulls the conscious mind, but not to complete unconsciousness. Good means of getting at the subconscious. See?"

"Sort of," said Pat. "If it only works!"

"Oh, it'll work if we can find—ah!" He seized a tiny cardboard box. "Scopolamine! This'll do the work."

He extracted a tiny glassy something from one or other of the boxes he held, and frowned down at it. He seized the carafe of water, plunged something pointed and shiny into it.

"Antiseptic," he muttered thoughtfully. He seized a brown bottle from the case, held it toward the light, and shook it. "Peroxide's gone flat," he growled. "Nothing but water."

He pulled a silver cigar-lighter from his pocket and snapped a yellow flame to it. He passed the point of the hypodermic rapidly back and forth through the little spear of fire. Finally he turned to Nick.

"Take off your coat," he ordered. "Roll up your shirt sleeve—the left one. And sit over there." He indicated the couch along the wall.

The youth obeyed without a word. The only indication of emotion was a long, miserable, wistful look at Pat as he seated himself impassively on the spot that the girl had so recently occupied.

"Now!" said the Doctor briskly, approaching the youth. "This will make you drowsy, sleepy. That's all it'll do. Don't fight the effect. Just relax, let the thing take its course, and I'll see what I can get out of you."

Pat gasped and Nick winced as he drove the needle into the bared arm.

"So!" he said. "Now relax. Lean back and close your eyes."

He stepped to the door, dragged in a battered chair from the hall, and occupied it. He sat beside Pat, watching the pale features of the youth, who sat quietly with closed eyes, breathing slowly, heavily.

"Long enough," muttered Horker. He raised his voice. "Can you hear me?" he called to the motionless figure on the couch. There was no response, but Pat fancied she saw a slight change in Nick's expression.

"Can you hear me?" repeated Horker in louder tones.

"Yes. I can hear you," came in icy tones from the figure on the couch. Pat started violently as the voice sounded. The eyes opened, and she saw in sudden terror the ruddy orbs of the demon!

CHAPTER THIRTY
The Demon Free

Pat emitted a small, startled shriek, and heard it echoed by a surprised grunt from Dr. Horker.

"Queer," he muttered. "The stuff must be mislabeled. Scopolamine doesn't act like this; it's a narcotic."

"He's—the other!" gasped Pat, while the being on the couch grinned sardonically.

"Eh? An attack? Can't be!" The Doctor shook his head emphatically.

"It's not Nick!" cried the girl in panic. "You're not, are you?" she appealed to the grim entity.

"Not your sweetheart?" queried the creature, still with his mocking leer. "A few hours ago you were lying here all but naked, confessing you were mine. Have you forgotten?"

She shuddered at the reference, and shrank back in her chair. She heard the Doctor's ominous, angry rumble, and the evil tittering chuckle of the other.

"Pathological or not," snapped Horker, "I can resent your remarks! I've considered several times varying my treatment with another solid cut to the jaw!" He rose from his chair, stamping viciously toward the other.

"A moment," said Nicholas Devine. "Do you know what you've done? Have you any idea what you've done?" He turned cool, mocking, red-glinting eyes on the Doctor.

"Huh?" Horker paused as if puzzled. "What I've done? What do you mean?"

"You don't know, then." The other gave a satiric smile. "You're stupid. I gave you the clue, yet you hadn't the intelligence to follow it. Do you know what I am?" He leaned forward, his eyes leering evilly into the Doctor's. "I'll tell you. I'm a question of synapses. That's all—merely a question of synapses!" He tittered again, horribly. "It still means nothing to you, does it, Doctor?"

"I'll show you what it means!" Horker clenched a massive fist and strode toward the figure, whose eyes stared, steadily, unwinkingly into his own.

"Back!" the being snapped as the great form bent over him. The Doctor paused as if struck rigid, his arm and heavy fist drawn back like the conventional fighting pose of a boxer. "Go back!" repeated the other, rising. Pat whimpered in abject terror as she heard Horker's surprised grunt, and saw him recede slowly, and finally sink into his chair. His bewildered eyes were still fixed on those of Nicholas Devine.

"I'll tell you what you've done!" said the strange being. "You've freed me! There was nothing wrong with your scopolamine. It worked!" He chuckled. "You drugged him and freed me!"

Horker managed a questioning grunt.

"I'm free!" exulted the other. "For the first time I haven't him to fight! He's here, but helpless to oppose me—he's feeble—feeble!" He gave again the horrible tittering chuckle. "See how weak the two of you are against my unopposed powers!" he jeered. "Weaklings—food for my pleasures!"

He turned his eyes, luminous and avid, on Pat. "This time," he said, "there'll be no interruptions. A witness to our experiment will add a delicate touch of pleasure—"

He broke off at the Doctor's sudden movement. Horker had snatched a glistening blue revolver from his pocket, held it leveled at the lust-filled eyes.

"Huh!" growled the Doctor triumphantly. "Do you think I come trailing a maniac without some protection? Especially a vicious one like you?"

Nicholas Devine turned his eyes on his opponent. He stared long and intently.

"Drop it!" he commanded at length. Pat felt a surge of chaotic terror as the weapon clattered to the floor. She turned a frightened glance on Horker's face, and her fright redoubled at the sight of his straining jaw, the perspiration-beaded forehead, and his bewildered eyes. The demon kicked the gun carelessly aside.

"Puerile!" he said contemptuously. He backed away from them, re-seating himself on the couch whence he had risen. He surveyed the pair in sardonic mirth.

"Pat!" muttered the Doctor huskily. "Get out of here, Honey! He's got some hellish trick of fascination that's paralyzed me. Get out and get help!"

The girl moved as if to rise. Nicholas Devine shifted his eyes for the barest instant to her face; she felt the strength drain out of her body, and she sank weakly to her chair.

"It's useless," she murmured hopelessly to the Doctor. "He's—he's just what I told you—a devil!"

"I guess you were right," mumbled Horker dazedly.

There was a burst of demonic mirth from the being on the couch. "Merely a matter of synapses," he rasped, chuckling. His face changed, took on the familiar coldness, the stony expression Pat had observed there before. "This palls!" he snapped. "I've better amusement—after we've rendered your friend merely an interested on-looker." He narrowed his red eyes as if in thought. "Take off a stocking," he ordered. "Tie his hands to the back of the chair."

"I won't!" said the girl. The eyes shifted to her face. "I won't!" she repeated tremulously as she kicked off a diminutive pump. She shuddered at the gleam in the evil eyes as she stripped the long silken sheath from a white, rounded limb. She slipped a bare foot into the pump and moved reluctantly behind the chair that held the groaning Horker. She took one of the clenched, straining hands, and drew it back, fumbling with shaking fingers as she twisted the strip of thin chiffon. The demon moved closer, standing over her.

"Loose knots!" he snarled abruptly. He knocked her violently away with a stinging slap across her cheek, and seized the strip in his own hands. He drew the binding tight, twisting it about the lowest rung of the chair's ladder back. Horker was forced to lean awkwardly to the rear; in this unbalanced position it was quite impossible to rise.

Nicholas Devine turned away from the straining, perspiring Doctor, and advanced toward Pat, who cowered against the shattered cabinet.

"Now!" he muttered. "The experiment!" He chuckled raspingly. "What delicacy of degradation! Your lover and your guardian angel—both helpless watchers! Excellent! Oh, very excellent!"

He grasped her wrist, drawing her after him to the center of the room, into the full view of the horrified, staring eyes of Horker.

"Always before," continued her tormentor, "these hands have prepared you for the rites—the ceremony that failed on two other occasions to transpire. Would it add a poignancy to the torture if I made you strip this body of yours with your own hands? Or will they suffer more watching me? Which do you think?"

Pat closed her eyes in helpless resignation to her fate. "Nick!" she moaned. "Oh, Nick dearest!"

"Not this time!" sneered the other. "Your friend and protector, the Doctor, has thoughtfully eliminated your sweetheart as a factor. He struggles too feebly for me to feel."

"Nick!" she murmured again. "Dr. Carl!"

But the Doctor, now pulling painfully at his bonds, could only moan in distraction, and curse the unsuspected strength of sheer chiffon. He writhed miserably at the chafing of his wrists; his strange paralysis had departed, but he was quite helpless to assist Pat.

"I think," said the cold tones of Nicholas Devine, "that the more delicate torture lies in your willingness. Let us see."

He drew her into his arms. He twisted a hand in her hair, jerked her head violently backward, and pressed avid lips to hers. She struggled a little, but hopelessly, automatically. At last she lay quite passive, quite motionless, supported by his arms, and making not the slightest response to his kiss.

"Are you mine?" he queried fiercely, releasing her lips. "Are you mine now?"

She shook her head without opening her eyes. "No," she said dully. "Not now, or ever."

Again he crushed her, while the Doctor looked on in helpless, bewildered, voiceless anger. This time his kiss was painful, burning, searing. Again that unholy fascination and unnatural delight in her own pain stirred her, and it took what little effort she was able to make to keep from responding. After a long interval, his lips again withdrew.

"Are you mine?" he repeated. She made no answer; she was gasping and tears glistened under her closed eyelids, from the pain of her crushed lips. Again he kissed her, and again the wild abandonment to evil suffused her. She was suddenly responding to his agonizing caress; she was clinging fiercely to his torturing lips, feeling an unholy exaltation in the pain of his tearing fingers in the flesh of her back.

"Yours!" she murmured in response to his query. She heard her voice repeat madly, "Yours! Yours! Yours!"

"Do you yield willingly?" came the icy tones of the demon.

"Yes—yes—yes! Willingly!"

"Take off your clothes!" sounded the terrible, overpowering voice. He thrust her from him, so that she staggered dizzily backward. She stood swaying; the voice repeated its command, the girl's eyes widened wildly; she had the appearance of one in an ecstasy, a religious fervor. She raised her hand with a jerky impulsive gesture to the neck of her frock, still pinned together in the makeshift repairs of the evening.

There came a strange interruption. The Doctor, helpless on-looker, had at length evolved an idea out of the bewilderment in his mind. He opened his mouth and emitted a tremendous, deep, ear shattering bellow!

Nicholas Devine sent the girl spinning to the floor with a vicious shove, and turned his blazing eyes on Horker, who was drawing in his breath for a repetition of his roar. "Quiet!" he rasped, his red orbs boring down at the other. "Quiet, or I'll muffle you!" Closing his eyes, the Doctor repeated his mighty shout.

The demon snatched the blanket from the couch, tossing it over the figure of the Doctor, where it became a billowing, writhing heap of brown wool. He turned his gaze on Pat, who was just struggling to her feet, and moved as if to advance toward her.

He paused. She had retrieved the Doctor's revolver from the floor, and now faced him with the madness gone out of her eyes, supporting the weapon with both hands, the muzzle wavering toward his face.

"Drop it!" he commanded. She felt a recurrence of fascination, and an impulse to obey. Out of the corner of her eye, she saw the Doctor's head emerging from the blanket as he shook it off.

"Drop it!" repeated Nicholas Devine.

She closed her eyes, shutting out the vision of his dominant vis-age. With a surge of terror, she squeezed the trigger, staggering back to the couch at the roar and the recoil.

She opened her eyes. Nicholas Devine lay in the center of the room on his face; a crimson spot was matting the hair on the back of his head. She saw the Doctor raise a free hand; he was working clear of his bonds.

"Pat!" he said softly. He looked at her pale, sickened features. "Honey," he said, "sit down till I get free. Sit down, Pat; you look faint."

"Never faint!" murmured the girl, and pitched backward to the couch, with one clad and one bare leg hanging in curious limpness over the edge.

CHAPTER THIRTY-ONE
"Not Humanly Possible"

Pat opened weary eyes and gazed at a blank, uninformative ceiling. It was some moments before she realized that she was lying on the couch in the room of Nicholas Devine. Somebody had placed her there, presumably, since she was quite unaware of the circumstances of her awakening. Then recollection began to form—Dr. Carl, the other, the roar of a shot. After that, nothing save a turmoil ending in blankness.

A sound of movement beside her drew her attention. She turned her head and perceived Dr. Horker kneeling over a form on the floor, fingering a white bandage about the head of the figure. Her recollections took instant form; she remembered the catastrophes of the evening—last night, rather, since dawn glowed dully in the window. She had shot Nick! She gave a little moan and pushed herself to a sitting position.

The Doctor glanced at her with a sick, shaky smile. "Hello," he said. "Come to, have you? Sorry I couldn't give you any attention." He gave the bandage a final touch. "Here's a job I had no heart for," he muttered. "Better for everyone to let things happen without interference."

The girl, returning to full awareness, noticed now that the bandage consisted of strips of the Doctor's shirt. She glanced fearfully at the still features of Nicholas Devine; she saw pale cheeks and closed eyes, but indubitably not the grim mien of the demon.

"Dr. Carl!" she whispered. "He isn't—he isn't—'

"Not yet."

"But will he—?"

"I don't know. That's a bad spot, a wound in the base of the brain. You'd best know it now, Pat, but also realize that nothing can happen to you. I'll see to that!"

"To me!" she said dully. "What difference does that make? It's Nick I want saved."

"I'll do my best for you, Honey," said Horker with almost a hint of reluctance. "I've phoned Briggs General for an ambulance. Your faint lasted a full quarter hour," he added.

"What can we tell them?" asked the girl. "What can we say?"

"Don't you say anything, Pat, I'm not on the board for nothing," He rose from his knees, glancing out of the window into the cool dawn. "Queer neighborhood!" he said. "All that yelling and a shot, and still no interest from the neighbors, that's Chicago, though," he mused. "Lucky for us, Pat; we can handle the thing quietly now."

But the girl was staring dully at the still figure on the floor. "Oh God!" she said huskily. "Help him, Dr. Carl!"

"I'll do my best," responded Horker gloomily. "I was a good surgeon before I specialized in psychiatry. Brain surgery, too; it led right into my present field."

Pat said nothing, but dropped her head on her hands and stared vacantly before her.

"Better for you, and for him too, if I fail," muttered the Doctor.

His words brought a reply. "You won't fail," she said tensely. "You won't!"

"Not voluntarily, I'm afraid," he growled morosely. "I've still a little respect for medical ethics, but if ever a case—" His voice trailed into silence as from somewhere in the dawn sounded the wail of a siren. "There's the ambulance," he finished.

Pat sat unmoving as the sounds from outdoors detailed the stopping of the vehicle before the house. She heard the Doctor descending the steps, and the creak of the door. Though it took place before her eyes, she scarcely saw the white-coated youths as they lifted the form of Nicholas Devine and bore it from the room on a stretcher, treading with carefully broken steps to prevent the swaying of the support. Dr. Horker's order to follow made no impression on her; she sat dully on the couch as the chamber emptied.

Why, she wondered, had the thought of Nick's death disturbed her so? Wasn't it but a short time since they had both contemplated it. What had occurred to alter that determination? Nick was dying, she thought mournfully; all that remained was for her to follow. There on the floor lay the revolver, and on the table, glistening in the wan light, reposed the untouched lethal draft. That was the preferable way, she mused, staring fixedly at its glowing contour.

But suppose Nick weren't to die—she'd have abandoned him to his terrible doom, left him to face a situation far more ominous than any unknown terrors beyond death. She shook her head distractedly, and looked up to meet the eyes of Dr. Horker, who was watching her gravely in the doorway.

"Come on, Pat," he said gently.

She rose, followed him down the stairs and out into the morning light. The driver of the ambulance stared curiously at her disheveled bedraggled figure, but she was so weary and forlorn that even the effort of brushing away the black strands of hair that clouded her smoke-dark eyes was beyond her. She slumped into the seat of the Doctor's car and sighed in utter exhaustion.

"Rush it!" Horker called to the driver ahead. "I'll follow you." The car swept into motion, and the swift cool morning air beating against her face from the open window restored some clarity to her mind. She fixed her eyes on the rear of the speeding vehicle they followed.

"Is there any hope at all?" she queried despondently.

"I don't know, Pat. I can't tell yet. When you closed your eyes, he half turned, dodged; the bullet entered his skull near the base, near the cerebellum. If it had pierced the cerebellum, his heart and breathing must have stopped instantly. They didn't, however, and that's a mildly hopeful sign. Very mildly hopeful, though."

"Do you know now what that devil—what the attack was?"

"No, Pat," Horker admitted, "I don't. Call it a devil if you like; I can't name it any better." His voice changed to a tone of wonder. "Pat, I can't understand that paralyzing fascination the thing exerted. I—any medical man—would say that mental dominance of that sort doesn't exist."

"Hypnotism," the girl suggested.

"Bah! Every psychiatrist uses hypnotism in his business; it's part of some treatments. There's nothing of fascination about it; no dominance of one will over another, despite the popular view. That's natural and understandable; this was like—well, like the exploded claims of Mesmerism. I tell you it's not humanly possible—and yet I felt it!"

"Not humanly possible," murmured Pat. "That's the answer, then, Dr. Carl. Maybe now you'll believe in my devil."

"I'm tempted to."

"You'll have to! Can't you see it, Dr. Carl? Even his name, Nick—that's a colloquialism for the devil, isn't it?"

"And Devine, I suppose," said Horker, "refers to his angelic ancestry. Devils are only fallen angels, aren't they?"

"All right," said Pat wearily. "Make fun of it. You'll see!"

"I'm not making fun of your theory. Honey, I can't offer a better one myself. I never saw nor heard of anything similar, and I'm not in position to ridicule any theory."

"But you don't believe me."

"Of course I don't, Pat. You're weaving an intricate fairy tale about a pathological condition and a fortuitous suggestiveness in names. Whatever the condition is—and I confess I don't understand it—it's something rational, and those things can be treated."

"Treated by exorcism," said the girl. "That's the only way anyone ever succeeded in casting out a devil."

The Doctor made no answer. The wailing vehicle ahead of them swung rapidly out of sight into an alley, and Horker halted his car before the gray facade of Briggs General.

"Come in here," he said, helping Pat to alight. "You'll want to wait, won't you?"

"How long," she queried listlessly, "before—before you'll know?"

"Perhaps immediately. The only chance is to get that bullet out at once—if there's still time for it."

She followed him into the building, past a desk where a white-clad girl regarded her curiously, and up an elevator. He led her into a small office.

"Sit here," he said gently, and disappeared.

She sat dully in the chair he had indicated, and minutes passed.

She made no attempt to think; the long, cataclysmic night had exhausted her powers. She simply sat and suffered; the deep scratches of fingernails burned in the flesh of her back, her cheek pained from the violent slap, and her head and jaw ached from that first blow, the one that had knocked her unconscious last evening. But these twinges were minor; they were merely physical, and the hurts of the demon had struck far deeper than any physical injury. The damage to her spirit was by all odds the more painful; it numbed her mind and dulled her thoughts, and she simply sat idle and stared at the blank wall.

She had no conception of the interval before Dr. Horker returned. He entered quietly, and began rinsing his hands at a basin in the corner.

"Is it over?" she asked listlessly.

"Not even begun," he responded. "However, it isn't too late. He'll be ready in a moment or so."

"I wish it were over," she murmured. "One way or the other."

"I too!" said the Doctor. "With all my heart, I wish it were over! If there were anyone within call who could handle it, I'd turn it to him gladly. But there isn't!"

He moved again toward the door, leaning out and glancing down the hall.

"You stay here," he admonished her. "Don't try to find us; I want no interruptions, no matter what enters that mind of yours!"

"You needn't worry," she said soberly. "I'm not fool enough for that." She leaned wearily back in the chair, closing her eyes. A long interval passed; she was vaguely surprised to see the Doctor still standing in the doorway when she opened her eyes. She had fancied him already in the midst of his labor.

"What will you do?" she asked.

"About what?"

"I mean what sort of operation will it need? Probing or what?"

"Oh," he said, "I'll have to trephine him. Must get that bullet."

"What's that—trephine?"

He glanced down the hall. "They're ready," he said, and turned to go. At the door he paused. "Trephining is to open a little door in the skull. If your devil is in his head, we'll have it out along with the bullet."

His footsteps receded down the hall.

CHAPTER THIRTY-TWO
Revelation

"Is it over now?" Queried Pat tremulously as the Doctor finally reappeared, the interminable waiting had left her even more worn, and her pallid features bore the marks of strain.

"Twenty minutes ago," said Horker. His face too bore evidence of tension; moreover, there was a puzzled, dubious expression in his eyes that frightened Pat. She was too apprehensive to risk a question as to the outcome, and simply stared at him with wide, fearful, questioning eyes.

"I called up your home," he said irrelevantly. "I told them you left with me early this morning. Your mother's still in bed, although it's after ten." He paused. "Slip in without anyone seeing you, will you, Honey? And rumple up your bed."

"If I haven't lost my key," she said, still with the question in her eyes.

"It's in the mailbox. Magda found it on the porch this morning. I talked to her."

She could bear the uncertainty no longer. "Tell me!" she demanded.

"It's all right, I think."

"You mean—he'll live?"

The Doctor nodded. "I think so." He turned his puzzled eyes on her.

"Oh!" breathed Pat. "Thank God!"

"You wanted him back, Honey, didn't you?" Horker's tone was gentle.

"Oh, yes!"

"Devil and all?"

"Yes—devil and all!" she echoed. Suddenly she sensed something strange in the other's manner. She perceived the uncertainty in his visage, and felt a rising trepidation. "What's the matter?" she queried anxiously. "You're not telling me everything! Tell me, Dr. Carl!"

"There's something else," he said. "I'm not sure, Pat, but I think—I hope—you've got him back without the devil!'

"He's cured?" Her voice was incredulous; she did not dare accept the Doctor's meaning.

"I hope so. At least I located the cause."

"What was it?" she demanded, an unexpected vigor livening her tired body. "What was that devil? Tell me! I want to know, Dr. Carl—"

"I think the best name for it is a tumor," he said slowly. "I told them in there it was a tumor. I wish I knew myself."

"A tumor! I don't understand!"

"I don't either, Pat—not fully. It's something on or beyond the border of medical knowledge. I don't think any living authority could classify it definitely."

"But tell me!" she cried fiercely. "Tell me!"

"Well, Honey—I'll try." He paused thoughtfully. "Cancers and tumors—sarcomas—are curious things, dear. Doctors aren't at all sure just what they are. And one of their peculiarities is that they sometimes seem to be trying to develop into separate entities, trying to become human by feeding like parasites on their hosts. Do you understand?"

"No," said the girl. "I'm sorry, Dr. Carl, but I don't."

"I mean," he continued, "that sometimes these growths seem to be trying to develop into—into organisms. I've seen them, for instance—every surgeon has—with bones developing. I've seen one with a rather perfect jaw-bone, and little teeth, and hair. As if," he added, "it were making a sort of attempt to become human, in a primitive, disorganized fashion. Now do you see what I mean?"

"Yes," said the girl, with a violent shudder. "Dr. Carl, that's horrible!"

"Life sometimes is," he agreed. "Well," he continued slowly, "I opened up our patient's skull at the point where the fluoroscope indicated the bullet. I trephined it, and there, pierced by the shot, was this—" He hesitated. "—this tumor."

"Did you—remove it?"

"Of course. But it wasn't a natural brain tumor. It was a little cerebrum, apparently joined to a Y-shaped branch of the spinal cord. A little brain, Pat—no larger than your small fist, but deeply convoluted, and with the pre-Rolandic area highly developed."

"What's pre-Rolandic, Dr. Carl?" asked Pat, shivering.

"The seat of the motor nerves. The home, you might say, of the will. This brain was practically all will—and I wonder," he said musingly, "if that explains the ungodly, evil fascination the creature could command. A brain that was nothing but pure willpower, relieved by its parasitic nature of all the distractions of a directing body! I wonder—" He fell silent.

"Tell me the rest!" she said frantically.

"That's all, Honey. I removed it, and I guess I'm the only surgeon in the world who ever removed a brain from a human skull without killing the patient! Luckily, he had two of them!"

"Oh God!" murmured the girl faintly. She turned to Horker. "But he will live?"

"I think so. Your shot killed the devil, it seems." He frowned. "I said it was a tumor; I told them it was a tumor, but I'm not sure. Perhaps, just as some people are born with six fingers or toes on each member, he was born with two brains. It's possible; one developed normally, humanly, and the other—into that creature we faced last night. I don't know!"

"It's what I said," asserted Pat. "It's a devil, and what you've just told me about tumors proves it. They're devils, that's all, and someday some student is going to cut one loose and raise it to maturity outside a human body, and you'll see what a devil is really like! And go ahead and laugh!"

"I'm not laughing, Pat. I'd be the last one to laugh at your theory, after facing that thing last night. It had satanic powers, all right—that paralyzing fascination! You felt it too; it wasn't just a mental lapse on my part, was it?"

"I felt it, Dr. Carl! I'd felt it before that; I was always helpless in the presence of it."

"Could it," he asked, "have imposed its will actively on yours? I mean, could it have made you actually do what it asked there at the end, just before I recovered enough sense to let out that bellow?"

"To take off—my dress?" She shivered. "I don't know, Dr. Carl— I'm afraid so." She looked at him appealingly. "Why did I yield to it so?" she cried. "What made me find such a fierce pleasure in its kisses—in its blows and scratches, and the pain it inflicted on me? Why was that, Dr. Carl?"

"Why," he countered, "do gangsters' girls and apache women enjoy the cruelties perpetrated on them by their men? There's a little masochism in most women, and that—creature was sadistic, perverted, abnormal, and somehow dominating. It took an unfair advantage of you. Pat, don't blame yourself."

"It was—utterly evil!" she muttered. "It was the ultimate in everything unholy."

"It was an aberrant brain," said Horker. "You can't judge it by human standards, since it wasn't actually human. It was, I suppose, just what you said—a devil. I didn't even keep it," he added grimly. "I destroyed it."

"Do you know what it meant by saying it was a question of synapses?" she asked.

"That was queer!" The Doctor's voice was puzzled. "That remark implies that the thing itself knew what it was. How? It must have possessed knowledge that the normal brain lacked."

"Was it a question of synapses?"

"In a sense it was. The nerves from the two rival brains must have met in a synaptic juncture. The oftener the aberrant brain gained control, the easier it became for it to repeat the process, as the synapse, so to speak, wore thin. That's why the attacks intensified so horribly toward the end; the habit was being formed."

"Last night was the very worst!"

"Of course. As the thing itself pointed out, I made the mistake of drugging the normal brain and giving the other complete control of the body. At other times, there'd always been the rivalry to weaken whichever was dominant."

"Does that mean," asked Pat anxiously, "that Nick's character will be changed now?"

"I think so. I think you'll find him less meek, less gentle, than heretofore. More spirited, perhaps, since his energies won't be drained so constantly by the struggle."

"I don't care!" she said. "I'd like that, and anyway, it doesn't make a bit of difference to me as long as he's just—*my* Nick."

The Doctor gave her a tender smile. "Let's go home," he said, pinching her cheek in his great hand.

"Can you leave him?"

"I'll run back after a while, Honey. I think he'll do." He took her hand, drawing her after him. "Don't forget to slip in unseen, Pat, and rumple up your bed."

"Rumple it!" She gave him a weary smile. "I'll be in it!"

"Good idea. You look a bit worn out, Honey, and we can't have you getting sick now, or even pull a temporary faint like that one last night."

"I didn't faint!"

"Maybe not," grinned Horker. "Perhaps the proceedings grew a little boring, and you just lay down on the couch for a nap. It *was* a dull evening."

THE END

CERTAIN DEATH AT THE HANDS OF A BEAUTIFUL WITCH

Corun—deposed prince of Conahur, and condemned pirate—languished in his cell, awaiting execution. But when the evil wizard Shorzon approached him, and made him a proposition, Corun thought perhaps there was a chance—however slim—to avoid an early and painful death. It seemed so simple: He would guide Shorzon to the lair of the Xanthi, and teach him their language, Corun would then be freed and his kingdom restored.

But Shorzon had other plans, and they did not involve restoring Conahur to its former glory, nor did he intend to let Corun just walk away a free man. He wanted ultimate power, power only beings of dark magic could grant…

Join science fiction and fantasy master Poul Anderson as he spins a swashbuckling tale of alien sorcery.

CAST OF CHARACTERS

CORUN OF CONAHUR
Though considered a blackguard by the conquering kingdom of Achaera, this pirate was a hero to many.

CHRYSEIS
The daughter of a king and a witch, she was as powerful and treacherous as she was beautiful.

PERIAS
Only the hard-hearted princess of Achaera could earn the devotion and protection of this widely feared erineye.

SHORZON
This evil wizard would use anyone to become a god—even his own granddaughter.

CAPTAIN IMAZU
He was a mercenary from Umlotu, and it wasn't just the taskmaster's whip that earned respect.

TSATHU
King of the Xanthi, a reptilian race who lived just as comfortably under water as men lived on land.

KHROMAN
He was a wiser ruler than his ancestors, and though he respected Corun, he couldn't grant clemency.

WITCH OF THE DEMON SEAS

By
POUL ANDERSON

ARMCHAIR FICTION
PO Box 4369, Medford, Oregon 97504

CHAPTER ONE

KHROMAN THE CONQUEROR, Thalassocrat of Achaera, stood watching his guards bring up the captured pirates. He was a huge man, his hair and square-cut beard jet-black despite middle age, the strength of his warlike youth still in his powerful limbs. He wore a plain white tunic and purple-trimmed cloak; the only sign of kingship was the golden chaplet on his head and the signet ring on one finger. In the gaudy crowd of slender, chattering courtiers, he stood out with a brutal contrast.

"So they've finally captured him," he rumbled. "So we're finally rid of Corun and his sea-going bandits. Maybe now the land will have some peace."

"What will you do with them, sire?" asked Shorzon the Sorcerer.

Khroman shrugged heavy shoulders. "I don't know. Pirates are usually fed to the erinyes at the games, I suppose, but Corun deserves something special."

"Public torture, perhaps, sire? It could be stretched over many days.""

"No, you fool! Corun was the bravest enemy Achaera ever had. He deserves an honorable death and a decent tomb. Not that it matters much, but—"

Shorzon exchanged a glance with Chryseis, then looked back toward the approaching procession.

THE CITY TAUROS was built around a semicircular bay, a huge expanse of clear green water on whose surface floated ships from halfway round the world—the greatest harbor for none knew how many empty sea-leagues, capital of Achaera which, with its trade and its empire of entire archipelagoes, was the mightiest of the thalassocracies. Beyond the fortified sea walls at the end of the bay, the ocean swelled mightily to the clouded horizon, gray and green and amber. Within, the hulls and sails of ships were a bright confusion up to the stone docks.

The land ran upward from the bay, and Tauros was built on the hills, a tangle of streets between houses that ranged from the clay huts of the poor to the marble villas of the great. Beyond the city walls on the landward side, the island of Achaera lifted still more steeply, a gaunt rocky country with a few scattered farms and herds. Her power came all from the sea.

A broad straight road lined with sphinxes ran straight from the harbor up to the palace, which stood on the highest hill in the city. At its end, wide marble stairs lifted toward the fragrant imperial gardens in which the court stood.

Folk swarmed about the street, mobs straining to see the soldiers as they led their captives toward the palace. The word that Corun of Conahur, the most dangerous of the pirates, had finally been taken had driven merchants to ecstasy and brought insurance rates tumbling down. There was laughter in the throng, jeers for the prisoners, shouts for the king.

Not entirely so, however. Most of the crowd were, of course, Achaerans, a slim dark-haired folk clad generally in a light tunic and sandals, proud of their ancient might and culture. They were loudest in shouting at the robbers. But there were others who stood silent and glum-faced, not daring to voice their thoughts but making them plain enough. Tall, fair men from Conahur itself, galled by Achaeran rule; fur-clad barbarians from Norriki, blue-skinned savages from Umlotu, with a high professional regard for their fellow pirate; slaves from a hundred islands, who had not ceased dreaming of home and remembered that Corun had been in the habit of freeing slaves when he captured a ship or a town. Others might be neutral, coming from too far away to care, for Corun had only attacked Achaeran galleys; the black men from misty Orzaban, the copper-colored Chilatzis, the yellow wizards from mysterious Hiung-nu.

The soldiers marched their prisoners rapidly up the street. They were mercenaries, blue Umlotuans in the shining corselets, greaves, and helmets of the Achaeran forces, armed with the short sword and square shield of Achaera as well as the long halberds which were their special weapon. When the mob came too close, they swung the butts out with bone-snapping force.

The captive pirates were mostly from Conahur, though there were a number of other lands represented. They stumbled wearily along, clad in a few rags, weighted down hand and foot by their chains. Only one of them, the man in the lead, walked erect, but he strode along with the arrogance of a conqueror.

"That must be Corun himself, there in the front of them," said Chryseis.

"It is," nodded Shorzon.

THEY MOVED FORWARD for a better look. Imperceptibly, the court shrank from them. Khroman's advisor and daughter were feared in Tauros.

Shorzon was tall and lean and dry, as if the Heaven-Fire beyond the eternal clouds had fallen on him and seared all moisture out of the gaunt body. He had the noble features of the old Achaeran aristocracy, but his eyes were dark and sunken and smoldering with strange fires. Even in the warmth of midday, he wore a black robe falling to his feet, and his white beard streamed over it. Folk knew that he had learned sorcery in Hiung-nu, and it was whispered that for all Khroman's brawling strength it was Shorzon who really dominated the realm.

Khroman had married Shorzon's daughter—none knew who her mother had been, though it was thought she was a witch from Hiung-nu. She had not lived long after giving birth to Chryseis, whose grandfather thus came to have much of her upbringing in his hands. Rumor had it that she was as much a witch as he a warlock.

Certainly she could be cruel and ungovernable. But she had a strange dark beauty over her that haunted men; there were more who would die for her than one could readily count...and, it was said, *had* died after a night or two.

She was tall and lithe, with night-black hair that streamed to her waist when unbound. Her eyes were huge and dark in a face of coldly chiseled loveliness, and the full red mouth denied the austere, goddess-like fineness of her countenance. Today she had not affected the heavy gold and jewels of the court; a white robe hung in dazzling folds about her—and there might as well not have been another woman present.

The prisoners came through the palace gates, which clashed shut behind them. Up the stairs they went and into the fragrance of green trees and bushes, blooming plants, and leaping fountains that was the garden. There they halted, and the court buzzed about them like flies around a dead animal.

Khroman stepped up to Corun. "Greeting," he said, and there was no mockery in his voice.

"Greeting," replied the pirate in the same even tones.

They measured each other, the look of two strong men who understood what they were about. Corun was as big as Khroman, a fair-skinned giant of a man in chains and rags. Weather-bleached yellow hair hung to his shoulders from a haughtily lifted head, and his fire-blue eyes were unwavering on the king's. His face was lean, long-jawed, curve-nosed, hardened by bitterness and suffering and desperate unending battle. A chained erinye could not have looked more fiercely on his captors.

"It's taken a long time to catch you, Corun," said Khroman, "You've led us a merry chase. Once I almost had the pleasure of meeting you myself. It was when you raided Serapolis—remember? I happened to be there, and gave chase in one of the war-galleys. But we never did catch you."

"One of the ships did." Corun's voice was strangely soft for so big a man. "It didn't come back, as you may recall."

"How did they finally catch you?" asked Khroman.

CORUN SHRUGGED, and the chains about his wrists rattled. "You already know as much as I care to talk about," he said wearily. "We sailed into Iliontis Bay and found a whole fleet waiting for us. Someone must finally have spied out our stronghold." Khroman nodded, and Corun shrugged a shoulder.

"They blocked off our retreat, so we just fought till everyone was dead or captured. These half-hundred men are all who live. Unfortunately, I was knocked out during the battle and woke up to find myself a prisoner. Otherwise—" his blue gaze raked the court with a lashing contempt. "I could be peacefully feeding fish now, instead of your witless fish-eyes."

"I won't drag out the business for you, Corun," said Khroman. "Your men will have to be given to the games, of course, but you can be decently and privately beheaded."

"Thanks," said the pirate, "but I'll stay with my men."

Khroman stared at him in puzzlement. "But why did you ever do it?" he asked finally. "With your strength and skill and cunning, you could have gone far in Achaera. We take mercenaries from conquered provinces, you know. You could have gotten Achaeran citizenship in time."

"I was a prince of Conahur," said Corun slowly. "I saw my land invaded and my folk taken off as slaves. I saw my brothers hacked down at the battle of Lyrr, my sister taken as concubine by your admiral, my father hanged, my mother burned alive when they fired the old castle. They offered me amnesty because I was young and they wanted a figurehead. So I swore an oath of fealty to Achaera, and broke it the first chance I got. It was the only oath I ever broke, and still I am proud of it. I sailed with pirates until I was big enough to master my own ships. That is enough of an answer."

"It may be," said Khroman slowly. "You realize, of course, that the conquest of Conahur took place before I came to the throne? And that I certainly couldn't negate it, in view of the Thalassocrat's duty to his own country, and had to punish its incessant rebelliousness?"

"I don't hold anything against you yourself, Khroman," said Corun with a tired smile. "But I'd give my soul to the nether fires for the chance to pull your damned palace down around your ears!"

"I'm sorry it has to end this way," said the king. "You were a brave man. I'd like to drain many beakers of wine with you on the other side of death." He signed to the guards. "Take him away."

"One moment, sire," said Shorzon. "Is it your intention to lock all these pirates in the same dungeon cell?"

"Why—I suppose so. Why not?"

"I do not trust their captain. Chained and imprisoned, he is still a menace. I think he has certain magical techniques—"

"That's a lie!" spat Corun. "I never needed your stinking woman's tricks to flatten the likes of Achaera!"

"I would not leave him with his men," advised Shorzon imperturbably. "Best he be given his own cell, alone. I know a place."

"Well—well, let it be so." Khroman waved a hand in dismissal.

As Shorzon turned to lead the guards off, he traded a long glance with Chryseis. Her eyes remained hooded as she looked after the departing captives.

CHAPTER TWO

THE CELL WAS NO LONGER than a man's height, a dripping cave hewed out of the rock under the palace foundations. Corun crouched on the streaming floor in utter darkness. The chains which they had locked to ringbolts in the wall clashed when he stirred.

And this was how it ended, he thought bitterly. The wild career of the exiled conqueror, the heave and surge of ships under the running waves, the laughter of comrades and the clamor of swords and the thrum of wind in the rigging, had come to this—one man hunched in a loneliness and darkness like a colder womb, waiting in timeless murk for the day when they would drag him out to be torn by beasts for the amusement of fools.

They fed him at intervals, a slave bringing a bowl of prison swill while a spear-armed guard stood well out of reach and watched. Otherwise he was alone. He could not even hear the voices of other captives; there was only the slow dripping of water and the harsh tones of iron links. The cell must lie below even the regular dungeons, far down in the very bowels of the island.

Vague images floated across his mind—the high cliffs about Iliontis Bay, the great flowers blooming with sullen fires in the jungle beyond the beach, the slim black corsair galleys at anchor. He remembered the open sky, the eternally clouded sky under which blew the long wet winds, out of which spilled rain and lightning and grew the eerie blue of dusk. He had often wondered what lay beyond those upper clouds.

Now and then, he remembered, one could see the vague disc of the Heaven-Fire, and he had heard of times when incredibly violent storms opened a brief rift in the high cloud layers to let through a shaft of searing brilliance at whose touch water boiled and the earth burst into flame. It made him think of the speculations of Conahur's philosophers, that the world was really a globe around which the Heaven-Fire swung, bringing day and night. Some had gone so far as to imagine that it was the world which did the moving, that the Heaven-Fire was a ball of flame in the middle of creation about which all other things revolved.

But Conahur was in chains now, he remembered, its folk bowed to the will of Achaera's greedy proconsuls, its art and philosophy the idle playthings of the conquerors. The younger generation was growing up with an idea that it might be best to yield, to become absorbed into the thalassocracy and so eventually gain equal status with the Achaerans.

But Corun could not forget the great flames flapping against a wind-torn night sky, the struggling forms at ropes' ends swaying from trees, the long lines of chained people stumbling hopelessly to the slave galleys under Achaeran lashes. Perhaps he had carried the grudge too long—no, by Breannach Brannor! There had been a family which was no longer. That was grudge enough for a lifetime.

A lifetime, he thought sardonically, which wouldn't be very much protracted now.

HE SIGHED WEARILY in the stinking gloom of the cell. There were too many memories crowding in. The outlaw years had been hard and desperate, but they'd been good ones too. There had been song and laughter and comradeship and gigantic deeds over an endless waste of waters—the long blue hush of twilight, the soft black nights, the gray days with a sea running gray and green and gold under squalls of rain, the storms roaring and raging, the eager leap of a ship—frenzy of battle at the taking of town or galley, death so close one could almost hear the beat of black wings, orgy of loot and vengeance—the pirate town, grass huts under jungle trees, stuffed with treasure, full of brawling bawdy life, the scar-faced swaggering men and the lusty insolent women, ruddy fire-light hammering back the night while the surf thundered endlessly along the beach—

Well, all things came to a close. And while he would have wished a different sort of death for himself, he didn't have long to wait in this misery.

Something stirred, far down the narrow corridor, and he caught the flickering glow of a torch. Scowling, he stood up, stooped under the low ceiling. Who in all the hells was this? It was too soon for feeding, unless his time sense had gone completely awry, and he didn't think the games could have been prepared in the few days since his arrival.

They came up to the entrance of the cell and stood looking in by the guttering red torchlight. A snarl twisted Corun's lips. Shorzon and Chryseis— "Of all the scum of Achaera," he growled, "I had to be inflicted with you."

"This is no time for insolence," said the sorcerer coldly. He lifted the torch higher. The red light threw his face into blood-splashed shadow. His eyes were pits of darkness in which smoldered two embers. His black robe blended with the surrounding shadow, his face and hands seemed to float disembodied in the dank air.

Corun's eyes traveled to Chryseis, and in spite of the hate that burned in him he had to admit she was perhaps the loveliest woman he had ever seen. Tall and slim and lithe, moving with the soundless grace of a Sanduvian pherax, the dark hair sheening down past the chill sculptured beauty of her marble-white face, she returned his blue stare with eyes of dark flame. She was dressed as if for action—a brief tunic that left arms and legs bare, a short black cloak, and high buskins—but jewels still blazed at throat and wrists.

Behind her padded a lean shadow at sight of which Corun stiffened. He had heard of Chryseis' tame erinye. Folk said the devil-beast had found a harder heart in the witch's breast and yielded to her; some said less mentionable things.

The slitted green eyes flared at Corun and the cruel muzzle opened in a fanged yawn. "Back, Perias," said Chryseis evenly.

Her voice was low and sweet, almost a caress. It seemed strange that such a voice had spoken the rituals of black sorcery and ordered the flaying alive of a thousand helpless Issarian prisoners and counseled some of the darkest intrigues in Achaera's bloody history.

She said to Corun, "This is a fine end for all your noble thoughts, man of Conahur."

"At least," he answered, "you credit me with having had them. Which is more than I'd say for you."

THE RED LIPS curved in a cynical smile. "Human purposes have a habit of ending this way. The mighty warrior, the scourge of the seas, ends in a foul prison cell waiting for an unimaginative death. The old epics lied, didn't they? Life isn't quite the glorious adventure that fools think it to be."

"It could be, if it weren't for your sort."" Wearily: "Go away, won't you? If you won't even let me talk with my old comrades, you can at least spare me your own company."

"We are here with a definite purpose," said Shorzon. "We offer you life, freedom—and the liberation of Conahur!"

He shook his tawny head. "It isn't even funny."

"No, no, I mean it," said Chryseis earnestly. "Shorzon had you put in here alone not out of malice, but simply to make this private talk possible. You can help us with a project so immeasurably greater than your petty quarrels that anything you can ask in return will be as nothing. And you are the one man who can do so.

"I tell you this so that, realizing you have some kind of bargaining position, you will meet as us as equal to equal, not as prisoner to captor. If you agree to aid us, you will be released this instant."

With a sudden flame within him, Corun tautened his huge body. O gods—O almighty gods beyond the clouds—if it were true—!

His voice shook: "What do you want?"

"Your help in a desperate venture," said Chryseis. "I tell you frankly that we may well all die in it. But at least you will die as a free man—and if we succeed, all the world may be ours."

"What is it?" he asked hoarsely.

"I cannot tell you everything now," said Shorzon. "But the story has long been current that you once sailed to the lairs of the Xanthi, the Sea Demons, and returned alive. Is it true?"

"Aye." Corun stiffened, with sudden alarm trembling in his nerves. "Aye, by great good luck I came back. But they are not a race for humans to traffic with."

"I think the powers I can summon will match theirs," said Shorzon. "We want you to guide us to their dwellings and teach us the language on the way, as well as whatever else you know about them. When we return, you may go where you choose. And if we get their help, we will be able to set Conahur free soon afterward."

Corun shook his head. "It's nothing good that you plan," he said slowly. "No one would approach the Xanthi for any good purpose."

"You did, didn't you?" chuckled the wizard dryly. "If you want the truth, we are after their help in seizing the government of Achaera, as well as certain knowledge they have."

"If you succeeded," argued Corun stubbornly, "why should you then let Conahur go?"

"Because power over Achaera is only a step to something too far beyond the petty goals of empire for you to imagine," said Shorzon bleakly. "You must decide now, man. If you refuse, you die."

Chryseis moved one slim hand and the erinye padded forward on razor-clawed feet. The leathery wings were folded back against the long black body, the barbed tail lashed hungrily and a snarl vibrated in the lean throat. "If you say no," came the woman's sweet voice, "Perias will rip your guts out. That will at least afford us an amusing spectacle for our trouble." Then she smiled, the dazzling smile which had driven men to their doom ere this. "But if you say yes," she whispered, "a destiny waits for you that kings would envy. You are a strong man, Corun. I like strong men—"

The corsair looked into the warm dark light of her eyes, and back to the icy glare of the devil-beast. No unarmed man had ever survived the onslaught of an erinye—and he was chained.

At thought of returning to the dark home of the Xanthi, he shuddered. But life was still wondrous sweet, and—once free to move about, he might still have some chance of escape or even of overpowering them.

Or—who knew? He wondered, with a brief giddiness, if the dark witch before him could be as evil as her enemies said. Strong and ruthless, yes—but so was he. When he learned the full truth about her soaring plans, he might even decide they were right.

In any case—to live! To die, if he must, under the sky!

"I'll go," he said hoarsely. "I'll go with you."

The low exultant laughter of Chryseis sang in the flare-lit gloom.

Shorzon came up and took a key from his belt. For a bare moment, the thought of snapping that skinny neck raged through Corun's mind.

The magician smiled grimly. "Don't try it," he said. "As a small proof of what we can do—"

Suddenly he was not there. It was a monster from the jungles of Umlotu standing in the cell with Corun, a scaled beast that hissed at him with grinning jaws and spewed poison on the floor.

SORCERY! Corun shrank back, a chill of fear striking even his steely heart. Shorzon resumed human shape and wordlessly unlocked the chains. They fell away and Corun stumbled out into the corridor.

The erinye snarled and slipped closer. Chryseis laid a hand on the beast's head, checking that gliding rush as if with a leash. Her smile and the faint sweet scent of her hair were dizzying.

"Come," she said. One hand slipped between his own fingers and the cool touch seemed to burn him.

Shorzon led the way, down a long sloping tunnel where only the streaming torch-flames had life. Their footsteps echoed hollowly in the wet black length of it.

"We go at once," he said. "When Khroman learns of your escape, all Tauros will be after us. But it will be too late then. We sail swiftly tonight."

Sail—whither?

"What of my men?" asked Corun.

"They're lost, I'm afraid, unless Khroman spares them until we get back," said Chryseis. "But we saved you. I'm glad of that."

A faint smell of fresh salty air blew up the tunnel. It must open on the sea, thought Corun. He wondered how many passages riddled the depth under Taurus.

They came out, finally, on a narrow beach under the looming western dills. The precipices climbed into the utter dark of night, reaching into the unseen sky. Before them lay open sea, swirling with phosphorescence. Corun drew deep lung-fulls of air. Salt and seaweed and wet wild wind—sand under his feet, sky overhead, a woman beside him—by the gods, it was good to be alive!

A galley was moored against a tiny pier. By the light of bobbing torches, Corun's mariner's eye surveyed her. She was built along the same lines as his own ship, a lean black vessel with one square sail; open-decked save at stem and stern, rower's benches lining the sides with a catwalk running between. There would be quarters for the men under the poop and forecastle decks, supplies in the hold beneath. A cabin was erected near the waist, apparently for officers, and there was a ballista mounted in the bows—otherwise no superstructure. A carved sea monster reared up for figurehead, and the sternpost curved back to make its tail. He read the name on the bows: *Briseia*. Strange that that dark vessel should bear a girl's name.

About a fifty-man capacity, he judged. And she would be fast.

The crew members were getting aboard—they must have come down the cliffs along some narrow trail. They were all Umlotuan blues, he noticed, a cutthroat gang if ever he saw one but silent and well disciplined. It was shrewd to take only the mercenary warriors along; they had no patriotic interest in what happened to Achaera, and their reckless courage was legendary.

A burly one-eyed officer came up and saluted. "All set, sir," he reported.

"Good," nodded Shorzon. "Captain Imazu, this is our guide, Captain Corun."

"The raider, eh?" Imazu chuckled and shook hands in the manner of the barbarians. "Well, we could hardly have a better one, I'm sure. Glad to know you, Corun."

The pirate murmured polite phrases. But he decided that Imazu was a likeable chap, and wondered what had led him to take service under anyone with Shorzon's reputation.

They went aboard. "The Sea of Demons lies due north," said Shorzon. "Is that the right way to sail?"

"For the time being," nodded Corun. "When we get closer, I'll be able to tell you more exactly."

"Then you may as well wash and rest," said Chryseis. "You need both." Her smile was soft in the flickering red light.

Corun entered the cabin. It was divided into three compartments—apparently Imazu slept with his men, or perhaps on deck as many men preferred. His own tiny room was clean, sparsely furnished with a bunk and a washbowl. He cleaned himself eagerly and put on the fresh tunic laid out for him.

When he came back on deck the ship was already under way. A strong south wind was blowing, filling the dark sail, and the *Briseia* surged forward under its thrust. The phosphorescence shone around her hull and out on the rolling waters. Behind, the land faded into the night.

He'd certainly been given no chance to escape, he thought. Barring miracles, he had to go through with it now—at least until they reached the Sea of Demons, after which anything might happen.

He shivered a little, wondering darkly whether he had done right, wondering what their mission was and what the world's fate was to be as a result of it.

Chryseis slipped quietly up to stand beside him. The erinye crouched down nearby, his baleful eyes never leaving the man.

"Outward bound," she said, and laughter was gay in her voice.

He said nothing, but stared ahead into the night.

"You'd better sleep, Corun," she said. "You're tired now, and you'll need all your strength later." She laid a hand on his arm, and laughed aloud. "It will be an interesting voyage, to say the least."

Rather! he thought with wry humor. It occurred to him that the trip might even have its pleasant aspects.

"Goodnight, Corun," she said, and left him.

Presently he went back to his room. Sleep was long in coming, and uneasy when it did arrive.

CHAPTER THREE

WHEN HE CAME OUT ON DECK in the early morning, there was only a gray emptiness of waters out to the gray horizon. They must have left the whole Achaeran archipelago well behind them and be somewhere in the Zurian Sea now.

There was a smell of rain in the air, and the ship ran swiftly before a keening wind over long white-maned rollers. Corun let the tang of salt and moisture and kelp, the huge restless vista of bounding waves, the creak and thrum of the ship and the thundering surge of the ocean, swell luxuriously up within him, the simple animal joy of being at home. The sea was his home now, he realized vaguely; he had been on it so long that it was his natural environment—his, as much as that of the laridae wheeling on white wings in the cloud-flying heavens.

He looked over the watch. It seemed to be well handled—the sailors knew their business. There were armored guards at bow and stern, and the rest—clad in the plain loincloth of ordinary seamen the world over—were standing by the sail, swabbing the decks, making minor repairs and otherwise occupying themselves. Those off duty were lounging or sleeping well out of the watch's way. The helmsman kept his eye on the compass and held the tiller with a practiced hand—good, good.

Captain Imazu padded up to him on bare feet. The Umlotuan wore helmet and corselet, had a sword at his side, and carried the whip of authority in one gnarled blue hand.

His scarred, one-eyed face cracked in a smile. "Good morning to you, Captain Corun," he said politely.

The Conahurian nodded with an amiability he had not felt for a long time. "The ship is well handled," he said.

"Thanks. I'm about the only Umlotuan who's ever skippered anything bigger than a war-canoe, I suppose, but I was in the Achaeran fleet for a long time." Again the hideous but disarming smile. "I nearly met you professionally once or twice before, but you always showed us a clean pair of heels. Judging from what happened to ships that did have the misfortune to overhaul you, I'm just as glad of it." He gestured to the tiny galley below the poop deck. "How about some breakfast?"

OVER FOOD which was better than most to be had aboard ship, they fell into professional talk. Like all captains, Imazu was profoundly interested in the old and seemingly insoluble problem of finding an accurate position. "Dead reckoning just won't do," he complained. "Men's estimates always differ, no matter how good they may be. There isn't even a decent map to be had anywhere."

Corun mentioned the efforts of theorists in Achaera, Conahur, and other civilized states to use the Heaven-Fire's altitude to determine position north and south of a given line. Imazu was aware of their work, but regarded it as of little practical value. "You just don't see it often enough," he objected. "And most of the crew would consider it the worst sort of impiety to go aiming an instrument at it. That's one reason, I suppose, why Shorzon shipped only Umlotuans. We don't worship the Heaven-Fire—our gods all live below the clouds." He cut himself a huge quid of liangzi and stuffed it into his capacious mouth. "Anyway, it doesn't give you east and west position."

"The philosophers who think the world is round, say we could solve that problem by making an accurate timepiece," said Corun.

"I know. But it's a lot of gas, if you ask me. A sand-glass or a water-clock can only tell time so close and no closer, and those mechanical gadgets they've built are worse yet. I knew an old skipper from Norriki once who kept a joss in his cabin and got his position in dreams from it. Only had one wreck in his life." Imazu grinned. "Of course, he drowned then."

"Look," said Corun suddenly, "do you know where the hell we're going, and why?"

"To the Sea of Demons is all they told me. No reason given." Imazu studied Corun with his sharp black eye. "You don't know either, eh? I've a notion that most of us won't live to find out."

"I'm surprised that any crew could be made to go there without a mutiny."

"This gang of bully boys is only frightened of Shorzon and his witch granddaughter. They—" Imazu shut up. Looking around, Corun saw the two approaching.

In the morning light, Chryseis did not seem the luring devil-woman of the night. She moved with easy grace across the rolling deck, the wind blowing her tunic and her long black hair in careless billows, and there was a girlish joy and eagerness in her. The pirate's heart stumbled and began to race.

She chattered gaily of nothing while she and the old man ate. Shorzon remained silent until he was through, then said curtly to the two men, "Come into the cabin with us."

They filled Corun's tiny room, sitting on bunk and floor. Shorzon said slowly, "We may as well begin now to learn what you know, Corun. What is the truth about your voyage to the Xanthi?"

"It was several seasons ago," replied the corsair. "I got the thought you seem to have had, that possibly I could enlist their help against my enemies." He smiled mirthlessly. "I learned better."

"What do we know of them, exactly?" said Shorzon methodically. He ticked the points off on his lean fingers. "They are an amphibious non-human race dwelling in the Sea of Demons, which is said to grow grass so that ships become tangled there and never escape."

"Not so," said Corun. "There's kelp on the surface, but you can sail right through it. I think the Sea is just a dead region of water around which the great ocean currents move."

"I know," said Shorzon impatiently, and resumed his summary: "Generations ago, the Xanthi, of whose presence men had only been vaguely aware before, fell upon all the islands in their sea and slew the people living there. They had great numbers, as well as tamed sea monsters and unknown powers of sorcery, so that no one could stand against them. Since then, they have not gone beyond their borders, but they ruthlessly destroy all human vessels venturing inside. King Phidion III of Achaera sent a great fleet to drive the Xanthi from their stolen territory. Not one ship returned. Men now shun the whole region as one accursed."

Imazu nodded. "There's a sailor's legend that the souls of the damned go to the Xanthi," he offered.

Shorzon gave him an exasperated look. "I'm only interested in facts," he said coldly. "What do you know, Corun?"

"I know what you just said, as who doesn't?" answered the Conahurian. "But I think they must have limits to their powers, and be reasonable creatures—but the limits are far beyond man's, and their reason is not as ours.

"I didn't try an invasion, of course. I took one small fast boat manned with picked volunteers and waited outside the Sea for a storm that would blow me into it. When that came, we ran before it—fast! In the rain and wind and waves, I figured we could get undetected far into their borders. So, it seemed, we could, and in fact we made it almost to the largest island inside. Then they came at us.

"They were riding cetaraea, and driving sea serpents before them. They had spears and bows and swords, and there were hundreds of them. Anyone of the snakes could have smashed our boat. We ran for land and barely made it.

"'We hadn't come to fight, so we held up our hands as the Xanthi leaped ashore and wondered if they'd just hack us down. But, as I'd hoped, they wanted to know what we were there for. So they took us to the black castle on the island."

MOMENTARILY Corun was cold as the memory of that wet dark place of evil shuddered through his mind. "I can't tell you much about it. They have great powers of sorcery, and the place seemed somehow unreal, never the same— always wrong, always with something horrible just beyond vision in the shadows. I remember the whole time as if it were a dream. There were treasures beyond counting. I saw gold and jewels from the sea bottom, mixed in with human skulls and the figureheads of drowned ships. The light was dim and blue, and there was always fog, and noises for which we had no name hooting out in the gloom. It stank, with the vile fishy smell they have. And the walls seemed to have a watery unreality, as I said, shifting and fading like smoke. You could smell sorcery in the very air of that place.

"They kept us there for many ten-days. We'd brought rich gifts, of course, which they accepted ungraciously, and they housed us in a dungeon under guard. They didn't feed us so badly, if you like a steady fish diet. And they taught us their language."

"How does it sound?" as Chryseis.

"I can't make it come out right. No human throat can. Something like this—" They stiffened at the chill hissing that slithered from Corun's lips. "It has words for things I never did understand, and it lacks many of the commonest human words—fear, joy, hope, adventure—" His glance slid to Chryseis. "Love—"

"Do they have a word for hate?" asked Shorzon.

"Oh, yes," Corun grinned without humor. After a moment he went on: "They wanted to know more of the outside world. That was why they spared our lives. When we knew the language well enough, they began to question us. How they questioned us! It got to be torture, those unending days of answering the things that hissed and gabbled at us in those shadowy rooms. It was like a nightmare, where mad happenings go on without ever ending. Politics, science, philosophy, art, geography—they wanted to know it all. They pumped us dry of knowledge. When we came to something they didn't understand, such as—love, say—they went back and forth over the same ground, over and over again, until we thought we'd go crazy.

And at last they'd give up in bafflement. I think they believe humans to be mad.

"I made my offer, of course—the loot of Achaera in exchange for the freedom of Conahur. They—I might almost say they laughed. Finally they answered in scorn that they could take whatever they wanted, the whole world if need be, without my help."

Shorzon's eyes glittered. "Did you find out anything of their powers?" he asked eagerly.

"A little. They put any human magician to shame, of course. I saw them charm sea monsters to death just to eat them. I saw them working on a new building on the island—they planted a little package somewhere, and set fire to it, and great stones leaped into the air with a bang like thunder. I saw their cetaraea cavalry, their tamed war-snakes—oh, yes, they have more powers than I could name. And their numbers must be immense. They live on the sea bottom, you know—that is, their commoners do. The leaders have strongholds on land as well. They farm both sea and land, and have great smithies on the islands.

"Well, in the end they let us go. They were going to put us to death for our trespass, I think, but I did some fast talking. I told them that we could carry word of their strength back to humans and overawe our race with it, so that if they ever wanted to collect tribute or something of the sort, they'd never have to fight for it. Probably that carried less weight than the fact that we had, after all, done no harm and been of some use. They had no logical reason to kill us—so they didn't." Corun smiled grimly. "We were a pretty tough crew, prepared to take a few Xanthi to death with us even if we were disarmed. Their killing-charms seem to work only on animals. That was another reason to spare us.

"One of their wizards was for having me, at least, slain. He said he'd had a prevision of my return with ruin in my wake. But the others—laughed?—at him, at the very thought of a human's being dangerous to them. Moreover, they pointed out, if that was to be the case then there was nothing they could do about it; they seem to believe in a fixed destiny. But the idea amused them so much that it was still another reason for letting us go." Corun shrugged. "So we sailed away. That's all. And never till now did I have any smallest thought of returning."

He added bleakly after a moment when silence had been heavy: "They have all they want to know from my visit. There will be no reason for them to spare us this time."

"I think there will," said Chryseis.

"There'd better be," muttered Imazu.

"You can start teaching us their language," said Shorzon. "It might not be a bad idea for you to learn too, Imazu. The more who can talk to them, the better."

The Umlotuan made a wry face. "Another tongue to learn! By the topknot of Mwanzi, why can't the world settle on one and end this babble!"

"The poor interpreters would starve to death," smiled Chryseis.

She took Corun's arm. "Come, my buccaneer, let's go up on deck for a while. There's always time to learn words."

THEY FOUND a quiet spot on the forecastle deck, and sat down against the rail. The erinye settled his long body beside Chryseis and watched Corun with sleepy malevolence, but he was hardly aware of the devil-beast. It was Chryseis. Chryseis, dark sweet hair and dark lambent eyes, utter loveliness of face and form, singing golden voice and light warm touch and—

"You are a strange man, Corun," she said softly. "What are you thinking now?"

"Oh—nothing." He smiled crookedly. "Nothing."

"I don't believe that. You have too many memories."

Almost without knowing it, he found himself telling her of his life, the long terrible struggle against overwhelming power, the bitterness and loneliness, the death of comrades one by one—and the laughter and triumphs and wild exultance of it, the faring into unknown seas and the dicing with fate and the strong, close bonds of men against the world. He mused wistfully about a girl who was gone—but her bright image was strangely fading in his heart now, for it was Chryseis who was beside him.

"It has been a hard life," she said at the end. "It took a giant of a man to endure it." She smiled, a small closed smile that made her look strangely young. "I wonder what you must think of this—sailing with your sworn foes to the end of the world on an unknown mission."

"You're not my foe!" he blurted.

"No—never your enemy, Corun!" she exclaimed. "We have been on opposite sides before—let it not be thus from this moment. I tell you that the purpose of this voyage, which you shall soon know, is—good. Great and good as the savagery of man has never known before. You know the old legend—that someday the Heaven-Fire will shine through opening clouds not as a destroying flame but as the giver of life—that men will see light in the sky even at night—that there will be peace and justice for all mankind? I think that day may be dawning, Corun."

He sat dumbly, bewildered. She was not evil—she was not evil. It was all he knew, but it sang within him.

Suddenly she laughed and sprang to her feet. "Come on!" she cried. "I'll race you around the ship!"

CHAPTER FOUR

RAIN AND WIND CAME. A lightning-shot squall in which the *Briseia* wallowed and bucked and men strained at oars and pumps. Toward evening it was over, the sea stilled and the lower clouds faded so that they saw the great dull-red disc of the Heaven-Fire through the upper clouds, sinking into the western sea. There was almost a flat calm, the glassy water was ruffled only by a faint breeze which half filled the sail and sent the galley sliding slowly and noiselessly northward.

"Man the oars," directed Shorzon.

"Give the men a chance to rest tonight, sir," begged Imazu. "They've all worked hard today. We can row all the faster tomorrow if we must."

"No time to spare," snapped the wizard.

"Yes, there is," said Corun flatly. "Let the men rest, Imazu."

Shorzon gave him a baleful glance. "You forget your position aboard."

Corun bristled. "I think I'm just beginning to remember it," he answered with metal in his voice.

Chryseis laid a hand on her grandfather's arm. "He's right," she said. "So is Imazu. It would be needless cruelty to make the sailors work tonight, and they will be better fitted by a night's rest."

"Very well," said Shorzon sullenly. He went into his room and slammed the door. Presently Chryseis bade the men goodnight and went to her quarters with the erinye trotting after.

Corun's eyes followed her through the deepening blue dusk. In that mystic light, the ship was a shadowy half-real background, a dimness beyond which the sea swirled in streamers of cold white radiance.

"She's a strange woman," said Imazu. "I don't understand her."

"Nor I," admitted Corun. "But I know now her enemies have foully lied about her."

"I'm not so sure about that—" As the Conahurian turned with a dark frown, Imazu added quickly, "Oh, well, I'm probably wrong. I never had much sight of her, you know."

They wandered up on the poop deck in search of a place to sit. It was deserted save for the helmsman by the dimly glowing binnacle, a deeper shadow in the thick blue twilight. Sitting back against the taffrail, they could look forward to the lean waist of the ship and the vague outline of the listlessly bellying sail. Beyond the hull, the sea was an arabesque of luminescence, delicate traceries of shifting white light out to the glowing horizon. The cold fire streamed from the ship's bows and whirled in her wake, the hull dripped liquid flame.

The night was very quiet. The faint hiss and smack of cloven water, creak of planks and tackle, distant splashing of waves and invisible sea beasts—otherwise there was only the enormous silence under the high clouds. The breeze was cool on their cheeks.

"How long till we get to the Sea of Demons?" asked Imazu. His voice was oddly hushed in the huge stillness.

"With ordinary sailing weather, I'd say about three tendays—maybe four," answered Corun indifferently.

"It's a strange mission we're on, aye, that it is." Imazu's head wagged, barely visible in the dark. "I like it not, Corun. I have evil feelings about it, and the omens I took before leaving weren't good."

"Why then did you sail? You're a free man, aren't you?"

"So they say!" Sudden bitterness rose in the Umlotuan's voice. "Free as any of Shorzon's followers, which is to say less free than a slave, who can at least run away."

"Why, doesn't he pay well?"

"Oh, aye, he is lavish in that regard. But he has his ways of binding servants to him so that they must do his bidding above that of the very gods. He put his geas on most of these sailors, for instance. They were simple folk, and thought he was only magicking them a good-luck charm."

"You mean they are bound? He has their souls?"

"Aye. He put them to sleep in some sorcerous way and impressed his command on them. No matter what happens now, they must obey him. The geas is stronger than their own wills."

Corun shivered. "Are you—Pardon. It's no concern of mine."

"No, no, that's all right. He put no such binding on me— I knew better than to accept his offer of a luck-bringing spell. But he has other ways. He lent me a slave-girl from Umlotu for my pleasure—but she is lovely, wonderful, kind, all that a woman should be. She has borne me sons, and made homecoming ever a joy. But you see, she is still Shorzon's and he will not sell her to me or free her—moreover, he did put his geas on her. If ever I rebelled, she would suffer for it." Imazu spat over the rail. "So I am Shorzon's creature too."

"It must be a strange service."

"It is. Mostly all I have to do is captain his bodyguard. But I've seen and helped in some dark things. He's a fiend from the lowest hell, Shorzon is. And his granddaughter—" Imazu stopped.

"Yes?" asked Corun roughly. His hand closed bruisingly on the other's arm. "Go on. What of her?"

"Nothing. Nothing. I really have had little to do with her." Imazu's face was lost in the gloom, but Corun felt the one eye hard on him. "Only—be careful, pirate. Don't let her lay her own sort of geas on you. You've been a free man till now. Don't become anyone's blind slave."

"I've no such intention," said Corun frostily.

"Then no more need be said." Imazu sighed heavily and got up. "I think I'll go to bed, then. What of you?"

"Not yet. I'm not sleepy. Goodnight."

"Goodnight."

CORUN sat back alone. He could barely discern the helmsman—beyond lay only glowing darkness and the whispering of the night. He felt loneliness like a cold hollow within his breast.

Father and mother, his tall brothers and his laughing lovely sister, the comrades of youth, the hard wild stout-hearted pirates with whom he had sailed for such a long and bloody time—where were they now? Where in all the blowing night were they?

Where was he and on what mission, sailing alone through a pit of darkness on a ship of strangers? What meaning and hope in all the cruel insanity of the world?

Suddenly he wanted his mother, he wanted to lay his head on her lap and cry in desolation and hear her gentle voice—no, by the gods, it wasn't her image he saw, it was a lithe and dark-haired witch who was crooning to him and stroking his hair—

He cursed tonelessly and got up. Best to go to bed and try to sleep his fancies away. He was becoming childish.

He went down the catwalk toward the cabin. As he neared it, he saw a figure by the rail darkly etched against a shimmering patch of phosphorescence. His heart sprang into his throat.

She turned as he came near. "Corun," she said. "I couldn't sleep. Come over here and talk to me. Isn't the night beautiful?"

He leaned on the rail, not daring to look at the haunting face pale—lit by the swirling sea-fire. "It's nice," he said clumsily.

"But it's lonely," she whispered. "I never felt so sad and alone before."

"Why—why, that's how I felt!" he blurted.

"Corun—"

She came to him and he took her with a sudden madness of yearning.

Perias the erinye snarled as they thrust him out of her cabin. He padded up and down the deck for a while. A sailor who stood watch near the forecastle followed him with frightened eyes and muttered prayers to the amulet about his neck.

Presently the devil-beast curled up before the cabin. The lids drooped over his green eyes, but they remained unwinkingly fixed on the door.

CHAPTER FIVE

UNDER A HOT SULLEN SKY, the windless sea swelled in long slow waves that rocked the tangled kelp and ocean-grass up and down, heavenward and hell ward. To starboard, the dark cliffs of a small jungled island rose from an angry muttering surf, but there were no birds flying above it.

Corun pointed to the shore. "That's the first of the archipelago," he said. "From here on, we can look for the Xanthi to come at any time."

"We should get as far into their territory as possible, even to the black palace," said Shorzon. "I will put a spell of invisibility on the ship."

"Their sorcerers can break that," said Chryseis.

"Aye, so. But when they come to know our powers, I think they will treat with us."

"They'd better!" smiled Imazu grimly.

"Steer on toward the island of the castle," said Shorzon to the pirate. "I go to lay the spell."

He went into his cabin. Corun had a glimpse of its dark interior before the door was closed-draped in black and filled with the apparatus of magic.

"He will have to be in a trance, physically, to maintain the enchantment," said Chryseis. She smiled at Corun, and his pulses raced. "Come, my dearest, it is cooler on the afterdeck."

The sailors rowed steadily, sweat glistening on their bare blue hides. Imazu paced up and down the catwalk, flicking idlers with his whip. Corun stood where he could keep an eye on the steersman and see that the right course was followed.

It had been utter wonder till now, he thought, unending days when they plowed through seas of magic, nights of joy such as he had never known. There had never been another woman such as Chryseis, he thought, never in all the world, and he was the luckiest of men. Though he died today, he had been more fortunate than any man ever dared dream.

Chryseis. Chryseis, loveliest and wisest and most valiant of women—and she was his, before all the jealous gods, she loved him!

"There has only been one thing wrong," he said. "You are going into danger now. The world would go dark if aught befell you."

"And I should sit at home while you were away, and never know what had happened, never know if you lived or died—no, no, Corun!"

He laid a hand on the sword at his waist. They had given him arms and armor again after she had come to him. Logical enough, he thought without resentment—he could be trusted now, as much as if he were one of Shorzon's ensorcelled warriors.

But if this were a spell too, the gods deliver him from ever being freed of it!

He blinked. There was a sudden breath of chill on him, and his eyes were blurring—no, no, it was the ship that wavered, ship and men fading— He clutched at Chryseis. She laughed softly and slipped an arm around his waist.

"It is only Shorzon's spell," she said. "It affects us too, to some extent. And it makes the ship invisible to anyone within seeing range."

Ghost ship, ghost crew, slipping over the slowly heaving waters. There was only the foggiest outline to be seen, shadow of mast and rigging against the sky, glimpses of water through the gray smoke of the hull, blobs of darkness that were the crewmen. Sound was still clear; he heard the mutter of superstitious awe, the crack of the whip, and Imazu's oaths that sent the oars creaking and splashing again. Corun's hand was a misty blur before his eyes. Chryseis was a shadow beside him.

She laughed once more, a low exultant throb, and pulled his lips down to hers. He ruffled the streaming fragrant hair and felt a return of courage. It was only a spell.

But what were the spells he wondered for the thousandth time? He did not hold with the simple theory that wizards were in league with gods or demons. They had powers, yes, but he was sure that somehow these powers came only from within themselves. Chryseis had always evaded his questions about it. There must be some simple answer to the problem, some real process, as real as that of making a fire, behind the performances of the sorcerers—but it baffled him to think what it might be.

Blast it all, it just wasn't reasonable that Shorzon, for instance, should have been able actually to change himself into a jungle monster many times his size. Yet he, Corun, had seen the thing, had felt its wet scales and smelled its reptile stink. How?

THE SHIP plowed slowly on. Now and then Corun looked at the compass, straining his eyes to discern the blurred needle. Otherwise they could only wait.

But waiting with Chryseis was remarkably pleasant.

It was at the end of a timeless time, perhaps half a day, that he saw the Xanthian patrol. "Look," he pointed. "There they come."

Chryseis stared boldly over the sea. The hand beneath his was steady as her voice. "So I see. They're—beautiful, aren't they?"

The cetaraea came leaping across the waves, big graceful beasts with the shapes of fish, their smooth black hides shining and the water white behind their threshing tails. Astride each was a great golden form bearing a lance. They quartered across the horizon and were lost to sight.

The crew mumbled in fear, shaken to their hardy souls by the terrible inhuman grace of the Xanthi. Imazu cursed them back to work. The ship went on.

Islands slipped by, empty of man-sign. They had glimpses of Xanthian works, spires and walls rearing above the jungle. These were not the white colonnaded buildings of Tauros or the timbered halls of Conahur—of black stone they were, with pointed towers climbing crazily skyward. Once a great sea serpent reared its head, spouted water, and writhed away. All creatures save man could sense the presence of wizardry and refused to go near it.

Night fell, an abyss of night broken only by faint glimmers of sea-fire under the carpeting weed. Men stood uneasy watch in full armor, peering blindly into the somber immensity. It was hot, hot and silent.

Near midnight the lookout shouted from the masthead: "Xanthi to larboard!"

"Silence, you fool!" called Imazu. "Want them to hear us?"

The patrol was a faint swirl and streaking of phosphorescence, blacker shadows against the night. It was coming nearer.

"Have they spotted us?" wondered Corun.

"No," breathed Chryseis. "But they're close enough for their mounts—"

There was a great snorting and splashing out in the murk. The cetaraea were refusing to go into the circle of Shorzon's spell. Voices lifted, an inhuman croaking. The erinye, the only animal who did not seem to mind witchcraft, snarled in saw-edged tones, eyes a green blaze against the night.

Presently the squad turned and slipped away. "They know something is wrong, and they've gone for help," said Corun. "We'll have a fight on our hands before long."

He stretched his big body, suddenly eager for action. This waiting was more than he could stand.

The ship drove on. Corun and Chryseis napped on the deck; it was too stiflingly hot below. The long night wore away.

In the misty gray of morning, they saw a dark mass advancing from the west. Corun's sword rasped out of the sheath. It was a long, double-edged blade such as they used in Conahur, and it was thirsty.

"Get inside, Chryseis," he said tightly.

"Get inside yourself," she answered. There was a lilt in her voice like a little girl's. He felt her quiver with joyous expectation.

The ghostly outlines of the ship wavered, thickened, faded again, flickered back toward solidity. Suddenly they had sight; the vessel lay real around them; they saw each other in helm and corselet, face looking into tautened face.

"They have a wizard along—he broke Shorzon's spell," said the Conahurian.

"We looked for that," answered Chryseis evenly. "But as long as Shorzon keeps fighting him, there will be a roiling of magic around us such that none of their beasts will approach."

She stood beside him, slim and boyish in polished cuirass and plumed helmet, short sword belted to her waist and a bow in one hand. Her nostrils quivered, her eyes shone, and she laughed aloud. "We'll drive them off," she said. "We'll send them home like beaten iaganaths."

Imazu blew the war-horn, wild brazen echoes screaming over the sea. His men drew in the oars, pulled on their armor, and stood along the rails, waiting.

"But did we come here to fight them?" asked Corun.

"No," said Chryseis. "But we've known all along that we'd have to give them a taste of our might before they'd talk to us."

The Xanthian lancers were milling about half a league away, as if in conference. Suddenly someone blew a harsh-toned horn and Corun saw half the troop slide from the saddle into the water. "So—they'll swim at us," he muttered.

THE ATTACK came from all sides, converging on the ship in a rush of foam. As the Xanthi neared, Corun saw their remembered lineaments and felt the old clutch of panic. *They weren't human.*

With the fluked tail, one of them had twice the length of a man. The webbed hind feet, on which they walked ashore, were held close to the body; the strangely human hands carried weapons. They swam half under water, the dorsal fins rising over. Their necks were long, with gills near the blunt-snouted heads; their grinning mouths showed gleaming fangs. The eyes were big, dark, alive with cold intelligence. They bore no armor, but scales the color of beaten gold covered back and sides and tail. They came in at furious speed, churning the sea behind them.

Chryseis' voice rose to a wild shriek. "Perias! Perias—kill!"

The erinye howled and unfolded his leather-webbed wings. Like a hurled spear he streaked into the air, rushed down on the nearest Xanthian like a thunderbolt—claws, teeth, barbed tail, a blinding fury of blood and death, ripping flesh as if it were parchment.

The ship's ballista *chunked* and balls of the ever-burning Achaeran fire were hurled out to fall blazing among the enemy. Chryseis' bow hummed beside Corun, a Xanthian went under with an arrow in his throat—the air was thick with shafts as the crew fired.

Still the Xanthi rushed on, ducking up and down, near impossible to hit. The first of them came up to the hull and sank their clawed fingers into the wood. The sailors thrust downward with pikes, howling in fear-maddened rage.

The man near Corun went down with a hurled javelin through him. At once a huge golden form was slithering over the rail, onto the deck. The sword in his hand flashed, another Umlotuan's weapon was knocked spinning from his hand and the reptile hewed him down.

Corun sprang to do battle. The swords clashed together with a shock that jarred the man backward. Corun spread his feet and smote out. His blade whirled down to strike the shoulder, gash the chest, and drive the hissing monster back.

With a rising cold fury, Corun followed it up. *That* for the long inquisition—*that* for being a horror out of the sea bottom—*that* for threatening Chryseis! The Xanthian writhed with a belly ripped open. Still he wouldn't die—he flopped and struck from the deck. Corun evaded the sweeping tail and cut off the creature's head.

They were pouring onto the ship through gaps in the line. Chryseis stood on the foredeck in a line of defending men, her bow singing death. Battle snarled about the mast, men against monsters, sword and halberd and ax belling in cloven bone.

A giant's blow bowled Corun off his feet, the tail of a Xanthian. He rolled over and thrust upward as the Sea Demon sprang on him. The sword went through the heart. Hissing and snapping, his foe toppled on him. He heaved the struggling body away and sprang back to his stance.

"To me!" bellowed Imazu. "To me, men!"

He stood wielding a huge battle ax by the mast, striking at the beasts that raged around him, lopping heads and arms and tails like a woodman. The scattered humans rallied and began to fight their way toward him, step by bloody step.

Perias the erinye was everywhere, a flying fury, ripping and biting and smashing with wing-blows. Corun loomed huge over the men who fought beside him, the sword shrieking and thundering in his hands. Imazu stood stolidly against the mast, smashing at all comers. A rush of Xanthi broke past him and surged against the foredeck. The defenders beat them off, Chryseis thrusting as savagely with her sword as any man, and they reeled back against the masthead warriors to be cut down.

A Xanthian sprang at Corun, wielding a long-shafted ax that shivered the sword in his hand. The Conahurian struck back, his blade darting past the monster's guard to stab through the throat. The Xanthian staggered. Corun wrenched the blade loose and brought it down again to sing in the reptile skull.

Before he could pull it loose, another was on him. Corun ducked under the spear he carried and closed his hands around the slippery sides. The clawed feet raked his legs. He lifted the thing and hurled it into another with bone-shattering force. One of them threshed wildly, neck broken—the other bounded at Corun. The man yanked his sword free and it whistled against the golden head.

BACK AND FORTH the struggle swayed, crashing of metal and howling of warriors. And the Xanthi were driven to the rails—they could not stand against the rallying human line in the narrow confines of the ship.

"Kill them!" roared Imazu. "Kill the misbegotten snakes!"

Suddenly the Xanthi were slipping overboard, swimming for their mounts beyond the zone of magic. Perias followed, harrying them, pulling them half out of the water to rip their throats out.

The ship was wet, streaming with human red and reptile yellow blood. Dead and wounded littered the decks. Corun saw the Xanthi cavalry retreating out of sight.

"We've won," he gasped. We've won—"

"No—wait—" Chryseis inclined her head sharply, seeming to listen, then darted past him to open a hatch. Light streamed down into the hold. It was filling—the bilge was rising. "I thought so," she said grimly. "They're below us, chopping into the hull."

"We'll see about that," said Corun, and unbuckled his cuirass. "All who can swim, after me!"

"No—no, they'll kill you—"

"Come on!" tapped Imazu, letting his own breastplate clang to the deck.

Corun sprang overboard. He was wearing nothing but a kilt now, and had a spear in one hand and a dirk in his teeth. Fear was gone, washed out by the red tides of battle. There was only a bleak, terrible triumph in him. Men *had* beaten the Sea Demons!

Underwater, it was green and dim. He swam down, down, brushing the hull, pulling himself along the length of the keel. There were half a dozen shapes clustered near the waist, working with axes.

He pushed against the keel and darted at them, holding the spear like a lance. The keen point stabbed into the belly of one monster. The others turned, their eyes terrible in the gloom. Corun took the dirk in his hand, got a grip on the next nearest, and stabbed.

Claws ripped his flanks and back. His lungs were bursting; there was a roaring in his head and darkness before his eyes. He stabbed blindly, furiously.

Suddenly the struggling form let go. Corun broke the surface and gasped in a lungful of air. A Sea Demon leaped up beside him. At once the erinye was on him. The Xanthian screamed as he was torn apart.

Corun dove back under water. The other seamen were down there, fighting for their lives. They outnumbered the Xanthi, but the monsters were in their native element. Blood streaked the water, blinding them all. It was a strange, horrible battle for survival.

In the end, Corun and Imazu and the others—except for four—were hauled back aboard. "We drove them off," said the pirate wearily.

"Oh, my dear—my dearest dear—" Chryseis, who had laughed in battle, was sobbing on his breast.

Shorzon was on deck, looking over the scene. "We did well," he said. "We stood them off, killed about thirty, and only lost fifteen men."

"At that rate," said Corun, "it won't take them long to clear our decks."

"I don't think they will try again," said Shorzon.

He went over to a captured Xanthian. The Sea Demon had had a foot chopped off in the battle and been pinned to the deck by a pike, but he still lived and rasped defiance at them. If allowed to live, he would grow new members—the monsters were tougher than they had a right to be.

"Hark, you," said Shorzon in the Xanthian tongue, which he had learned with astonishing ease. "We come on a mission of peace, with an offer that your king will be pleased to hear. You have seen only a small part of our powers. It is not beyond us to sail to your palace and bring it crumbling to earth."

Corun wondered how much was bluff. The old sorcerer might really be able to do it. In any case—he had nerve!

"What can you things offer us?" asked the Xanthian.

"That is only for the king to hear," said Shorzon coldly. "He will not thank you for molesting us. Now we will let you go to bear word back to your rulers. Tell them we are coming whether they will or no, but that we come in friendship if they will but show it. After all, if they wish to kill us it can be just as easily done—if at all—after they have heard us out. Now go!"

Imazu pulled the pike loose and the yellow-bleeding Xanthian writhed overboard.

"I do not think we will be bothered again," said Shorzon calmly. "Not before we get to the black palace."

"You may be right," admitted Corun. "You gave them a good argument by their standards."

"Friends?" muttered Imazu. "Friends with those things? As soon expect the erinye to lie down by the bovan, *I* think."

"Come," said Chryseis impatiently. "We have to repair the leak and clean the decks and get under way again. It is a long trip yet to the black palace."

She turned to Corun and her eyes were dark flames. "How you fought!" she whispered. "How you fought, beloved!"

CHAPTER SIX

THE CASTLE STOOD ATOP ONE of the high gray cliffs which walled in a little bay. Beyond the shore, the island climbed steeply toward a gaunt mountain bare of jungle. The sea rolled sullenly against the rocks under a low gloomy sky thickening with the approach of night.

The *Briseia* rowed slowly into the bay, twenty men at the oars and the rest standing nervous guard by the rails. On either side, the Xanthi cavalry hemmed them in, lancers astride the swimming cetaraea with eyes watchful on the humans, and behind them three great sea snakes under direction of their sorcerers followed ominously.

Imazu shivered. "If they came at us now," he muttered, "we wouldn't last long."

"We'd give them a fight!" said Corun.

"They will receive us," declared Shorzon.

The ship grounded on the shallows near the beach. The sailors hesitated. To pull her ashore would be to expose themselves almost helplessly to attack. "Go on, jump to it!" snapped Imazu, and the men shipped their oars and sheathed their weapons, waded into the bay and dragged the vessel up on the strand.

The chiefs of the Xanthi stood waiting for them. There were perhaps fifty of the reptiles, huge golden forms wrapped in dark flowing robes on which glittered ropes of jewels. A few wore tall miters and carried hooked staffs of office. Like statues they stood, waiting, and the sailors shivered.

Shorzon, Chryseis, Corun, and Imazu walked up toward them with all the slow dignity they could summon. The

199

Conahurian's eyes sought the huge wrinkled form of Tsathu, king of the Xanthi. The monster's gaze brightened on him and the fanged mouth opened in a bass croak:

"So you have returned to us. You may not leave this time."

"Your majesty's hospitality overwhelms me," said Corun ironically.

A stooped old Xanthian beside the king plucked his sleeve and hissed rapidly: "I told you, sire. I told you he would come back with the ruin of worlds in his train. Cut them all down now, before the fates strike. Kill them while there is time!"

"There will be time," said Tsathu.

His unblinking eyes locked with Shorzon's and suddenly the twilight shimmered and trembled, the nerves of men shook and out in the water the sea-beasts snorted with panic. For a long moment that silent duel of wizardry quivered in the air, and then it faded and the unreality receded into the background of dusk.

Slowly the Xanthian monarch nodded, as if satisfied to find an opponent he could not overcome.

"I am Shorzon of Achaera," said the man, "and I would speak with the chiefs of the Xanthi."

"You may do so," replied the reptile. "Come up to the castle and we will quarter your folk."

At Imazu's order, the sailors began unloading the gifts that had been brought: weapons, vessels and ornaments of precious metals set with jewels, rare tapestries and incenses. Tsathu hardly glanced at them. "Follow me," he said curtly. "All your people."

"I'd hoped at least to leave a guard on the ship," murmured Imazu to Corun.

"Would have done little good if they really wanted to seize her," whispered the Conahurian.

It did not seem as if Tsathu could have heard them, but he turned and his bass boom rolled over the mumbling surf. "That is right. You may as well relax your petty precautions. They will avail nothing."

IN A LONG FILE, they went up a narrow trail toward the black palace. The Xanthian rulers went first, with deliberately paced dignity, thereafter the human captains, their men, and a silent troop of armed reptile soldiery. *Hemmed in*, thought Corun grimly. *If they want to start shooting—*

Chryseis' hand clasped his, a warm grip in the misty gloom. He responded gratefully. She came right behind him, her other hand on the nervous and growling erinye.

The castle loomed ahead, blacker than the night that was gathering, the gigantic walls climbing sheer toward the sky, the spear-like towers half lost in the swirling fog. There was always fog here, Corun remembered, mist and rain and shadow; it was never full day on the island. He sniffed the dank sea-smell that blew from the gaping portals and bristled in recollection.

They entered the cavernous doorway and went down a high narrow corridor which seemed to stretch on forever. Its bare stone walls were wet and green-slimed, tendrils of mist drifted under the invisibly high ceiling, and he heard the hooting and muttering of unknown voices somewhere in the murk. The only light was a dim bluish radiance from fungoid balls growing on the walls, a cold unhealthy shadowless illumination in which the white humans looked like drowned corpses. Looking behind, Corun could barely make out the frightened faces of the Umlotuans, huddled close together and gripping their weapons with futile strength.

The Xanthi glided noiselessly through the mumbling gloom, tall spectral forms with faint golden light streaming from their damp scales. It seemed as if there were other presences in the castle, too, things flitting just beyond sight, hiding in lightless corners and fluttering between the streamers of fog. Always, it seemed, there were watching eyes, watching and waiting in the dark.

They came into a cavernous antechamber whose walls were lost in the dripping twilight. Tsathu's voice boomed hollowly between the chill immensities of it, "Follow those who will show you to your quarters."

Silent Xanthi slipped between the human ranks, herding them with spears—the sailors one way, their chiefs another. "Where are you taking the men?" asked Imazu with an anger sharpened by fear. "Where are you keeping them?" The echoes flew from wall to wall, jeering him—*keeping them, keeping them, them, them*—

"They go below the castle," said a Xanthian. "You will have more suitable rooms."

Our men down in the old dungeons— Corun's hand whitened on the hilt of his sword. But it was useless to protest, unless they wanted to start a battle now.

The four human leaders were taken down another whispering, echoing tunnel of a corridor, up a long ramp that seemed to wind inside one of the towers, and into a circular room in whose walls were six doors. There the guards left them, fading back down the impenetrable night of the ramp.

THE ROOMS were furnished with grotesque ornateness—huge hideously carved beds and tables, scaled tapestries and rugs, shells and jewels set in the mold-covered walls. Narrow slits of windows opened on the wet night. Darkness and mist hid Corun's view of the ground, but the faintness of the surf told them they must be dizzyingly high up.

"Ill is this," he said. "A few guards on that ramp can bottle us up here forever. And they need only lock the dungeon gates to have our men imprisoned below."

"We will treat with them. Before long they will be our allies," said Shorzon. His hooded eyes were on Chryseis. It was with a sudden shock that Corun remembered. Days and nights of bliss, and then the violence of battle and the tension of approach, had driven from his mind the fact that he had never been told what the witch-pair was really here for. It was *their* voyage, not his, and what real good could have brought them to this place of evil?

He shoved his big body forward, a tawny giant in the foggy chill of the central room. "It is near time I was told something of what you intend," he said. "I have guided you and taught you and battled at your side, and I'll not be kept blindfolded any longer."

"You will be told what I tell you—no more," said Shorzon haughtily. "You have me to thank for your miserable life— let that be enough."

"You can thank me that you're not being eaten by fish at the bottom of the sea right now," snapped Corun. "By Breannach Brannor, I've had enough of this!"

He stood with his back against the wall, sweeping them with ice-blue eyes. Shorzon stood black and ominous, wrath in the smoldering, sunken eyes. Chryseis shrank back a little from both of them, but Perias the erinye growled and flattened his belly to the floor and stared greenly at Corun. Imazu shifted from foot to foot, his wide blue face twisted with indecision.

"I can strike you dead where you stand," warned Shorzon. "I can become a monster that will rip you to rags."

"Try it!" snarled Corun. "Just try it!"

Chryseis slipped between them and the huge dark eyes were bright with tears. "Are we not in enough danger now, four humans against a land of walking beasts, without falling at each other's throats? I think it is the witchcraft of Tsagu working on us, dividing us—fight *him!*"

She swayed against the Conahurian. "Corun;" she breathed, "Corun, my dearest of all—you shall know, you shall be told everything as soon as we dare. But don't you see—you haven't the skill to protect yourself and your knowledge against the Xanthian magic?"

Or against your magic, beloved.

She laughed softly and drew him after her, into one of the rooms. "Come, Corun. We are all weary now, it is time to rest. Come, my dear. Tomorrow—"

CHAPTER SEVEN

DAY CREPT PAST IN A blindness of rain. Twice Xanthians brought them food, and once Corun and Imazu ventured down the ramp to find their way barred by spear-bearing reptiles. For the rest they were alone.

It ate at the nerves like an acid. Shorzon sat stiff, unmoving on a couch, eyes clouded with thought; his gaunt body could have been that of a Khemrian mummy. Imazu squatted unhappily, carving one of the intricate trinkets with whose making sailors pass dreamy hours. Corun paced like a caged beast, throttled rage mounting in him. Even Perias grew restless and took to padding up and down the antechamber, passing Corun on the way. The man could not help a half smile. He was growing almost fond of the erinye and his honest malevolence, after the intriguing of humans and Xanthi.

Only Chryseis remained calm. She lay curled on her bed like a big beautiful animal, the long silken hair tumbling darkly past her shoulders, a veiled smile on her red lips. And so the day wore on.

It was toward evening that they heard slow footfalls and looked out to see a party of Xanthi coming up the ramp. It was an awesome sight, the huge golden forms moving with deliberation and pride under the shimmering robes that flowed about them. Some were warriors, with saw-edged pikes flashing in their hands, but the one who spoke was plainly a palace official.

"Greeting from Tsathu, king of the Demon Sea, to Shorzon of Achaera," the voice boomed. "You are to feast with the lords of the Xanthi tonight."

"I am honored," bowed the sorcerer. "The woman Chryseis will come with me, for she is equal with me."

"That is permitted," said the Xanthian gravely.

"And we, I suppose, wait here," muttered Corun rebelliously.

"It won't be for long," smiled Chryseis softly. "After tonight, I think it will be safe to tell you what you wish to know."

She had donned banqueting dress carried up with her from the ship, a clinging robe of the light-rippling silk of Hiung-nu, a scarlet cloak that was like a rush of flame from her slim bare shoulders, barbarically massive bracelets and necklaces, a single fire-ruby burning at her white throat. Pearls and silver glittered like dewdrops in her night-black hair. The loveliness of her caught at Corun's throat. He could only stare with dumb longing as she went after Shorzon and the Xanthi.

She turned to wave at him. Her whisper twined around his heart: "Goodnight, beloved."

When they were gone, the erinye padding after them, Imazu gave Corun a rueful look and said, "So now we are out of the story."

"Not yet," answered the Conahurian, still a little dazed.

"Oh, yes, oh, yes. Surely you do not think that we plain sailormen will be asked for our opinions? No, Corun, we are only pieces on Shorzon's board. We've done our part, and now he will put us back in the box."

"Chryseis said—"

Imazu shook his scarred bald head sadly. "Surely you don't believe a word that black witch utters?"

Corun half drew his sword. "I told you before that I'd hear no word against Chryseis," he said thinly.

"As you will. It doesn't matter, anyway. But be honest, Corun. Strike me down if you will, it doesn't matter now, but try to think. I've known Chryseis longer than you, and I've never known anyone to change their habits overnight—for anyone."

"She said—"

"Oh, I think she likes you, in her own way. You make as handsome and useful a pet as that erinye of hers. But whatever else she is after, it is something for which she would give more than the world and not have a second thought about it."

Corun paced unhappily. "I don't trust Shorzon," he admitted. "I trust him as I would a mad pherax. And anything Tsathu plans is—evil.' He glared down the cavernous mouth of the ramp. "If I could, only hear what they say!"

"What chance of that? We're under guard, you know."

"Aye, so. But—" Struck with a sudden thought, Corun went over to the window. The rain had ceased outside, but a solid wall of fog and night barred vision. It was breathlessly hot, and he heard the low muttering of thunder in the hidden sky.

THERE WERE VINES growing on the wall, tendrils as thick as a man's leg. The broad leaves hung down over the sill, wet with rain and fog. "I remember the layout of the castle," he said slowly. "It's a warren of tunnels and corridors, but I could find my way to the feasting hall."

"If they caught you, it would be death," said Imazu uneasily.

Corun's grin was bleak. "It will most likely be death anyway," he said. "I think I'll try."

"I'm not as spry as I once was, but—"

"No, no, Imazu, you had best wait here. Then if anyone comes prying and sees you, he'll think we're both here—maybe."

Corun slipped off tunic and sandals, leaving only his kilt. He hung his sword across his back, put a knife in his belt, and turned toward the window.

"It may be all wrong," he said. "I should trust Chryseis—and I do, Imazu, but they might easily overpower her. And anything is better than this waiting like beasts in a trap."

"The gods be with you, then," said Imazu huskily. He shook a horny fist. "To hell with Shorzon! I've been his thrall too long. I'm with you, friend."

"Thanks." Corun swung out the window. "Good luck to both—to all of us, Imazu."

The fog wrapped around his eyes like a hood. He could barely see the shadowy wall, and he groped with fingers and toes for the vines. One slip, one break, and he would be spattered to red ruin in the courtyard below.

Down and down and down—Twigs clawed at him. The branches were slick in his hands, buried under a smother of leaves. His muscles began to ache with the strain. Several times he slipped and saved himself with a desperate clawing grip.

Something moaned in the night, under the deepening growl of thunder.

He clung to the wall and strained his eyes down. A breath of wind parted the fog briefly into ragged streamers through which winked the savage light of a bolt of lightning, high in the murky sky. Down below was the courtyard. He saw the metallic gleam of scales, guards pacing between the walls.

Slowly, he edged his way across the out jutting tower to the main wall of the castle. Slantwise, he crept over its surface until a slit of blackness loomed before him, another window. He had to squeeze to get through, the stone scraping his skin.

For a moment he stood inside, breathing heavily, the drawn sword in his hand. There was a corridor stretching beyond this room, on into a darkness lit by the ghostly blue fungus-glow. He saw and heard nothing of the Xanthi, but something scuttled across the floor and crouched in a shadowed corner, watching him.

On noiseless bare feet, he ran down the hall. Fog eddied and curled in the tenebrous length of it, he heard the dripping of water and once a shuddering scream ripped the dank air. He thought he remembered where he was in that labyrinth—left here, and there would be another ramp going down—

A huge golden form loomed around the corner. Before the jaws could open to shout, Corun's sword hissed in a vicious arc and the Xanthian's head leaped from his shoulders. He kicked the flopping body behind a door and sped on his way, panting.

Halfway down the ramp, a narrow entrance gaped, one of the tunnels that riddled the building through its massive walls. Corun slithered down its lightless wet length. It should open on the great chamber and—

Black against the dim blue light of the exit, a motionless form was squatting. Corun groaned inwardly. They had a guard against intruders, then. Best to go back now—no! He snarled soundlessly and bounded forward, clutching the sword in one hand and reaching out with the other.

Fingers rasping across the scaly hide, he hooked the thing's neck into the crook of his elbow and yanked the heavy body back into the tunnel with one enormous wrench. Blind in the darkness, he stabbed into the mouth, driving the point of his sword through flesh and bone into the brain.

The dying monster's claws raked him as he crouched over the body. He reflected grimly that no matter how benevolent the Xanthi might be, he would die for murder if they ever caught him. But he had no great fear of their suddenly becoming tender toward mankind. The bulk of the reptile race was peaceable actually, but their rulers were relentless.

The tunnel opened on a small balcony halfway up the rearing chamber wall Corun lay on his belly, peering down over the edge.

THEY SAT at a long table, the lords of the Demon Sea, and he felt a dim surprise at seeing that they were almost through eating. Had his nightmare journey taken that long? They were talking, and the sound drifted up to his ears.

At the head of the table, Tsathu and his councilors sat on a long ornate couch ablaze with beaten gold. Shorzon and Chryseis were reclining nearby, sipping the bitter yellow wine of the Xanthi. It was strange to hear the hideous hissing and croaking of the reptile language coming from Chryseis' lovely throat.

"—interesting, I am sure," said the king.

"More than that—more than that!" It seemed to Corun that he could almost see the terrible fire in Shorzon's eyes. The wizard leaned forward, shaking with intensity. "You can do it. The Xanthi can conquer Achaera with ease. Your sea cavalry and serpents can smash their ships, your devil-powder can burst their walls into the air, your legions can overrun their land, and your wizardry can blind and craze them. And the terror you will inspire will force the people to do our bidding."

"Possibly you overrate us," said Tsathu. "It is true that we have great numbers and a strong army, but do not forget that the Xanthi are actually a more peaceful race than man. Your kind is hard and savage, murdering even each other, making war simply for loot or glory or no real reason at all. Until the king-race arose, the Xanthi dwelt quietly on the sea bottom and a few small islands, without wish to harm anyone.

"They have not even the natural capacity for magic possessed, however undeveloped, by all humans. As a result they are much more susceptible to it than men. Thus, when the king-race was born with such powers, they were soon able to control all their people and make themselves the absolute masters of the Xanthi. But we, kings and wizards and lords of the Demon Sea, are all one interbred clan. Without us, the Xanthi power would collapse; they would go back to what they were.

"Even Xanthi science is all of our making. *We*, the king-race, developed the devil-powder and all that we have ever made is stored in the dungeons of this very building—enough to blow it into the sky."

TSATHU made a grimace which might have been a sardonic smile. "Do not read weakness into that admission," he said. "Even though all the lords who make Xanthian might are gathered in this one room, that power is still immeasurably greater than you can imagine. To show you how helpless you are—your men are locked into the dungeons and your geas has been lifted from their minds."

"Impossible!" gasped Shorzon. "A geas cannot be lifted—"

"But it can. What is it but a compulsion implanted in the brain, so deeply as to supersede all other habits? One mind cannot erase that imposed pattern, but several minds working in concert can do so, and that I and my councilors have done. As of today, your folk are free in soul, hating you for what you made them. You are alone."

The great scaled forms edged closer, menacingly. Corun's fist clenched about his sword. If they harmed Chryseis—

But she said coolly, "It does not matter. Our men were simply to bring us here, nothing else. We can dispense with them. What matters is our plan to impose magic control over Achaera."

"And I cannot yet see what benefit the Xanthi would get of it," said Tsathu impatiently. "Our powers of darkness are so much greater than yours already that—"

"Let us not use words meant to impress the ignorant among ourselves," said Chryseis scornfully. "Every sorcerer knows there is nothing of heaven or hell about magic. It is but the imposition of a pattern on other minds. It creates, by control of the senses, illusions of lycanthropy or whatever else is desired, or it binds the subject by the unbreakable compulsion of a geas. But it is no more than that—one mind reaching through space to create what impressions it wills on another mind. Your devil-powder, or an ordinary sword or ax or fist, is more dangerous—if the fools only knew."

Corun's breath hissed between his teeth. If—if that—O gods, if *that* was the secret of the magicians—

"As you will," said Tsathu indifferently. "What matters is that there are more of our minds than your two, and thus we can beat down any attempt you may make against us. So it comes back to the question, why should we help you seize and hold Achaera? What will we gain?"

"I should say nothing of its great wealth," said Shorzon. "But it is true, as you say, that many minds working together are immeasurably more powerful than one—more powerful, even, than the sum of all those minds working separately. I have worked with as many as a dozen slaves, having them concentrate with me, so that I could draw their mind-force through my own brain and use it as my own, and the results have amazed me. Now if the entire population of Achaera were forced to help us, all at one time—"

The Xanthi's eyes glittered and a low murmur rose among them. Shorzon went on, rapidly, "It would be power over the world. Nothing could stand before that massed mental force. With us, skilled sorcerers, to direct, and the soldiers of Xanthi to compel obedience, we could lay a geas on whole nations without even having to be near them. We could span immeasurable gulfs of space and contact minds on those other worlds which philosophers think exist beyond the upper clouds. We could, by thus heightening our own mental powers, think out the very problems of existence, find the deepest secrets of nature, forces beside which your devil-powder would be a spark. Drawing life-energy from other bodies, we would never grow old, we would live forever.

"Tsathu—Lords of Xanthi—I offer you a chance to become gods!"

THE STILLNESS was broken only by the muttering and whispering of the Xanthi among themselves. Mist drifted through the raw wet night of the hall. The walls seemed to waver, shift and blur like smoke.

"Why could we not do this in our own nation?" asked Tsathu.

"Because, as you yourself said, the Xanthi do not have the latent mental powers of humans—save for you few who are the masters. It must be mankind who is controlled, with the commoners of your race as overseers."

"And why could we not kill you and do this ourselves?"

"Because you do not understand humans. The differences are too great. You could never control human thoughts as Chryseis or I could."

Another Xanthian spoke, "But do you realize what this will do to the human race? Your Achaerans will become mindless machines under such control. Drained of life-energy, they will age and die like animals. I doubt that any will live ten seasons."

"What of that?" shrugged Chryseis. "There are other nations nearby to draw on—Conahur, Norriki, Khemri, ultimately the world. We will have centuries, remember—we will never die!"

"And you do not care for your own race at all?"

"It will no longer be our race," said Shorzon. "We will be gods, thinking and living and wielding such powers as they—as we ourselves right now—could never dream. Why, do what you will with our men here, to start. What does it matter?"

"But do not harm the yellow-haired man from Conahur," said Chryseis sharply. "He's mine—forever."

Tsathu sat thinking, like the statue of a Khemrian beast-god cast in shining gold. Slowly, at last, he nodded, and an eerie sigh ran down the long table as the lords of the Xanthi hissed agreement.

"It will be done," said Tsathu.

Corun stumbled back down the tunnel, reckless of discovery, blind and deaf with madness that roared in his skull. Chryseis—Chryseis—Chryseis—

It was not the horror of the scheme, the ruin that it would bring even if it failed, the revelation of how immeasurably powerful were the forces leagued against man. He could have stood that, and braced himself to fight it as long as there was breath in his lungs. But Chryseis—

She had been part of it. She had helped plan it, had coldly condemned her whole race to oblivion. She had lied to him, cheated him, betrayed him, used him, and now she wanted him for a toy, an immortal puppet—Witch! Witch! Witch!

Less human than the erinye at her feet, than the Xanthi themselves, mad with a cold madness such as he had never thought could be—*Chryseis, Chryseis, Chryseis, I loved you. With all my heart, I loved you.*

There was no hope in him, no longing for anything but the fullest revenge he could take before they hewed him to the ground. Had the old Xanthian wizard foretold he would bring death? Aye, by the mad cruel gods who ruled men's destinies, he would!

He reached the corridor and began to run.

CHAPTER EIGHT

DOWN A LONG CURVING RAMP that led into a pit of blackness—the dungeons could not be far, they lay this way—

He hugged himself into the shadows as a troop of guards went by. They were talking in their hoarse croaking language, and did not peer into the corners of the labyrinth. When they were past, Corun sped on his way.

The stone walls became rough damp tunnels, hewed out of the living rock under the castle. He groped through a blackness relieved only by the occasional dull glow of fungi. The darkness hissed and rustled with movements; he caught the glimmer of three red eyes watching, and something slithered over his bare feet. A far faint scream quivered down the hollow length of passages. It had shaken him when he was here before, but now—

What mattered? What was important, save to kill as many of the monsters as he could before they overwhelmed him?

The tunnel opened on a great cave whose floor was a pool of oily black water. As he skirted its rim along a narrow slippery ledge, something stirred, a misshapen giant thing darker than the night. It roared hollowly and swam toward him. A wave of foul odor came with it, catching Corun's throat in a sick dizziness.

He swayed on the edge of the pool and the swimmer began to crawl out of it toward him. Corun saw its teeth gleam wetly in the vague blue light, but there were no eyes—it was blind. He retreated along the ledge toward the farther exit. The ground trembled under the bulk of the creature.

Its jaws clashed shut behind him as he leaped free. Racing down the tunnel, he heard the bellowing of it like dull thunder through the reeking gloom. It wouldn't follow far, but that way of return would be barred to him.

No matter, no matter. He burst out into another open space. It was lit by a dim flickering fire over which crouched three armed Xanthi. Beyond, the red light glimmered on an iron-barred doorway, and behind that there were figures stirring. Men!

Corun bounded across the floor, the sword shrieking in his hand. It whirled down to crash through the skull-bones of one guard. Before he could free it, the other two were on him.

He ducked a murderous pike thrust and slipped close to the wielder, stabbing upward with his dagger. The Xanthian screamed and hugged Corun close to himself, fastening his jaws in the man's shoulder. Corun slashed wildly, ripping open the throat. They tumbled to the ground, locked in each other's arms, raging like beasts. Corun's knife glanced off the Xanthian's ribs and he felt the steel snap over. He got both hands into the clamped jaws, heedless of the fangs, and wrenched. The jawbone cracked as he forced the reptile's mouth open.

He rolled from beneath the still feebly struggling creature and glared around for the third. That one lay in a hacked ruin against the cell; he had backed up too close to the bars, and the men inside still had their weapons.

GASPING, Corun climbed to his feet. An eager baying of fierce voices rolled out from the cell; men gripped the bars and howled in maddened glee.

"Corun—Captain Corun—get us out of here—let us out to rip Shorzon's guts loose—Aaarrrgh!"

The Conahurian lurched over to a dead Xanthian at whose waist hung a bundle of keys. His hands shook as he tried them in the lock. When he got the door open, the men were out in a single tide. He leaned heavily on an Umlotuan's arm. "What happened to you?" he asked.

"The devils led us down here and then closed the door on us," snarled the blue man. "Later a group of them in rich dress came down—and suddenly we saw what a slavery we'd been in to Shorzon, suddenly it no longer seemed that obedience to him was the only possible thing—Mwanzi, let me at his throat!"

"You may have that chance," said the pirate. He felt strength returning; he stood erect and faced them in the flickering firelight. Their eyes gleamed back at him out of the shadows, fierce as the metal of their weapons.

"Listen," he said. "We might be able to fight our way out of here, but we'd never escape across the Demon Sea. But I know a way to destroy this whole cursed house and every being in it. If you'll follow me—"

"Aye!" The shout filled the cavern with savage thunder. They shook their weapons in the air, gleam of red-lit steel out of trembling darkness. "Aye!"

Corun picked up his sword and trotted down the nearest passageway. He was bleeding, he saw vaguely, but he felt little pain from it—he was beyond that now. The thing was to find the devil-powder. Tsathu had said it was somewhere down here.

They went along tunnel after winding tunnel, losing all sense of direction in the wet hollow dark. Corun had a sudden nightmare feeling that they might wander down here forever, blundering from cave to empty cave while eternity grayed.

"Where are we going?" asked someone impatiently. "Where are Xanthi to fight?"

"I don't know," snapped Corun.

They came suddenly into another broad cavern, beyond which was another barred door. Four Xanthi stood guard in front of it. They never had a chance—the air was suddenly full of hurled weapons, and they were buried under a pile of edged steel.

Corun searched the bodies but found no keys. In the murk beyond, he could dimly see boxes and barrels reaching into fathomless distances, but the door was held fast. Of course—Tsathu would never trust his men-at-arms with entrance to the devil-powder.

The corsair snarled and grabbed a bar with both hands. "Pull, men of Umlotu!" he shouted. "Pull!"

They swarmed close, thirty-odd big blue men with the strength of hate in them, clutching the cell bars, grabbing each other's waists, heaving with a force that shrieked through the iron. "Pull!"

The lock burst and they staggered back as the door swung wide. Instantly Corun was inside, ripping open a box and laughing aloud to see the black grains that filled it.

For a wild moment he thought of plunging a brand into the powder and going up in flame and thunder with the castle. Coldness returned—he checked himself and looked around for fuses. His followers would not have permitted him to commit a suicide that involved them. And after all— the longer he lived, the more enemies he'd have a chance to cut down personally.

"I've heard talk of this stuff," said one of the men nervously. "Is it true that setting fire to it releases a demon?"

"Aye." Corun found the long rope-like fuses coiled in a box. He knotted several together and put one end into the powder. The ignition of one container would quickly set off the rest—and the cavern was huge, and filled with many shiploads of sleeping hell.

"If we can fight our way to our ship, and get clear before the fire reaches the powder—" began the Umlotuan.

"We can try that, I suppose," said Corun.

He estimated the burning time of his fuse from memories of the use he'd seen the Xanthi make of the devil-powder. Yes, there would be a fair allowance for escape, though he doubted that they would ever reach the strand alive.

He touched a stick from the fire to the end of the fuse. It began to sputter, a red spark creeping along it toward the open box. "Let's go!" shouted Corun.

They pounded along the tunnel, heedless of direction. There should be an upward-leading ramp somewhere—ah! There it was!

Up its length they raced, past levels of the dungeons toward the main floor of the castle. At the end, there was a brighter blue light than they had seen below. Up—up!

Up—and out!

THE CHAMBER was enormous, a pillared immensity reaching to a ceiling hidden in sheer height; rugs and tapestries of the scaled Xanthian weave were strewn about, and their heavy, intricately carved furniture filled it. At the far end stood a towering canopied throne, on which sat a huge golden form. Other shapes stood around it, and there were pikemen lining the walls at rigid attention.

Through the haze of mist and twilight, Corun saw the black robe of Shorzon and the flame-colored cloak of Chryseis. He shrieked an oath and plunged for them.

A horn screamed and the guards sprang from the walls to form a line before the throne. The humans shocked against the Xanthi with a fury that clamored through the building.

Swords and axes began to fly. Corun hewed at the nearest grinning reptile face, felt the sword sink in and roared the war-cry of Conahur. He spitted the monster on his blade, lifted it, and pitch forked it into the ranks of the guards.

Tsathu bellowed and rose to meet him. Suddenly the Xanthian king was not there; it was a tentacled thing from the sea bottom that filled the room, a thing whose bloated dark body reared to the ceiling. Someone screamed—fear locked the battlers into motionlessness.

"Magic!" It was a sneering rattle in Corun's throat. He sprang into the very body of the sea creature.

He felt the shock of striking its solid form, the rasp of its hide against him, the overwhelming poisonous stench of it. One tentacle closed around him. He felt his ribs snapping and the air popping from his burst lungs.

It wasn't real, his mind gasped through the whirling agony. It wasn't real! He plowed grimly ahead, blind in the illusion that swirled around him, striking, striking.

Dimly, through the roaring in his nerves, he felt his blade hit something solid. He bellowed in savage glee and smote again, again, and again. The smashing pressure lifted. He sobbed air into himself and looked with streaming eyes as the giant form dissolved into smoke, into mist, into empty air. It was Tsathu writhing in pain at his feet, Tsathu with his head nearly chopped off. It was only another dying Xanthian.

Corun leaped up onto the throne and looked over the room. The guards and the sailors were still standing in shaken silence. "Kill them!" roared the pirate. "Strike them down!"

Battle closed again with a snarl and a clang of steel. Corun glared around after other Xanthi of the sorcerer breed. There were none in sight; they must prudently have fled into another part of the castle. Well—let them!

But other Xanthi were swarming into the chamber, battle horns were hooting and the guttural reptile voices crying a summons. If the humans were not to be broken by sheer numbers, they'd have to fight their way out soon...

And down in the dungeons a single red spark was eating its way toward a box of black powder.

Corun jumped down again to the floor. His sword leaped sideways, cut a Xanthian spine across, bit the tail from another. "To me!" he bawled. "Over here, men of Umlotu!"

The blues heard him and rallied, gathering into compact knots that slashed their way toward where his dripping sword whined and thundered. He never stopped striking; he drove the reptiles before him until they edged away from his advance.

The men formed into one group and Corun led it across the floor in a dash for the looming doorway. A red thought flashed across his brain: Where were Shorzon and Chryseis?

The Xanthi scattered before the desperate human rush. The men came out into a remembered hallway—it led to the outside, Corun recalled. By Breannach Brannor, they might escape yet!

"Corun! Corun, you sea devil! I knew it was your doing!"

The Conahurian turned to see Imazu bounding toward him with a bloody ax in one hand. Imazu—thank all the gods. Imazu was free!

"I heard a noise of fighting, and the tower guards went off toward it," gasped the Umlotuan captain. "So I came too. On the way I met Shorzon and Chryseis."

"What of them?" breathed Corun.

The blue warrior smiled savagely and flung a red thing down at Corun's feet. "There's Shorzon's scheming head. My woman is free!"

"Chryseis—"

Imazu leaned on his ax, panting.

"She launched her erinye at me. I ducked into a room and slammed the door in its face, then came here through another entrance."

Chryseis was loose—"We've got to get clear," said Corun. "The devil-powder is going to go off any time now."

The Xanthi were rallying. They came at the humans in another rush. Corun and Imazu and their best men filled the corridor with a haze of steel, backing down toward the outer portal.

It was a crazy blur of struggle, hewing at faces that wavered out of night, slapping down thrusts and reaching for the life of the enemy. Men fell, and others took their places in the line. Down the corridor they retreated, fighting to get free, and they left a trail of dead.

The end of the passage loomed ahead. And the monstrous iron door was swinging shut.

Chryseis stood in the entrance. A wild storm-wind outside sent her cloak flapping about her, red wings beating in the lightning-shot darkness about the devil's rage of the goddess face.

"Stay here!" she screamed. "Stay here and be cut down, you triple traitor!"

The nearest Umlotuan sprang at her. The door clashed shut in his face—they heard the great bolt slam down outside. They were boxed in the end of the hall, and the Xanthi need only shoot them down with arrows.

Down in the dungeons, the fuse burned to its end. A sheet of flame sprang up in the opened-box of powder, reaching for the stacks around it.

CHAPTER NINE

THE FIRST EXPLOSION CAME as a muffled roar. Corun felt the floor tremble under his feet. Men and Xanthi stood motionless, looking at each other with widening eyes in which a common doom arose.

So it ended. Shorzon and Tsathu and their wizard cohorts would be gone, but Chryseis, mad, lovely Chryseis, was loose, and the gods knew what hell she could brew among the leaderless Xanthi.

The walls groaned as another boom echoed down their length.

Well, death came to every man, and he had not done so badly. Corun began to realize how weary he was; he was bleeding from wounds and breath was raw in his lungs.

The Umlotuans hammered on the door in panic. But the twenty or fewer survivors could never break it down.

The devil-powder roared. The floor heaved sickeningly under Corun's feet. He heard the crash of collapsing masonry.

Wait—wait—one chance! One chance, by the gods!

"Be ready to run out when the walls topple," he shouted. "We'll have a little time—"

The Xanthi were fleeing in terror. The humans stood alone, waiting while the explosions rolled and banged around them. Cracks zigzagged across the walls, dust choked the dank air.

Crash!

Corun saw the nearer wall swaying, toppling. The floor lifted and buckled and he fell to the lurching ground. All the world was an insanity of racket and ruin.

The lintel caved in, the portal sagged. Corun leaped for the opening like a pouncing erinye. The men swarmed with it, out through the widening hole while the roof came down behind them.

Someone screamed, a faint lost sound in the grinding fury of sundering stone. Rocks were flying—Corun saw one of them crack a man's head like a melon. Wildly he ran as the outer facade came down.

There was a madness of storm outside, wind screaming to fill the sky, driving solid sheets of rain and hail before it. The incessant blinding lightning glared in a cold shadowless brilliance, the bawling thunder drowned the roar of exploding devil-powder. They fought out through the courtyard, past the deserted outer gate.

There came a blast which seemed to crack the sky. Corun was knocked down as by a giant's fist. He lay in the mud and saw a pillar of flame lift toward the heavens with the castle fountaining up on its wings. Thunder roared over the earth, shouting to the storm that raged in the heavens.

Corun picked himself up and leaned dizzily against a tree stripped clean by the blast. Rain slanted across the ground, churning the mud beneath his feet, the livid lightning-glare blazing above. Vaguely, through ringing, deafened ears, he heard the wild clamor of the sea. Looking down the cataract which the upward trail had become, he saw the *Briseia* rocking in the wind where she lay on the beach.

He gestured to Imazu, who staggered up to join him. His voice was barely audible over the shouting wind: "Take the men down there. We can't sail in this storm, but make the ship fast, stand guard over her. If I'm not back when the storm is done, start for home."

"Where are you going?" cried the Umlotuan.

"I'll be back—maybe. Stay with the ship!"

Corun turned and slogged across the ground toward the jungle.

WEARINESS was gone. He was like a machine running without thought or pain until it burned out. Chryseis would have fled toward high ground, he thought dully.

Behind him, Imazu started forward, then checked himself. Something of the ultimate loneliness that was in Corun must have come to the Umlotuan. It was not a mission on which any other man might go. And they had to save the ship. He gestured to his few remaining men and they began the slow climb down to the beach.

The castle was a heap of shattered rock, still moving convulsively as the last few boxes of devil-powder exploded. The rain boiled down over it, churning through the fragments. Lightning flamed in the berserk heavens.

Corun pushed through underbrush that clutched at his feet and clawed at his skin. The sword was still hanging loosely in one hand, nicked and blunted with battle. He went on mechanically, scarcely noticing the wind-whipped trees that barred his way.

It came to him that he was fighting for Khroman, the thalassocrat of Achaera, ruler by right of conquest over Conahur. But there were worse things than foreign rule, if it was human, and one of the greater evils had fled toward the mountain.

Presently he came out on the bare rocks above the fringe of jungle growth. The rain hammered at him, driven by a wind that screamed like a maddened beast. Thunder boomed and rolled overhead, a roar of doom answering the thud of his heart. The water rushed over his ankles, foaming down toward the sea.

She stood waiting for him atop a high bare hill. Her cloak was drawn tightly about her slender body, but the wind caught at it, whipped and tore it. Her rain-wet hair blew wild.

"Corun," she called under the gale. "Corun."

"I am coming," he said, not caring if she heard him or not. He struggled up to where she stood limned against the sheeted fire in heaven. They faced each other while the storm raged around them.

"Corun—"

She read death in his eyes as he lifted the sword. Her form blurred, the outlines of a monster grew to his eyes.

He laughed bitterly. "I know what your magic is," he said. "You saw me kill Tsathu."

She was human again, human and lovely, a light-footed spirit of the hurricane. Her face was etched white in the lightning-glare.

"Perias!" she screamed.

The erinye crept forth, belly to the ground, tail lashing. Hell glared out of the ice-green eyes. Corun braced himself, sword in hand.

Perias sprang—not straight at the man, but into the air. His wings caught the wind, whirling him aloft. Twisting in midflight, he arrowed down. Corun struck at him. The erinye dodged the blow and one buffeting wingtip caught the man's wrist. The sword fell from Corun's hand. At once the erinye was on him.

Corun fell under that smashing attack.

The erinye's fangs gleamed above his throat; the claws sank into his muscles. He flung up an arm and the teeth crunched on it, grinding at the bone.

Corun wrapped his legs in a scissor-lock around the gaunt body, pressing himself too close for the clawed hind feet to disembowel him. His free hand reached out, gouging—he felt an eyeball tear loose, and the erinye opened his mouth in a thin scream. Corun pulled his torn arm free. He struck with a balled fist at the devil-beast and felt his knuckles break under the impact. But bone snapped. Perias' jaw hung suddenly loose.

The erinye sprang back and Corun lurched to hands and knees. Perias edged closer, stiff-legged. Corun stumbled erect and Perias charged. One great wing smashed out, brought the man toppling back to earth. Perias leaped for his exposed belly.

Corun lashed out with both feet. The thud was dull and hollow under the racketing thunder. Perias tumbled back and Corun sprang on him. The barbed tail slashed, laying Corun's thigh open. He fell atop the struggling beast and got his free hand on the throat.

The mighty wings threshed, half lifting man and erinye. Corun pulled himself over on the writhing back. He locked legs around the body, arms around the neck, and heaved.

The erinye yowled. His wings clashed together with skull-cracking force, barely missing the head of the man who hugged his back. His tail raked against Corun's back, seeking the vitals. Corun gave another yank. He felt the supple spine bending. Heave!

Perias lifted a brassy scream. The strange dry sound of snapping vertebrae crackled out. Corun rolled away from the threshing form.

Perias gasped, lifted his broken head, and looked with filming green eyes at Chryseis where she stood unmoving against the white fire of the sky. Slowly, painfully, he dragged himself toward her. Breath rattled in and out of his blood-filled lungs.

"Perias—" Chryseis bent over to touch the great head. The erinye sighed. His rough tongue licked her feet. Then he shuddered and lay still.

"Perias."

Corun climbed to his feet and stood shaking. There was no strength left in him—it was running out through a dozen yawning wounds. The ground whirled and tilted crazily about him. He saw her standing against the sky and slowly, slowly, he came toward her.

Chryseis picked up a stone and threw it. It seemed to take an immense time, arcing toward him. Some dim corner of his buckling consciousness realized that it would knock him out, that she could then kill him with the sword and escape into the hills.

It didn't matter. Nothing mattered. The stone crashed against his skull and the world exploded into darkness.

CHAPTER TEN

HE WOKE UP, SLOWLY AND painfully, and lay for a long time in a state of half-awareness, remembering only confused fragments of battle and despair.

When he opened his eyes, he saw that the storm was dying. Lightning was wan in the sky, and thunder mumbled farewell. The wind had fallen, the rain fell slow and heavy down on him.

He saw her bending over him. The long wet hair tumbled past her face to fall on his breast. He was wrapped in her cloak, and she had ripped bandages from her robe for his hurts.

He tried to move, and could only stir feebly. She laid a hand on his cheek. "Don't," she whispered. "Just lie there Corun."

His head was on her lap, he realized dimly. His eyes questioned her. She laughed softly under the falling rain.

"Don't you see?" she said. "Didn't you think of it? Shorzon's geas was put on me as a child. I was always under his will. Even when he was dead, it was strong enough to drive me along his road.

"But I love you, Corun. I will always love you. My love warred with Shorzon's will even as I tried to kill you. And when I saw you lying there helpless, after such a fight as no man has ever waged since the gods walked the earth—

"I tried to stab you. And I couldn't. Shorzon's geas was broken."

Her hands stroked his hair. "You aren't too badly hurt, Corun. I'll get you down to the ship. With my witch's powers, we can win through any Xanthi who try to stop us—not that I think they will, with their leaders destroyed. We can get safely to Achaera."

She sighed. "I will see that you escape my father's power, Corun. If you will return to the pirate life, I will follow you."

He shook his head. "No," he whispered. "No, I will take service under Khroman, if he will have me."

"He will," she vowed softly. "He needs strong men. And someday you can be thalassocrat of the empire—"

It wasn't so bad, thought Corun drowsily. Khroman was a good sort. A highly placed Conahurian could gradually ease the burdens of his people until they had full equality with Achaera in a united and peaceful domain.

The menace of the Xanthi was ended. To be on the safe side, Achaera had better make them tributary; an expedition which he, Corun, could lead. After that, there would be enough to keep a man busy. As well as the loveliest and best of women for wife.

He slept. He did not waken when Imazu led a squad up in search of him. Chryseis laid a finger on her lips and a flash of understanding passed between her and the captain. He nodded, smiling, and clasped her hand with sudden warmth.

They bore the sleeping warrior back through the rain, down to the waiting ship.

THE END

If you've enjoyed this book, you will not want to miss these terrific titles…

ARMCHAIR SCI-FI & HORROR DOUBLE NOVELS, $12.95 each

D-131 **COSMIC KILL** by Robert Silverberg
BEYOND THE END OF SPACE by John W. Campbell

D-132 **THE DARK OTHER** by Stanley Weinbaum)
WITCH OF THE DEMON SEAS by Poul Anderson

D-133 **PLANET OF THE SMALL MEN** by Murray Leinster
MASTERS OF SPACE by E. E. "Doc" Smith & E. Everett Evans

D-134 **BEFORE THE ASTEROIDS** by Harl Vincent
SIXTH GLACIER, THE by Marius

D-135 **AFTER WORLD'S END** by Jack Williamson
THE FLOATING ROBOT by David Wright O'Brien

D-136 **NINE WORLDS WEST** by Paul W. Fairman
FRONTIERS BEYOND THE SUN by Rog Phillips

D-137 **THE COSMIC KINGS** by Edmond Hamilton
LONE STAR PLANET by H. Beam Piper & John J. McGuire

D-138 **BEYOND THE DARKNESS** by S. J. Byrne
THE FIRELESS AGE by David H. Keller, M. D.

D-139 **FLAME JEWEL OF THE ANCIENTS** by Edwin L. Graber
THE PIRATE PLANET by Charles W. Diffin

D-140 **ADDRESS: CENTAURI** by F. L. Wallace
IF THESE BE GODS by Algis Budrys

ARMCHAIR SCIENCE FICTION & HORROR CLASSICS, $12.95 each

C-58 **THE WITCHING NIGHT**
by Leslie Waller

C-59 **SEARCH THE SKY**
by Frederick Pohl and C. M. Kornbluth

C-60 **INTRIGUE ON THE UPPER LEVEL**
by Thomas Tempel Hoyne

ARMCHAIR SCI-FI & HORROR GEMS SERIES, $12.95 each

G-15 **SCIENCE FICTION GEMS, Vol. Eight**
Keith Laumer and others

G-16 **HORROR GEMS, Vol. Eight**
Algernon Blackwood and others